Tangled Want

TANGLED SERIES

SOPHIE ANDREWS

Content Note

Tangled Want is an open door romance between a train wreck celebrity and a bookish middle school teacher with plenty of angst, a big, loud family, and lots of spice. There are also discussions of conservative religion, biphobia, and parental abandonment.

For all the short kings, I see you.

CHAPTER ONE

Bronte

After two days together, we should have been used to it, but Willow's wail could wake the dead, and I twitched from my position on the couch, where I'd been sprawled out.

Laney snorted a laugh. "Maybe she'll be a good singer when she's older."

Sam discreetly reached for the remote, raising the volume of the *Golden Girls* episode we were watching as Gem stood up.

But then Jason's voice called down from upstairs. "Don't move, Gemma! I got her!"

She plopped back down and offered me a sad smile. "Happy birthday."

I waved my fork, covered in blue icing from the cake. "There's never been a better one. I'm with my best friends, and I got the flower."

It was true. As long as I was with my girls, I didn't care what we did. Even if that meant listening to an unhappy baby.

Gem wrinkled her nose as Willow continued to cry upstairs. "I'm sorry we aren't out getting drunk or something," she said, all forlorn. "I feel so old."

"You kinda are." Sam pointed the remote at her. "You're a mom now."

I agreed as a twinge of jealousy settled into my bones when Jason plodded down the stairs, his daughter wrapped up in a monkey print muslin blanket. He cringed at Gem while Willow cried against his shoulder. "I think she wants her mama."

We all laughed, proving Sam's point.

Jason Mitchell, Gem's fiancé, was dressed casually in sweatpants and a T-shirt. He was a tall, muscular, preppy type and totally opposite of the guy I imagined wild child Gem would end up with, if any at all. But here she was, in a brand-new home with a beautiful, screeching baby. Even though I think we all assumed I'd be the first one of us to settle down.

Jason passed Willow off to Gem, asking, "Do you need anything? More water?" When she nodded, he grabbed her gigantic aluminum water bottle before pointing to the rest of us. "Ladies? Anything? More wine? Cake? Pretzels, chips?"

Laney lifted her glass with a few drops of pink wine left in it. "I wouldn't be opposed if you guys want to open another bottle."

Sam and I both looked to each other and then shrugged. Jason took that as his answer. "'Nother bottle coming up."

Sam settled her back against the couch. "This is great."

Laney shifted over to comb her fingers through Sam's rose-gold hair, separating it into three groups to braid. "What is?"

"This." She gestured around the room.

"This?" Gem asked, popping out her boob to feed Willow.

A look of horror crossed Sam's face. "No, not that. I mean..." She circled her arm again. "You built this whole family, and it's really nice to be here."

"I somehow convinced you three to stay in my house with my ten-week-old under the guise of Bronte's birthday weekend, but really, it was so I could remember what the *before* times were like." A ghost of a smile tugged at Gem's lips. "Don't lie and tell me you're enjoying this tiny banshee."

"I'm not lying. Being in this house is like living in a sign from Target, you know?" Sam lifted her hand as if reading it on the wall. "Love lives here."

Gem mumbled out a, "Dork," as she tamped down a smile.

"No, it's true." I placed my plate and fork on the table. Unlike Gem, who had been raised by a single mom, and Sam, who struggled with her parents' divorce, I was really close to my siblings and parents, and I couldn't wait to have my own family. I was so happy for Gem and Jason, but I was also envious of what they'd built here.

"We should be out celebrating, but instead…" Gem trailed off, adjusting her hold on Willow.

I flicked the thought away. "We had our spa day and went out to dinner last night. I'm having fun with my girls here."

Willow whimpered as if to say *Me too!* and we all laughed.

Jason reappeared from the kitchen, carrying a bottle of wine and Gem's water bottle, which he gave to her first before refilling all our wineglasses.

"We even have our own handsome butler." Laney lifted her wine in a salute.

"Pleasure to be of service." Jason grinned then plopped down next to Gem, dropping an arm around her shoulders.

"It's still weird sometimes," she said. "Like, Willow will wake up in the middle of the night, and for a second, I forget where I am and *who* I am. It takes me a minute to remember I have a kid now."

"You forget about me too?" Jason quipped, towing Gem in closer to him.

"I could never," she said saccharine sweet. "You snore too loud to ignore."

Jason jostled her, whispering something in her ear that made her cheeks flame as she smiled. She elbowed him away to scoop Willow from her breast and onto her shoulder.

Laney finished Sam's hair with a clap and leaped up. "Bobby snores too, but no matter what, I can never wake him up to stop."

Sam lifted her hands above her head, stretching. "That's why I enjoy sleeping alone."

Laney grabbed her phone, always one to document everything, a social media queen. "Jason, if you please?"

He accepted her phone, while Laney, Sam, and I all found seats on either side and in front of Gem and Willow.

"On three," Jason said, positioning the phone up.

"Happy birthday, Bronte," Sam said from her seat on the floor.

"One."

"Hope it's a good year for you." Laney tugged on my ponytail from the other side of Gem.

"Two."

"And all your wishes come true," Gem added.

"Three."

Jason snapped a few pictures then handed Laney her phone back in exchange for Willow from Gem. "I'll leave you ladies to it." He kissed Gem's forehead. "I'll take the midnight feeding, okay? You've got enough milk stored."

It was only eight o'clock, but I suspected he planned on staying upstairs the rest of the night with the baby so Gem could have the last few hours with us.

"It was nice finally meeting you in person, and I'm really glad you guys could come for the weekend," he said to the group. "Our guest rooms are open whenever you want them."

A chorus of gratitude rang out and barely audible sighs of appreciation when he pivoted around with Willow in his arms, his long, confident strides on display as he walked away. After a few moments of silence, Laney, Sam, and I all turned our attention to Gem, who blushed with a laugh. "I know, right? He's perfect."

"Like a dream!" Laney crowed.

Sam grabbed the remote once again. "A literal real-life Ken doll."

"I'm happy for you," I said, holding Gem's hand. We'd come a long way since meeting on our college campus the first day as roommates. I had been a mess, crying and homesick, while Gem was excited to be out of her home state and away from her mother's "douchebag boyfriend." A few days later, we'd met Sam and Laney in a humanities class, but it wasn't until two weeks after that we had solidified our friendship at a party when some scum of the earth slipped something into Gem's drink. The three of us immediately swooped in to help her, and the rest was history. Best friends for life.

Gem glowed, her eyes watering, as she squeezed my hand in return, bringing me back to the present. "Life is good."

My eyes watered too because I was physically incapable of not crying when someone else cried. "I can tell."

"Are you happy?"

I coasted my gaze around Gem and Jason's living room, the walls a bold but soothing orange with pops of gray and green in the furniture and plants everywhere, and my friends scattered about but close enough to touch. Laney with her foot resting against Gem's thigh and her head on the arm of the sofa, next to Sam, both of them laughing about something on Laney's phone. This was the first time we'd been able to be together in person in over a year, and it was well worth the wait.

"Yeah," I said in answer. I may have been envious of Gem and what she had in this house, but these three girls were as close to me as my own family. This weekend was the happiest I'd been in a long time. "I'm happy."

"Well," Laney started, lifting the wine toward Gem. "Since Jason's called dibs on the midnight feeding, that means you can have a drink, right?"

"You're damn right." She wiggled her fingers, and Laney passed her the wine. She drank right from the bottle—like the lady she was—and we all giggled, telling stories until after two when Gem finally had to go upstairs to pump. Instead of separating into different bedrooms, Laney, Sam, and I piled into one bed, where we slept crammed together until exactly six o'clock in the morning.

That's when Willow's howl roused us. Time for breakfast. Like clockwork, that tiny one was. A girl after my own heart.

CHAPTER TWO

Chris

It was exactly fourteen minutes until takeoff, and I was cutting it close. I couldn't recall the last time I'd had a layover, let alone traveled on a commercial airline.

Still catching my breath, I shuffled down the jetway toward the plane, fixing my well-worn baseball cap over my brow. At the entrance of the plane, I inhaled a deep breath, attempting to calm my racing heart, as I passed those really tempting first-class seats on the way to the cramped and overcrowded ones behind. Almost everyone was already in place with heads bowed over a book or cell phone. Some inspected their cramped surroundings, but no one took any extra notice of me.

No one stared. No one made a fuss, pointed, asked for a picture. Nothing.

Between the gate agent not recognizing me and this, I was sure my star status had not only fallen, but imploded into a black hole.

I shook the thought from my head. This was what I wanted, what I needed. To avoid attention.

I made my way to the back of the plane and turned toward my row, blocked by someone already in the aisle seat. "Excuse me, can I…"

A pair of startlingly blue eyes blinked up at me expectantly. "Do you need to get in?"

"Yeah."

The young woman stood, allowing me to slide in. I settled in my seat with a sigh and, out of the corner of my eye, caught her movements as she sat back down. Opening a magazine, she leaned back into her seat, getting comfortable.

As if that was possible.

I buckled the seat belt nice and tight. Not that it mattered. If the plane went down, a thin strip of cloth across my lap wasn't going to save me. I flopped my head back with a groan when one of the flight attendants began the safety speech over the loudspeaker.

"Hey, um, sir, are you okay?"

I slanted my gaze to my neighbor. "I'm a little..."

"Don't like flying?"

"No. Not really." Understatement of the year. I didn't normally fly without assistance with some drug or alcohol, but I'd learned from my first flight that they didn't serve drinks until we were up in the air, and those tiny bottles of vodka were crazy expensive. Didn't stop me from ordering the limit, two, but still. Flying coach was for the birds.

"A few more hours, that's it," I whispered to myself.

"What?"

"Nothing, only trying to calm down." This was why I took private planes on the rare occasion I had to fly anywhere, so I could get drunk or high and no one would care. Though, Wes clearly didn't want to give me even that luxury of having a panic attack in private.

"You can talk to me, if you want. I mean, if it'll help," my seatmate said.

"Okay," I agreed, my body rigid and unmoving, save for a bouncing knee.

The engines roared as the plane taxied toward the runway, and my blood pounded in my ears.

"I'm reading this magazine. Do you want to take a quiz? It's to find your workout personality."

I glanced to her hands which held brightly colored pages with ads for sneakers and sports bras before I faced front again where a flight attendant demonstrated how to put on an oxygen mask.

That must have been enough of an answer for her because she cleared her throat. "What are you most likely to be doing on a Saturday night? A, unwinding with a book and bubble bath. B, going for a run to outdo your best time. C, challenging your friends to a game of poker or Scrabble."

Obvious choice. "High stakes poker, C."

"Poker," she repeated, checking off the letter with her pen. "At work, you have a reputation for being... A, the independent and sometimes hard-nosed one, who strives for personal best. B, the laid-back one to organize projects on your own. Or C, the social butterfly who energizes everyone."

"Social butterfly, I guess." As if that wasn't the exact reason I'd been sent on this sojourn.

She checked off the box. "Last one. After a bad day, what would cheer you up most? Indulging in your favorite dessert, the knowledge you can overcome any obstacle, or a pep talk from a friend?"

The pilot called for the flight attendants to have a seat and prepare for takeoff. "Can the pep talk be naked?"

"Sure. All pep talks are better naked," she answered with a trace of laughter. "Okay, according to your answers, you're the fun seeker. You're social, noncompetitive, and are primarily driven by the fun factor activities offer. Your main fitness road-block may be a lack of commitment. You find it hard to stick with a regimen once the novelty wears off. Mix it up with outdoor activities like hiking or cycling to have fun and burn calories.”

I chanced a look to my left and found her staring at me with a curious smile.

“Right.” The plane sped up, and so did my breathing.

She frowned. “So, are you leaving on a trip or on your way home?”

“I...” I dropped my gaze to her hand when she moved it next to mine on the armrest. I wasn’t exactly going on vacation, but I wasn’t going home either. “I’m escaping.”

“Escaping to Pennsylvania?”

My voice wavered as the plane tilted up. “Ye-yes.”

“Did you rob a bank or something?”

“No. No bank robbing.”

“Too bad. I could really use some extra cash.”

My grip was white-knuckled. “Who says I’d give you any?”

“Just a little neighborly donation. Goodwill, karma. All that.”

“I could use some good karma.”

The wheels picked up off the ground, and the plane shifted, soaring into the sky. With the drop of my stomach, I snapped my eyes shut.

“Hey, you’re okay,” she said with a pat to my wrist, urging me to relax. I slowly released my stranglehold on the armrest, and she turned my hand palm up, pressing two fingers on my wrist. “Your heartbeat is really fast. You need to breathe.”

Eventually, I gathered enough nerve to open my eyes, and she nodded reassuringly. “Breathe with me.”

She inhaled and exhaled audibly, an example to follow. And I did. My gaze drifted from her shoulders to her chest, which rose and fell with each of her breaths. As we breathed in unison, the intimate contact between us didn’t seem to bother her even though we were complete strangers.

She offered my hand an encouraging squeeze. "We're flying."

I peeked out the window, through the white clouds. It was amazing, really, if I didn't think about being in a death trap too long.

The pilot's voice filtered through the plane, informing the passengers that we were at cruising altitude and would be flying for about two hours.

"You doing okay?" the woman asked.

When I nodded, she turned in her seat, lifting the armrest so there was nothing separating us. Mimicking her movements, I rested my left shoulder on the seat and finally got a good look at my personal anxiety panacea.

Her hair was a dark brown, almost black, and hung down to her shoulders, framing a pale face with cheeks that dimpled and eyes the color of the clear sky outside the window next to me.

"You were scaring me there for a bit." How had I missed her voice before? Low and raspy and sexy as hell. "My name's Bronte."

"Bronte?"

"Like the sisters? My dad's a literature professor, and my mom's a librarian. They wanted us to have strong, literary names. My brother's name is Fitzgerald."

At my blank face, she tried again.

"Like F. Scott. You know, *The Great Gatsby*."

I shook my head.

"You've never read it? It's a classic high school read."

"Didn't do much reading in high school," I said, bypassing the fact that I'd been homeschooled and the only things I read now were scripts. "But Fitzgerald's quite a name."

"Yeah, we call him Fitz. My sister's name is Shelley. Familiar with *Frankenstein*?"

"Yeah, I've seen a couple different Frankenstein films."

Bronte smiled like I was an adorable idiot. "They're based on Mary Shelley's book."

"Of course." Who knew this flight would come with an English test as well? "And what about your name?"

"The Brontës are three sisters who wrote a few books in the early nineteenth century, like *Jane Eyre* and *Wuthering Heights*, but they all died young in their twenties and thirties."

"Yikes." I pressed my head into my seat, ignoring Wes's voice in the back of my mind, reminding me that the brightest flames always seemed to burn out the fastest. I might have been hailed as a genius in my craft, but Wes had said that didn't mean I had to go out in a blaze of glory.

I pushed all that away and focused on the woman next to me. "Bronte is unusual, beautiful. It suits you."

Her porcelain complexion turned pink. "Thank you...? I'm sorry, I didn't even get your name."

My stage name, CJ, almost dropped from my tongue, but I swallowed it. She clearly didn't recognize me, and I wasn't about to spoil it. "Chris."

Bronte stuck out her hand. "Nice to meet you, Chris."

I liked hearing my real name after being CJ for so long. And it wasn't because she was saying it. That fact had nothing to do with it.

Or, maybe, a tiny bit to do with it.

"My pleasure, Bronte." My thumb caressed the back of her hand for a moment before I let go, and if she twitched in response, I pretended not to notice. "What were you doing in Chicago?"

"One of my best friends lives about an hour outside. She had a baby two months ago, and I went out there for my birthday, along with my two other friends."

I smiled. "It's your birthday?"

"It was Saturday. Turned twenty-six."

"Happy birthday."

She nodded her thanks. "The four of us try to get together as much as we can, but with Gemma having the baby and all of us living all over the place, it's been impossible lately."

"You spent your birthday with a two-month-old?"

"Yeah, it was great. Gem felt bad, but..." She shrugged. "Those girls are my best friends. Hell or high water, we're getting together. Plus, I'm totally a type A personality, and it was relaxing for me to go there and do some dishes for her."

"You did the dishes?"

"Well..." She laughed. It was breathy and kind of embarrassed, and it was the loveliest sound I'd heard in a long time. "Her fiancé has it pretty much covered, but yeah. I don't mind. I've got a bunch of nieces and nephews, so I'm used to the baby panic."

"How many?"

"My brother has three, and my sister is pregnant with baby number two."

My eyebrows shot up. "Quite a brood."

"Mm-hmm. Do you have any?"

"Nieces and nephews?" I asked.

"Yeah. Or kids, too, I guess."

For a second, I was tempted to give her some family history, but I tossed the idea out as quickly as it came in. "Nope. None of the above."

"Yeah, me neither." Her gaze skated away from a moment, and I could almost see her mind working on something, before she met my eyes again. "So, if you aren't a bandit, what is it you do, Chris?"

That was the question. It was now or never.

CHAPTER THREE

Chris

I turned my attention to the overhead buttons, playing with the air vent. The thought of Bronte knowing who I was and looking at me differently killed me. I wasn't ready to break whatever good thing we had going on. "Are you hot? I'm kind of hot."

"Uh, no. I'm good," she said, obviously not falling for my piss-poor distraction.

I sighed and dropped my hand to my lap. "I'm taking a break right now."

"A break? From what?"

"Life." I returned the question before she could press for more details. "What do you do?"

"I'm a teacher."

"I hear that's pretty stressful."

She spread out her hands, motioned down the length of the plane. "Hence the weekend getaway."

"What grade do you teach?"

"I'm in special education, so I don't teach a certain grade. I have a range of kids in middle school."

"What... Are they...? Never mind."

"No, it's okay. I know what you're trying to ask. My kids have mild to moderate developmental delays."

My shoulders sank. Here she was with this incredibly meaningful job, while I was a so-called movie star with a penchant for trouble. "What do you teach them?"

"Mostly, we work on life skills, reading and math, and they go to different classrooms for all the other subjects."

"Do you like it?"

"I love it."

My own smile grew as her face lit up. "I can tell. It's nice to see someone doing some good for this world."

"You don't see much good where you're from?"

She stared at me with such interest and sincerity, I felt compelled to tell her the truth. Maybe not the whole truth, but at least some of it. "It wasn't my idea."

"What wasn't?"

"This trip I'm taking."

"I thought you were escaping," she teased.

"I am. I'm escaping my life for a while."

"What happened? If you don't mind my asking."

I avoided her steady scrutiny and cast my eyes down, playing with the safety instructions tucked into the pocket of the seat. "I've...been a dick," I said, waiting to see if her posture toward me would change. It didn't, and I went on, my attention back on the blue leather of the seat in front of me. "I've been a real asshole for the past couple years, arrogant and spoiled. And now, I'm taking a break. Hoping people forget that particular side of me."

"Time heals all wounds."

"Does it?" My eyes met hers, and I couldn't turn back now. "I wrapped my car around a tree, and I was arrested for DUI."

I waited as Bronte soaked in the information. I waited for

her disgust or disappointment, but her reaction was far from it.

She only studied me for a few moments. "Seems like you know that was a bad decision, though."

I rubbed at my neck. "Really stupid. It wasn't the only stupid thing I've done these last few years, but..."

"What happened?" she asked, empathy emanating from those big blue eyes of hers, and she inched closer to me. I followed as if I was a magnet, my body and words unable to resist.

Avoiding any particulars, I explained, "I like cars. I like driving fast, and that night, I got some bad news and decided to go for a drive. Even though I thought I was okay to get behind the wheel, I shouldn't have. Went around a curve, and bam. Thankfully, I didn't hurt anyone." I stopped, flinching at the possibility of what might have happened. "The court fined me, and I was ordered to do some community service, and after I finished, my friend thought it might be a good idea if I got away for a while." Never mind the paparazzi stalking me, the constant calls for interviews.

She smiled softly. "I'm proud of you for knowing you made a mistake and trying to make up for it."

"You don't even know me."

"Yes, I do." She tipped her head back as if offended and wagged a finger, a small tilt of her pretty pink lips at the corner. "I see you. I see the nervous tic of your leg, the way your fingers can't keep still—" her face softened, eyes burning into me "—your honesty."

And in that second, I was sure Bronte could see more than I wanted her to. All my fears and insecurities, but weirdly enough, I wanted her to. And *that* had some emotion clawing up inside me that I couldn't yet name.

I moved so my back was against the window, our knees

touching. "Well, you know so much about me, and I don't know anything about you."

"There's not much to tell."

"No drugs, rehab, or illicit past?"

She made a face, as if afraid to admit it. "I smoked pot a few times in high school."

"Well, that's it. I don't think we can be friends anymore. I can't have such a bad influence around me."

"Rude." She laughed, reaching to flick my arm, but I grabbed her wrist in defense. Her grin immediately faded when our eyes met.

For the length of a heartbeat, panic rose in my chest, assuming she'd figured out who I was, but as I felt her rapid pulse against my fingertips, I knew whatever it was that passed between us had nothing to do with my celebrity status.

"Sorry," she said, recoiling out of my grasp as if she'd been burned.

I wanted to apologize too, for whatever it was I did to make her uncomfortable, but she was so stiff sitting next to me now that I was afraid to push it. For a few minutes, I did nothing but listen to the hum of the engines. It was only when the flight attendant stood next to us with the refreshments cart that we fell back into an easier rhythm.

With sodas in hand, Bronte and I passed the time by asking each other questions about everything and nothing in particular. Favorite memory? Mine was when I got my first guitar for Christmas at ten years old. Hers was the family trip across the country in an old station wagon. Our stance on organized religion and politics? I'd been raised in a strict Christian home, attending church and bible study multiple times a week. While she said she was a registered independent but leaned left. I loved cold weather and hated mayonnaise. She loathed social media and adored her monthly book club meetings, where she was usually one of the few who read the book. The others, she told me with a smile, went for the wine and cheese.

I answered her questions truthfully, though not completely honestly. And I was sure I'd feel guilty about it for a long time.

Before I knew it, the pilot's voice returned, signaling the descent into Lehigh Valley International Airport, and with the sudden dip of the plane, I gripped the armrest.

Bronte leaned into me. "You okay?"

Surprisingly... "Yeah. I'm okay."

The plane touched down with a bumpy landing, and her head bounced into my shoulder. She frowned, touching the tiny red spot below her right eye. I brushed my thumb over her cheekbone. "Sorry."

She leaned ever so slightly into my touch, and when the aircraft rumbled to a stop, the passengers stood in a wave, reaching for their carry-ons. Bronte and I stayed in our seats, faces inches from each other. Not quite close enough to kiss, but definitely close enough to smell the cinnamon-flavored gum she had been chewing to keep her ears from popping.

When the rest of the passengers surged forward, forming a line to exit, she sat up. "Guess we better..."

I hated to leave our cramped, cozy bubble. I didn't want to let go of this yet. I didn't want to let go of *her*.

"Yeah," I agreed, slow to get up.

Bronte walked ahead of me, but as soon as she stepped onto the jetway, she peeked over her shoulder. I was stuck behind an elderly couple, and she stopped, waiting for me to catch up. She clearly didn't want our time to end yet either.

We leisurely made our way to baggage claim in easy silence, every once in a while catching each other's eyes with a sly smile. And more than once, I kept my fingers from wrapping around her hand as she pointed out which way to go.

When we reached the luggage carousel, she moved to grab

her small suitcase, but I beat her to it, setting it down at her feet.

"So," I began.

"So."

"Do you have a ride?" I asked, hoping I could offer her one.

"My dad's picking me up."

I nodded, desperate to fill up this new expanse of space between us. All around, people greeted one another with hugs and lugged bags onto carts. But it was white noise as I concentrated solely on Bronte.

She fidgeted, her hands jumping from her suitcase to push her hair behind her ears, back to her suitcase, and then finally settling in the pockets of her jacket. "I'm glad you were sitting next to me."

"Me too. It must have been fate," I said, then reconsidered, shaking my head. "But if fate were any good, I would have met you a long time ago."

"Chris, I…" She shifted from foot to foot, her attention on the floor.

"Hey. It's better late than never, right?" When she picked her head up, my gaze roamed over her features, wondering if this instant connection was a fluke. It had to be. Stuff like this only happened in movies. I would know.

Giving in to the kind of reckless behavior I'd been used to, I curved my palm around her jaw, my focus on the tip of her tongue as it slipped out, wetting her lips, and I'd bet anything her kisses were as sweet as she was. But before I could find out, she stepped away from me with a sharp intake of breath.

"I'm sorry, that—"

"What's wrong?" When I reached for her hand, she folded her fingers into a fist.

"Don't. Please, Chris, don't."

"All right." I stepped away, managing a meager half smile. "Can I at least get your number, or—"

"It was nice meeting you." She backed away, her hand to her throat. "Take care of yourself."

A dull ache filled my chest as she walked away from me, recognizing that unidentifiable emotion from before as hope, and I watched as it was lost among the sea of travelers. I'd had an intense couple of hours seated next to Bronte, and I could tell it was crazy intense for her too.

Then again, that was the problem. I was used to crazy. She was not.

She'd come to her senses, probably realizing this thing between us was too good to be true. And then I'd tried to kiss her, and the warning bells went off.

With a sardonic laugh at myself, I readjusted the baseball hat on my head. Fucking up something before I even had it in my grasp was par for the course, I supposed.

I turned my back on the spot Bronte had occupied to grab my things from the luggage carousel. Once I had my duffel bag in hand and guitar case slung over my shoulder, I headed toward the rental car counter for my very sensible four-door Chrysler. I snorted when I saw the white automobile. After I demolished my special edition Aston Martin, replicated from the original James Bond car, Wes would never arrange for anything other than a very safe four-cylinder for me to drive. I hopped in and typed the address for my temporary home into the GPS: Allentown, Pennsylvania.

Wes had been my manager—but really more friend—for the past ten years and had stuck by me, cleaning up my messes. Although his patience had understandably worn thin, he'd gladly extended me his childhood home for some rest and relaxation. "A time to read some scripts and think about what you really want," Wes had said as he'd pushed the keys into my hand back in Los Angeles.

In the fifteen-minute drive to the house, the sun began setting, lighting the trees on fire in varying degrees of red and orange. With the windows rolled down, I caught the scent of crisp autumn leaves in the cool wind and started to loosen up. I slowed at a stop sign and took in the sights around me. Oak-tree-lined streets. Homes decorated for Halloween with pumpkins and scarecrows. Kids riding their bikes in the dying twilight.

I pulled up to my temporary address, parking in front of a little two-story brick house, and gathered my stuff before heading into my makeshift home. Wes had mentioned his parents had moved down to Florida a couple of years ago, and he had taken the place over, renting it out, which explained why it was so barren, with beige walls and a few pieces of furniture.

I had just finished checking the house out, tossing my hat and duffel on the bed, when the doorbell rang. I opened the front door to a smiling woman. She appeared to be in her late fifties or early sixties, lines of gray streaking her dark hair, with a pair of square glasses over her light-blue eyes.

"Hi, I'm Pattie Hollinger. I live next door. Wes called and asked me to look in on you."

A moment of alarm passed before I answered. "Oh, you don't have to—"

"I made you a potato casserole. I figured you'd be famished and wouldn't know your way around to find anything." She held up a covered dish.

I tried to argue, but at that moment, my stomach decided to speak up in a loud growl. When she raised her eyebrow as if her point had been proven, I accepted the large glass container. "Thank you."

"Wes explained everything to me."

"Explained everything?"

"Don't worry." She tapped the side of her nose and winked. "I know you're here to hide out."

I reluctantly opened the door wider for Pattie to enter. Once inside, she took the casserole and headed right to the kitchen, knowing her way around. She pressed a few buttons and slid the food into the oven. "It has to be reheated for a few minutes."

I leaned against the counter, eyeing the woman. "So, Mrs. Hollinger, how do you know Wes?"

"Pattie," she corrected, waving her hands in the air. "I've known Wes for a long time. He and my son were good friends growing up and practically lived in my house. They were always getting into trouble," she said with a laugh as she rolled her eyes. "Once got suspended in high school for stealing a sign as a senior prank."

"Wes was like one of the family, huh?"

"Oh yes. That's why he called me." She pointed to the table. "Well, come on, have a seat." Setting a place at the table, she continued, "Listen, honey, I may know you're CJ Cunningham, but I'm not going to treat you any differently." She pushed me toward the chair. "No wild parties, no speeding around the neighborhood, no big-time celebrity act. Got it?"

I blinked, taken aback by her motherly tone. "Right, yeah, of course." I sat down and looked up at her. "And since I'm not a big-time celebrity, can you call me Chris?"

She patted my shoulder, and I surprised myself by enjoying the touch. My relationship with my own mother was nonexistent, but Pattie seemed to slide so easily into the role. Even if it was only for a dinner. She scooped me out a big serving of the potato casserole, and I dug in, scarfing down the mix of cheesy hash browns and crunchy flakes.

"This is so good," I told her between bites.

"I'm glad you like it." She fixed her glasses on her nose. "I'll leave you to get settled, but let me know if you need anything."

I nodded, my mouth full.

"You're welcome to come on over whenever." She waved and saw herself out of the house.

After I finished another helping of the casserole, I cleaned up the kitchen and trudged upstairs to the bedroom.

I threw myself on the bed, my eyes on the ceiling as I thought back to earlier in the day. My work had taken me all over the world, and I'd met lots of people, but fame was insular. Especially in LA. Once a person "made it," there really wasn't anywhere else for them to go. I only ever saw the same people, worked within the Hollywood sphere of actors, directors, and producers. It wasn't often I could meet someone who truly didn't care that I was CJ Cunningham.

I didn't know what it was about Bronte—as if there was something inside me that knew I needed something inside her —that excited me so much. A kind of dangerous, heart-stuttering excitement. I'd never experienced it before.

And probably never would again.

CHAPTER FOUR

Bronte

My cell phone rang as I changed pajamas, and the name on the screen had my pacing the floor. Up until that moment, I could pretend the earlier episode with Chris hadn't happened, but now with the blaring trill of the incoming call, I had to face it.

At first, I'd only wanted to comfort the man who looked so miserable, but then he'd tipped his hat back and I'd caught sight of him. His deep brown eyes, aged, and filled with something I didn't understand yet desperately wanted to. Beneath all the dark scruff was a mouth that seemed a tad too big for his face, and when he'd smiled, it'd been familiar in a way I hadn't been able to quite put my finger on. Even after only that short time together, I couldn't deny the instant and unsettling attraction to him. But I wasn't a romantic. I was a realist, and I certainly didn't believe in love, or even lust, at first sight. Which was why I was amazed to find myself so unable to ignore Chris.

With his straggly hair and flannel shirt, he was sort of sexy. In the lumberjack kind of way. And I'd wanted to kiss him. Damn, had I wanted to kiss him. I wanted to feel the rough hair of his beard, know the taste of his lips, and memorize the look in his eyes right before he leaned into me.

I'd been close to kissing him. Too close.

Technically, I hadn't cheated, but there was a nagging tug deep down as if I'd crossed a line I wasn't supposed to.

But what was it?

When I'd touched his hand?

When we'd sat close, heads bent together, whispering?

When I'd accidentally-on-purpose brushed my hand against his thigh?

Fortunately, I would never see him again, so there was no chance of a repeat performance. Chris was a blip on the radar, a fleeting memory, while Hunter was a reality currently on the other end of the phone call.

I answered with a nervous twitch. "Hi, Hunt."

"Brontosaurus! How are you?"

I forced a smile even though he couldn't see it. "Good. How was your weekend?"

"Busy. I'm sorry I couldn't pick you up from the airport. I couldn't get out there tonight with all this work."

"I know. I know." I picked at my cotton pants. "Did you make any headway on that bill?"

"Yeah." He sighed. "I'm exhausted, but I don't want to talk about that. I want to talk about you. I miss you."

"I miss you too," I said, although I wasn't one hundred percent sure if I missed my boyfriend or the idea of him.

"When are you going to come visit me?"

I flopped onto my bed. "When are you going to come visit *me*? If you'd picked me up tonight, you could've stayed over."

"Bronte." He only ever used my real name when he was annoyed. "I told you I was sorry. There's nothing I can do about my schedule. If you'd move in with me, then—"

"I thought you wanted to talk about how much you miss me, not argue about moving."

"It's part of the same conversation. I miss you, and I want

you to move in with me. I don't want to argue about it. I want you to say yes."

"You can't expect me to pick up and move," I said with a huff.

"Why not? It's not like I'm asking you to move to another state. It's an hour and a half away."

"Because I like living here, and I don't want to leave my job."

"You can teach anywhere."

"And what about you?" I swiped my arm through the air, proving a point to the empty room. "You can be a lawyer anywhere."

"Come on, Bronte. You know that's not true. I've worked too hard to get where I am. I'm not going to give up my position here."

"And I'm not going to give up my kids."

He snorted. "Like they know the difference."

I shot up ramrod straight, Hulk-level anger radiating from me. "Don't say that."

"I'm only telling you how I feel."

"And I'm telling you, you're acting like an asshole."

"I'm sorry. I didn't mean it." He let out an audible breath. "I'm frustrated that we keep having the same conversation all the time. I love you and want you with me."

"I'm frustrated too," I said. Hunter knew all the buttons to push to make me feel bad, and after what happened with Chris, guilt weighed heavy on my heart, but I didn't have it in me to play the patient and understanding girlfriend tonight. "I'm pretty beat. I think I'm going to go to bed."

"I'll talk to you tomorrow."

"Okay, night." I hung up and stalked into the bathroom to brush my teeth and wash my face before crawling into bed with the book I'd bought at the airport. It was a rather bland memoir of a female human rights activist. I got a few chapters in before falling asleep with the lights still on.

I dreamed about the beach. Lying on the warm sand with the water lapping at my feet while a man hovered above me. His taut, muscular arms boxed me in as he caressed my jaw, throat, and collarbone with his lips. The air was thick with heat, our bare skin slick, sliding along each other in a tease of what was to come. I combed my fingers into the man's hair, pulling his mouth up to mine so I could finally see into his eyes.

It was Chris.

And I woke with a start, my heart racing and skin tingling. It had been a few weeks since I'd seen Hunter, and even longer since I'd been satisfied by him. The sky was still dark outside my bedroom window as I reached over to shut off the light and pull the comforter higher up my shoulders. Under the covers, I found the aching spot between my legs with my fingers while my brain conjured up the image of Chris, picking up where my dream left off. Whether it was right or wrong, he made me feel good, and I wasn't ready to forget it quite yet.

———

My alarm sounded at six o'clock, and I blindly reached out to silence it. After a few minutes of hiding under the sheets, I stretched out my arms and legs, teasing some life into my limbs before slinking off into the bathroom. My morning routine was efficient and never-changing. Brush teeth, shower, dress, makeup, hair, coffee, car.

Mrs. Soto, another special education teacher from down the hall, knocked on the doorframe before entering my room. "Morning."

"Hey, Rach. Brought a goodie?" I tipped my chin to the small brown bag Rachel held.

"It was buy one, get one." She handed me the bag containing a donut with orange icing and black sprinkles. "How was your trip?"

"Good," I mumbled around a bite. "We mostly hung out at my friend's house, but we went out to eat and had a spa day."

Rachel slumped into a seat at one of the kids' desks. "That sounds nice."

"Mm-hmm. I got a chocolate wrap."

"A what?"

"Like a mud wrap, but chocolate." I licked icing from my finger. "It was the best and worst way to waste chocolate."

"Oh yeah? Did you waste any of the chocolate with Hunter?" She waggled her eyebrows twice, a lewd smile slanting across her face, but I only wiped my hands of donut crumbs before pulling up a file on my computer to print. "What does that mean? You guys arguing again?"

Again. It was all so stupid.

She sucked air through her teeth. "Remind me how long you've been together."

I did the mental math. "About eight years, on and off. You'd think he'd have learned by now I'm a homebody." When Rachel offered a sympathetic smile, I continued, "Did I ever tell you he was in a frat?"

At her horrified face, I laughed. "I know. He was the stereo-typical college guy with the polo and sunglasses, but there was something about him. He was older, charismatic, smart. Everybody on campus loved him." I blinked away the memories and glanced at my friend with a shrug. "Back then, my choices seemed so obvious. But now, I'm not so sure."

"You? Not sure?" She pointed a long finger at me. "Has the

left side of your brain stopped working? Should I make a quick Excel spreadsheet for you?"

I smiled despite myself. "No, I'm good."

"Do you have an IEP today?" she asked as I grabbed the stack of papers from the printer and stapled together.

"Meeting's at two."

"Still coming to the gym tonight?"

"Yep."

We both stood as loud screeches and a stampede of footsteps sounded outside. Time for the day to begin.

It was after four thirty when I finally left school and headed home to change into some workout gear, barely making it to the gym in time for the dance cardio class I attended with Rachel. After an hour of sweating and swearing at her for making fun of my clumsiness, I met my mom and sister for dinner.

Shelley pointed to my sweat-slicked hair. "Looking good, Bean."

In turn, she nodded at Shelley's pregnant belly. "You too. Where's Mom?"

"She was at a doctor's appointment with Dad. Should be here soon, though." Right then, Shelley's phone rang. "Speak of the devil. Hey, Mom," she said into the phone. "Oh, okay... Well, how did it go?" I leaned across the table, trying to listen in, as my sister replied, "That's because he eats all that garbage. And you know he sneaks cigarettes when he's at school."

Bronte mouthed "What happened?" at my sister, but she waved me off.

"Okay, I guess we'll see you this weekend, then. Bye."

"What did she say?"

Shelley dropped her phone into her purse. "They're sending Dad for an EKG."

I shook my head and grabbed my own cell phone to text Gem, Laney, and Sam a quick message about my dad's test. I'd need their positive energy. "Between the smoking and his diet, I'm surprised he hasn't had problems earlier."

"I know. And he doesn't get any exercise. He needs to get out, start taking walks." Shelley stood up to go to the counter to order. "Mom said she's making dinner Saturday night."

Almost immediately, the girls responded to my text with good luck emojis, and I put my phone away to follow Shelley. We ordered then stopped for drinks and napkins before returning to our seats with trays of burritos. Shelley popped a tortilla chip into her mouth. "Are you going to bring Hunter along?"

"I'll see if he can come," I said, and she made a face. *That* face. "What?"

"I think...I..."

"What?"

She lifted one shrewd eyebrow. "What's the point of being together if you aren't together? He's over there, you're here, and it's weird—"

"Stop."

"You guys fall into this same pattern over and over again."

I opened the aluminum foil of my burrito with an irritated flick of my wrist. "We're working it out, okay?"

"Fine," she relented. "But I'll be shocked if he shows up on Saturday, that's all."

I eyed my sister, who made another face then took a gigantic bite of her burrito.

CHAPTER FIVE

Bronte

Saturday night at the Hollinger house was raucous, but it always was when the whole gang got together. Hunter and I were the last to arrive, with Zoe opening the door to us.

"Aunt Bean!" she squawked, and I picked up my four-year-old niece, blowing raspberries on her neck before placing her back down. We walked hand in hand into the living room, Hunter trailing behind, sidestepping children's shoes and jackets.

It was a minefield. Toys and bodies strewn everywhere.

Zoe dragged me over to a very small princess table with a purple tea set on top. Tommy had his legs shoved underneath.

I grinned at my brother-in-law. "How's the food?"

"Cookies are a bit stale," he said, knocking the plastic chocolate chip cookie on the table. He disentangled himself from his seat to kiss my cheek, then shook Hunter's hand. We exchanged a few pleasantries before Zoe yanked her dad back down to his seat. His tea was getting cold.

A few more steps, and we found my dad and Matty sculpting figurines with Play-Doh. When my father started to stand, I held out my hand. "Don't get up, Dad. Hi, Matty."

My nephew held up a green lump. "It's Nuwse Wached."

"Who?" Hunter asked.

"Nuwse Wached and McMuwphy," he repeated, picking up a bluish figure.

"Nurse Ratched? McMurphy? Dad," I chided, "are you teaching him *One Flew Over the Cuckoo's Nest*?"

He fixed his wire-rimmed glasses more firmly on his nose. "I might be."

"He's three!"

"Never too young to hear a good story."

I scoffed then greeted my brother, who sat with his oldest son, Caleb, watching football highlights on ESPN. I high-fived both of them and headed for the staircase leading upstairs. Luke sat on the bottom step, rocking back and forth, holding some kind of gaming system in his lap.

"Hi, Luke." I knelt down, attempting to meet his gaze. "How are you?" He mumbled something under his breath. "How was school this week?" He lifted his eyes ever so slightly in my direction. "Remember Hunter?"

Hunter waved. "How's it going?"

Amanda, my sister-in-law, made her way down the steps. "Luke, honey, I think it's time you put that away." He didn't move, and she held out her palm. "All done."

"All done," he repeated evenly as he handed over the game.

Amanda let out a breath, her shoulders drooping, before facing me and Hunter with a tired smile. "How are you guys?"

"Good," I said. "How are you?"

She sighed. "It's been a rough week. Still having a hard time transitioning."

"First grade is a lot different from kindergarten." I curled my arm around her shoulders. "Anytime you need a break, you know you can call me, right? Let's go see if they need help in the kitchen. Come on, Luke."

"Come on," Luke repeated. "Come on." He dragged out the

last word as he followed us to the kitchen, where Shelley pulled some plates from a cupboard.

"Tell everyone dinner's ready," my mom called from outside.

"Dinner's ready!" Shelley shouted practically in my ear.

I shoved her shoulder, but before we could fight, the family herd charged out to the backyard, sitting down at two picnic tables pushed together. I greeted my mom with a hug and a kiss then nudged Hunter forward to do the same.

"What's that?" I pointed at the casserole dish.

"Whole wheat vegetable lasagna. Don't tell your father," she whispered as she waved to someone behind my back. "There you are! I was about to come get you."

I glanced over my shoulder to see whom my mother was talking to.

A mirage.

A hallucination.

A dream.

I pinched myself. Nope, it was real. *He* was real. And walking toward me.

The moment Chris's eyes met mine, there was a slight hitch in his step, but my mom didn't notice as she ushered him toward the family.

"Come meet everybody." Starting with my dad, she gestured around the table. "You know Steven already. This is Shelley and her husband, Thomas, and Zoe. Zoe, honey, you need to sit on your bottom, not on your feet. And my son, Fitzgerald, he's the one I told you about."

"What?" Fitz asked, poking his head around Mom's shoulder. "What are you saying about me?"

I watched in shock as my mother explained how Wes, Fitz's old friend, had set up Chris in the house next door.

"Man, I haven't talked to him in a while," Fitz said. "I've been so busy. How's he doing?"

Chris's eyes flickered to mine before he answered. "He's doing good. I heard you two were pretty tight back in the day."

"That we were." Fitz grinned impishly then introduced his family. "This is my wife, Amanda, and those three running around are Caleb, Luke, and Matthew. Boys, time to eat." He whistled through his teeth. "Let's go." The three brothers made their way to the table with Luke lagging behind, flapping his hands back and forth.

Mom finally turned to me, and I froze as Chris's gaze wandered over my face as if he had discovered some long-lost artifact. "And this is my youngest—"

"Bronte." He smiled, and I lost my breath. Lost my mind.

"You know each other?" Mom asked.

"We were on the same plane coming back from Chicago," he said, closing the gap between us. "I can't believe it."

Hunter held out his hand. "What a small world. I didn't catch your name."

Chris stared down at his hand for a few moments before shaking it. "Chris."

Hunter pulled his hand away and dropped it around my shoulders. "Chris, nice to meet you. I'm Bronte's boyfriend, Hunter."

My eyes darted between the two men. Hunter, tall and clean-cut in his crisp button-down sweater and perfectly styled crew cut, next to Chris, only a couple inches taller than my own five foot seven inches. With his shaggy hair, scruffy beard, and dark clothes, Chris and Hunter couldn't be more different.

Conventional wisdom would say I belonged with Hunter. He was the model boyfriend by most standards—handsome, good job, nice family. Yet, when I considered Chris, I didn't care about any of that. The mental checklist I'd made for the "right guy" didn't have any boxes for mysterious brown eyes, alluring charm, or a mouth I couldn't stop staring at. There was nothing about Chris that I should have been attracted to. I barely knew him, and yet...

God, I wanted to kiss those lips. Lips that were slightly turned down into a frown now.

I met Chris's gaze for only a fraction of a second before his eyes moved past me as he cleared his throat. "Well, it's nice to meet everybody. I'm gonna get going."

Mom shook her head. "I thought you would eat dinner with us."

"I don't want to impose."

I was rooted to the ground as my dad indicated an open spot next to him. "Nonsense. We have enough to feed an army. Have a seat."

Chris sat down, and I couldn't believe this was happening. It couldn't be any worse.

Until my mom rubbed his back, smiling warmly at him.

And it was officially way worse.

Chris was welcomed into the family, and what I thought was a slight fissure in my relationship with Hunter had the potential to develop into a huge chasm.

"Come on, Brontosaurus." Hunter tugged me into a seat next to him. "I'm starving."

"So, you're from Los Angeles, Chris?" Fitz asked as he dug into the asparagus.

"Not originally, no. I'm from Indiana."

"Oh, yeah?" Dad bristled when Mom took the butter dish out of his hands. "Where in Indiana? I have a cousin in Indianapolis."

"I'm from Fort Wayne."

Fitz intercepted Matty's cup before juice spilled all over the table, his eyes on Chris. "What are you doing over here?"

I stopped myself from turning to the opposite end of the table as I forked salad onto my plate, my cheeks heating up from the glances I knew Chris threw my way.

"Just...getting away for a while."

"Who'd want to get away from LA?" Hunter said. "Big city, nice weather, beautiful people, bet it's amazing."

"Not always," Chris mumbled.

Hunter let out a skeptical huff, one which always irritated me. I chanced a peek up, my eyes locking on Chris's. His gaze wavered between me and my boyfriend before finally settling back on me, heavy yet guarded.

Tommy, thankfully, called Chris's attention away with a question. "What do you do?"

"I'm, um, in the entertainment industry."

"You seem kind of familiar," Amanda said, trying to settle Luke.

Shelley pointed her fork in Chris's direction. "Yeah, you do."

He shook his head, yanking his hat lower, clearly uncomfortable. I knew how awkward it was to be under examination by the whole family.

"Do you know anybody famous?" Shelley asked.

Mom thumped her water glass on the table. "Shell, come on. Not everyone who lives in California is famous."

Dad rapped his knuckles on the table twice. "Let's forget about the Hollinger Inquisition for now and let Chris eat, shall we? Caleb, tell everybody about your soccer game today."

And like that, said inquisition was over. The conversation never ended, though, as everyone spoke over one another, chatting about school, Halloween costumes, the overgrown rosebushes, pumpkin picking, and the new swing set Grampy set up at the back of the yard.

"Bean, remember when you broke your arm?" Fitz asked, elbowing Matty. "Ask Aunt Bean how she broke her arm."

"Aunt Bean, how you bweak ya awm?"

I leaned over as if imparting a secret to him. "I was on the swing, and your daddy pushed me."

Fitz slapped the table with a guffaw. "Liar."

"You definitely pushed me."

"I did not. You jumped off."

"You convinced me I could fly, and Shelley counted to three —" I pointed at my sister for backup, but the traitor only sipped at her water. "—but before she got to three, you pushed me off."

"You did have a vivid imagination, Beanie Baby," Dad piped up. "I remember you spent an entire day in the tub one time, thinking it would make you a mermaid."

"Never did work," I said as Zoe climbed into my lap.

"Aunt Bean, I'm a mermaid."

"You are? Where're your fins?"

She wiggled her feet. "Right here."

I tickled her toes and sides, hugging her close. "Who's the prettiest girl in the world?"

Zoe grinned ear to ear. "Aunt Bean is!"

"Yes." I kissed her cheeks, then stage-whispered, "Good answer." I'd been training her to say that for quite a while now and earned a few laughs, including one from Chris. Not that I had taken much notice.

"All right," Mom said with a clap of her hands for every-one's attention. "Guess what I bought today?"

I risked yet another glance in Chris's direction and found him staring at me as guesses rang out from my niece and neph-ews. Something about s'mores and a fire pit was mentioned, but I couldn't grasp the conversation, feeling as though I was in a vortex with Chris. Only him and those dark, unnerving eyes, peering straight into me.

What were the possible odds that in all of the towns in America, he would show up in mine? Math was never my strong suit, but I could guess they were pretty slim. Then again, the odds I would pass out from the effects of high blood pressure were rising by the second.

The sky had darkened, and the temperature dropped, ushering in a cold breeze. I stepped inside the house to grab a hoodie, and as I pushed my head through, Chris appeared in front of me.

"Hi."

"Hey." I tugged the sweatshirt down, hoping my insides would stay inside and not be hurled at his feet.

"So, Bean, is it?" He tilted his head, folding his arms over his chest. "I don't believe we've ever met." When I didn't say anything, he jutted a stubborn chin out at me. "You lied to me."

The hint of anger in his voice spurred my indignation, pushing the nausea aside. "My name is Bronte. I live in Allentown, Pennsylvania. My parents are Steve and Pattie Hollinger. I have two siblings, one niece, and three nephews, with one on the way. I'm a special education teacher, and I met you on a plane coming back from a long weekend in Chicago. Did I miss anything?"

"The part about you having a boyfriend. It's a pretty big thing to forget to tell someone. Especially when—"

"Nothing happened."

He took one step closer. "Yeah, but—"

"No." I cut him off, stepping back with heavy feet. I didn't want to hear him say what I suspected, that he felt this pull too.

Until tonight, I had hoped it was my imagination getting

the best of me, that I'd somehow concocted Chris's magnetism. But no. Whatever it was about him that drew me to him, our attraction was real, and hadn't faded since our first meeting.

He narrowed his eyes, crushing the bill of his baseball hat between his hands. "So, you're going to ignore it?"

"I didn't mean to give you the wrong impression."

His eyebrows shot up, disappearing under his hair. "The wrong impression? You're telling me—"

Voices filtered in from the kitchen, and I trained my eyes in their direction. "We can't talk about this now. I can't do this."

I brushed by him, apologizing under my breath, and nearly ran to the backyard. With the fire burning bright, the kids roasted marshmallows, while Shelley ate them straight out of the bag. I took a seat next to her and occupied myself by making a s'more.

Chris sauntered back outside a minute later, flanked by my brother and mother. "I'm going to head home." I kept my eyes glued to the marshmallow I held over the fire as Chris said, "Thanks for letting me crash your dinner, Steve."

"You're welcome anytime," Dad said in his usual friendly tone.

Then after a few seconds, in which I tried my best not to look up, Chris finally took his leave, saying, "It was nice meeting everybody."

I was so busy tuning him out I didn't feel Hunter place his arm on the back of my chair. "You almost ready to go?"

I ignored the question.

CHAPTER SIX

Chris

I didn't believe in fate or destiny. People weren't born sinners or saints; they were made, formed not by some heavenly hand but by individual choice and personal responsibility.

That was why seeing Bronte tonight was some insane, serendipitous shit. For the second time in a matter of days, fate had gone and plunked her down right in front of me, only to slap me in the face with her jerk-off boyfriend. What kind of Alanis Morrisette irony was that?

I couldn't have gotten out of the Hollingers' house any faster.

"You mind if I talk to you a minute?"

I startled, not having heard Fitz sidle up to me. I shook my head, although I didn't really have a choice since Fitz was already next to me. "What's up?"

We stopped outside of my back door, and Fitz lowered his voice. "Look, Wes and I go way back. I know he works with a pretty big actor." I didn't acknowledge anything, and he continued, "I don't care one way or another who you are, but what exactly are you doing here?"

What was with this family? How did they all know? "Wes

said nobody would bother with me here. I could lie low for a while."

His eyes narrowed slightly as if deciding whether I was a problem or not. Finally, he relaxed. "Nobody else knows?"

"Your mom."

Nodding, he stuck his hands in his pockets. "I guess you can tell my family is pretty—"

"Loud?"

"Yeah, that's one way to put it." He chuckled. "Piece of advice, though. Stay away from Shelley if you can. She's the motormouth in the family."

"You think she suspects anything?"

"Hard to say. But my wife..." He squinted in thought. "Mandy really liked that James Dean movie you did." As if he had a sudden thought, he held his hands up. "I mean, not to say I don't like it. It's... I like movies with stuff that blows up, you know? No offense."

I laughed and gave Fitz a friendly slap on the back. "None taken."

We shook hands, and he pointed his thumb back to his parents' backyard. "I'll try to keep everybody off the scent."

"I'd appreciate it," I said and opened my screen door.

"And oh, CJ, I mean, Chris. Sorry. What's up with you and my sister?"

I pivoted back, one leg already inside the house. "Huh?"

"You and Bean."

"Nothing," I said quickly. Maybe too quickly. "We sat next to each other coming back from Chicago. We talked. That's it."

"That's it?"

I needed to work on my acting skills because I was dying under Fitz's big-brother stare. "Yeah, why?"

"Felt like there was some weird tension going on there or something."

I shrugged it off with a hasty goodbye. No sense in continuing the act when I was doing a shit job of it.

———

The next morning, I woke up relatively early, changed into sweats, and took a ride to a sporting goods store where I purchased some workout equipment. Nothing major, a jump rope and dumbbells, enough to try to lose the weight I'd put on the last few months. At 5'9", I was already at a slight disadvantage compared to some of the guys in my acting bracket—the ones who were over six feet with muscles on muscles, they were the ones who scored the huge deals for superhero movies—and no one was going to hire me with a beer belly.

After trying out my new purchases, I showered, changed, and headed outside with my guitar. The neighborhood was quiet, being late Sunday morning, and I positioned myself on a freestanding hammock, strumming away on my guitar until Pattie appeared.

"That sounds wonderful, Chris."

"I was only fooling around." I noted she was dressed in a skirt and jacket. "You look nice. Are you headed out somewhere?"

"We just got back from church."

Church.

That word alone still made my teeth snap together, although she didn't seem to notice, continuing, "I make brunch every Sunday, but no one could make it today. Seems like they all got enough of one another last night. Are you interested in something to eat? I have bacon and eggs, bagels, fruit?"

I really liked Mr. and Mrs. Hollinger and was happy to

make some friends here. Even if the Bronte connection was weird and fraught with rejection. "If you don't mind."

"Of course not."

I set my guitar in the house before taking the short walk next door.

Steven stood at the counter, in front of the coffee machine. "Chris, how are you today? Do you want a cup?"

"Sure."

He handed me a mug as Pattie placed a dish in front of me. "Help yourself. We don't serve in this house."

With my plate piled high, I learned my neighbors had met while Steven was earning his PhD and Pattie had worked at the college library. They asked me a few questions about Indiana and how it compared to Pennsylvania, taking genuine interest in anything I had to say. It was nice they cared so much and, even more, humbling.

After we finished eating, they ushered me into the living room, where I perused the enormous bookshelf, overflowing with worn paperbacks. "Did you read all these?" I asked, thumbing through a few.

"Between the whole family, they've all been read," Pattie answered. "Probably a few times over."

Steven motioned to the book in my hand. "Ah, that one's my favorite."

I opened the cover of *The Great Gatsby*. "Bronte told me you named Fitz after the author?"

He nodded.

"Do you mind if I borrow it?"

"Not at all."

I moved on to admiring the family photos along the wall, in varying degrees of ages and number of people. I pointed to a particularly awkward school picture of Bronte with braces and a short bowl cut. "Why Bean?"

Pattie found a photo album and held it open, flipping through pictures so I could see. Fitz, tall and athletic, in football and baseball uniforms. Shelley, with auburn hair, singing on a stage and smiling in the middle of a group of cheerleaders. And, finally, Bronte, posing with Minnie Mouse at Disney World. "Fitz is the jock, Shelley's the performer, and Bronte is our bean pole. All elbows and chicken legs."

"Still is." Steven curled his arm around his wife's waist. "Skinny as a bean pole. Takes after her mom."

I smiled when Pattie flipped to a picture of Bronte in a cast and on crutches. "I think that's when she tried to skateboard."

I took the album from her hands to page through it. Bronte's whole life was laid out for me from kindergarten to college graduation, but instead of answering any of my questions about her, it only raised more.

Like, did she ever master skateboarding? Did she always want to be a teacher? What was it like to grow up in this family, in this support system?

Passing the album back to Pattie, I shook the thoughts from my head.

I couldn't wonder about Bronte. I couldn't daydream about her. I couldn't give in to the fantasy of her—that she was somehow the woman for me—because she wasn't. She had a boyfriend, a whole life here.

And I was only passing through.

"I'm going to head out."

"Make sure you come back." Steven walked me to the door, tapping the book in my hand. "I want to hear what you think."

"I will. Thanks."

He slapped me once more on the back and grinned. "Good to have you around."

CHAPTER SEVEN

Bronte

My favorite time of year was fall. I loved the cool nip in the air, the reds and oranges of the trees, and the ever-present smell of pumpkin spice everything. I only lived ten minutes from my parents and had a ritual of going to my favorite hole-in-the-wall coffee shop a few blocks from their house on my way to the park, where I'd find a bench to read or get some work done while soaking up vitamin D with a view.

It was Wednesday afternoon, and the place was relatively quiet, with a handful of people scattered among the mismatched tables and chairs. I stepped up to the counter, greeted Kira, the surly barista, and perused the blackboard menu above my head, as if I didn't already know what I was going to get.

"What'd you like?" Kira asked, as if *she* didn't already know the answer.

"Medium cinnamon pumpkin latte with skim milk, please. To go."

As usual, Kira rolled her eyes, muttering under her breath about how basic I was as she made the drink. This was the game we played—Kira pretending she didn't kind of like me, and me continually leaving a big tip until she gave in. I laughed to myself, shaking my head. I—

Chris?

There was Chris.

I'd know that beard anywhere. And hands, for that matter. Golden skin with blunt fingertips, the slightly crooked pinkie finger on his right hand.

He was hidden in the corner with a rumpled beanie over his head, and with his attention focused on a book, I could blatantly ogle him. He was turned slightly in his chair, kind of curled up into himself. His brow furrowed in concentration as his lips moved ever so slightly, reading to himself, while his fingers absently played with the upper corner of the page.

I was tempted to take a picture. A hot guy reading in public was like spotting a wolf in the wild.

Instead of reaching for my phone, I loosened the scarf around my neck, a tad overheated. It'd been a few days since he'd been sprung on me at my parents' home, but I hadn't forgotten what it was like to see him sitting next to my dad, talking like they'd known each other for years.

That was the thing with Chris. It *was* like he'd been around for years. Though unsettling, that thought wasn't completely unwelcome. Especially when he pulled at his bottom lip with his thumb and index finger.

"Bronte!" Kira called out, even though I stood only two feet to the left. Out of the corner of my eye, I saw Chris's head snap up, and my plans for studying him from a distance were dashed. I had to say something now. But what? What did you say to the guy who knocked your world off its axis?

I grabbed the coffee, took a deep breath, and started in Chris's direction, greeting him with a small wave. "Hey."

He tilted his head to the side, his eyes briefly drifting down my body. "Fancy meeting you here."

There was a definite pattern forming between us, and I nodded. "Yeah, coincidental."

"Is it, though?" he asked after three long seconds and then kicked out the chair in front of me with his foot. When I didn't move, he raised his eyebrows in a dare.

Possessed by those eyebrows, I plunked down and lifted the lid of my drink. "What's that supposed to mean?"

He leaned over, leveling me with a playful gaze that had me momentarily stunned. "We keep having these 'coincidences.' It makes me think they aren't so coincidental after all."

I cleared my throat and shifted in my seat, keenly aware of how close we were as I pursed my lips and blew across the top of my coffee. His eyes dropped to my mouth while steam curled between us and didn't move until I sipped my drink and placed it back down on the table. When his eyes finally found their way back up to mine, they were heated with something much more than a friendly gaze.

"I have a boyfriend."

"So you've said."

Yet here I sat across from Chris, who was very much not my boyfriend.

"What's with this?"

"What?"

He pressed his thumb lightly against the inside of my left eyebrow. "This little crease. What are you thinking about?"

Unwrapping my scarf completely from around my neck, I sat all the way back in my chair, putting much-needed space between us to clear my head and cool off. Avoiding the truth of what I was really thinking—that I'd like to feel the press of his thumb somewhere else—I yanked a book from my purse to show it to him. It was a thin textbook on classroom behavior strategies. "Homework."

He swiped a hand over his dubious smile. "Sure."

"What are you reading?" I asked, and he held up the book. "*Slaughterhouse-Five*. Really?"

"Yeah. Now what's this face for?"

I sipped my coffee. "You don't strike me as a Vonnegut fan."

"Your dad suggested it. He's helping me with a quest."

"Quest?"

His face filled with worry as if he were going to slay a dragon. "I'm trying to read every book on your parents' bookshelves."

There were hundreds of books stacked up on all those shelves. That was one hell of a dragon. "How many have you gotten through so far?"

"This'll be number two." He grinned. "Slow and steady wins the race," he said, his foot moving next to mine, his leg resting along my own.

"Why is it so hard for me to believe you're the slow and steady type?"

He took off his beanie to run a hand over his wavy hair then tugged it back down. "I'm not usually. But I could be."

There was more to those two sentences than their face value. He wasn't flirting or playing anymore. His voice was deep yet soft, and he spread out the words like a promise.

He could be slow and steady.

His dark eyes, the color of his coffee, pinned me in place as he waited patiently for me to collect my scattered thoughts.

When I finally gathered them all together, they told me to flee. "Well, I gotta go."

"You gotta go?" The spell was broken, and he leaned back. "Where?"

"I've got to read this before my online class tonight," I said, slinging my book in my purse before wrapping my scarf around my neck. I didn't usually procrastinate like this.

"What was that?"

I stopped in the middle of looping my purse over my shoulder. I hadn't realized I'd said that out loud. "Nothing." Only that I never waited so long to do my homework. I was a get-it-done-as-soon-as-it-was-assigned student, not the push-it-off-until-tomorrow kind I had turned into lately.

"I guess I'll see you Saturday, then?" he said.

"Saturday?"

"Luke's birthday party."

I should have known. My mom mentioned Chris had been spending a lot of time at their house, but it never occurred to me that I'd be seeing him so often. How was I supposed to forget him when he hung around my favorite coffee shop and family dinners?

Leaping up from my chair, I noisily pushed it in to the table and stepped backward. "Yeah, I guess so."

He licked his lips and unleashed a wicked smile. "Have a good day, Bronte."

His book was open, yet his eyes were on me, and the heat in them had my heart racing faster than my feet as I practically sprinted out of there.

Chris was trouble with a capital T, and I was capital T tempted to give in. But if I did, my whole world would change, and I had never been good with change.

CHAPTER EIGHT

Chris

Saturday afternoon, I found myself outside on the hammock with my guitar once again, strumming a familiar tune, "Amazing Grace." It was one of the first songs I'd learned, one I'd often played at church. Then again, most of the songs I had played back then were church songs. The others, the popular tunes I'd taught myself, I only played when no one else could hear. Funny that now no one else was around, I was back to playing those old hymns.

Something rustled to my left, and I glanced up to find Luke standing in the Hollingers' yard, staring at me.

"Hey, Luke. Happy birthday." When he didn't move, I went back to playing.

After a few minutes, I looked up again when I heard leaves crunching under slight steps. Luke was slowly crossing the yard to me, his eyes locked on my fingers as they glided over the strings. I stopped strumming when he stood about a foot away. "So, how old are you today? Seven?"

No answer.

"Seventeen, then. Got your driver's license and everything, huh? Going to go out and cause some trouble?"

Luke only stared at the instrument in my hands.

"Interested in the guitar?"

Nothing.

"Do you want me to play something for you?"

Finally, his eyes flickered from the guitar to me and back.

"I'll take that as a yes. What do you want to hear?" I flipped through my mental rolodex of songs. Admittedly, it was not very long. I was an actor not a musician, but I could play something for Luke. "You like the Beatles?"

I began "Blackbird," and Luke's eyes got a bit brighter, his fingers settled from their slight flapping. As I sang, he tilted his head forward, intent on listening, although as soon as the song was over, he started shuffling.

"Do you want to hear it again?" I asked.

He nodded.

"All right." I held out my hand, motioning him over. "But this time, do you want to stand next to me? You can help me play."

He followed my direction, a smile threatening his lips.

"You're a Paul McCartney fan, huh? Me too. Okay, buddy, do you want to hold the pick? Is it okay if I put my hands on yours?" I gently placed my fingers over Luke's so we could strum together.

With the help of my new friend, I began again, and some-time during the second chorus, Luke started humming, leaning in closer to me, almost allowing our shoulders to touch.

A noise sounded somewhere in front of me, but I ignored it, too caught up in the moment. Luke's voice was barely above a whisper, though his lips imitated every note I sang, and by the end, he was full-out smiling.

"That was great. Really, really great," I said, reaching a hand out to his shoulder.

He didn't shy away from the touch, and I finally looked up, away from Luke, my grin immediately dropping when I spied the entire Hollinger clan, mouths gaping open. I gently nudged Luke aside, handing him the guitar pick, and stood. "Uh, hey, everybody, we were..." My eyes drifted down to Luke, who'd taken to shuffling and flapping. "Jamming."

Fitz and Amanda scooped up Luke for a hug as Pattie walked over to me. "That was beautiful. I think we're all amazed, to say the least."

"It wasn't that big of a deal." I forced a laugh past the lump in my throat. "Everybody loves the Beatles."

Pattie rubbed my back. "Looks like it. Let's all go back inside. Time for cake. What do you think, Lukie-poo?"

Luke didn't answer, but his eyes did move over to the guitar in my hand.

"Maybe we can play again another day," I offered.

"'Nother day," he repeated.

Fitz patted his son's head and escorted him back to the yard as Pattie invited me over. "No encore necessary."

Everyone followed Pattie back inside except for Shelley and Bronte, and when I strolled over, zipping up my hoodie, Shelley angled her head, eyeing me suspiciously.

I greeted her with a wave, my nerves rattled by her stare.

"Hey." She pursed her lips, appearing as if she was about to give the game away but stopped when Zoe shouted something from inside the house. Shelley threw me one last raise of her brow over her shoulder as she ambled inside, leaving me and Bronte alone.

"Well, that was unexpected," she said, holding a half-eaten cookie in one hand.

"Yeah. Luke was—"

"You play the guitar."

I laughed at her accusatory tone. "Yeah."

"And you have a really good voice." She wielded the cookie at me. "Like, really good."

"Uh, thanks." I scratched the back of my head. The guitar and my voice had landed me my first big role in *The Travellers*, a made-for-TV movie about a band from the 1950s who time traveled to present-day. It was touted as *Back to the Future* meets *High School Musical* and spawned two sequels.

I only hoped the jig wasn't up. I was really starting to like it here, and I'd hate to have to go back home to Los Angeles if word got out about who I was. "Thanks. I guess."

We started back to the house, but Bronte's eyes stayed on me. "You were incredible."

I, for the first time in a very long time, felt myself blush at her compliment.

"Luke's on the autism spectrum. He's never like that with people he doesn't know."

"He liked the music, that's all."

"No." She shook her head, reaching her fingers out as if she wanted to touch my arm, but she stopped herself and dropped her hand. "We know he likes music, but that was different. He was communicating with you, looking you in the eyes. It's... I can't believe it."

I held the back door open for Bronte and, since I had no such qualms about being bold, briefly touched her back as she walked past me. I flattened my hand against her thin blue sweater and guided her into the dining room, where everyone gathered around the table. We settled next to each other in the corner as Steven lit the candles on the homemade cake in front of Luke and turned off the lights. All at once, the family started singing "Happy Birthday," and I glanced over at the woman next to me. Her eyes shone in the reflection of the lit candles, her dimples prominent in the shadows, and without thinking, I reached for my phone, snapping a picture.

"What're you doing?"

I positioned the phone toward Luke, surrounded by his brothers and parents as they helped him blow out the candles. "Taking pictures."

I snapped a few in quick succession before showing them to her. "They're really cute," she said. "Can you send them to me?"

I handed over my cell so she could plug her number into it, and I shouldn't have been so excited. But here I was, like a twelve-year-old with his first crush.

Pattie held out a piece of cake to Bronte. "Do you want to take a piece for Hunter?"

"No, that's okay."

I wasn't at all impressed by what I'd seen of Bronte's boyfriend so far, and I couldn't help but be curious about him. I tried to sound as nonchalant as possible when I asked, "Why isn't he here? He's missing out on good cake."

Bronte averted her eyes. "He lives in Harrisburg and works a lot of hours, so it's hard for him to find time to visit."

"But it's okay for her to go there all the time," Pattie mumbled under her breath. She evidently wasn't warm toward the guy, and I tried not to be too happy about it.

I forked a piece of cake into my mouth. "How long is the drive there?"

"An hour and a half on a good day. And speaking of," Bronte started, setting her piece of cake on the table, "I should get going." She said goodbye to each of her family members, and I waited for her to acknowledge me somehow, disappointed when all I got was a slight tilt of her chin over her shoulder. "See you guys later."

Pattie took Bronte's place beside me and helped herself to

the cake left on the table. "I love all my kids, but sometimes you want to kick them in the pants." Then she nudged my shoulders with hers, saying, "I'm so happy you're living next door. Steven loves having another boy in the house again."

I looped my arm around her. "I'm happy I'm here too."

CHAPTER NINE

Bronte

I plunked my head back on the headrest. I was stalled on I-78, stuck between a pickup truck with a slobbering dog hanging out of the passenger window staring at me and two young guys on my right side, who would randomly shout insults at the yet-to-be-seen accident clogging up the interstate.

My cell phone buzzed with a text message alert, and I picked it up from the cup holder, smiling when the picture of Luke popped up.

UNKNOWN NUMBER
This one is my favorite.

Caleb had his arms around both of his brothers, Luke was staring off into space, and Matty had a huge grin plastered across his face while he poked one finger in the cake.

My stomach gave in to a somersault knowing who was texting me. With my car parked for the foreseeable future, I typed out a message.

I think I'll frame it.

UNKNOWN NUMBER
Texting & driving? Rule-breaker.

I was on my way to see my boyfriend, not exactly the best time to send a flirtatious text back to another man. I saved his contact.

> Never. I'm not the rule-breaking kind. I'm stuck in traffic.

CHRIS

Well then. Something to keep you busy.

A few more pictures showed up.

> Thanks.

After about half an hour into the standstill, I sent my friends the **SOS** message to FaceTime. If I was going to live on this highway now, I at least needed some company. Laney and I were from Pennsylvania and had met Gem and Sam at the University of Pittsburgh, but now that we were all spread to the four corners of the country, we kept in touch daily with texts and occasional group FaceTimes.

Within a minute, their faces all appeared on my screen.

"What's up, buttercup?" Laney asked, her golden hair in its naturally curly state.

"I'm stuck in traffic and bored."

"You're going to see Hunter?" Sam asked, and from the AirPods and blue sky behind her, I assumed she was out for a walk.

"Yeah."

"So, everything's all right?" Laney asked.

"Mm-hmm. Yep. All good."

Gem kept her gaze on Willow as she wiped her baby's face with a cloth, deadpanning, "That didn't sound suspicious at all."

Sam snickered. "What's the problem?"

After a moment of gathering my courage, I said, "It's normal to be attracted to other people when you're in a relationship, right?"

Sam paused her movement, her face completely still as Gem stared straight at her camera, her eyes narrowed. Laney lifted her head. "Attracted?"

I swallowed thickly. "Yeah, that's normal, right? Tell me that's normal."

"It's, uh…" Gem repositioned Willow to her shoulder. "I mean, I think other guys besides Jason are cute, so yeah."

"What do you mean by attracted?" Sam asked. "Like, I think Chris Evans is hot—or, like, I want to find Chris Evans and fuck him?"

I rolled my eyes. I should have kept my mouth shut.

"What happened?" Laney asked, peering into her screen and thus into my soul, until I told my best friends the whole sordid tale, from meeting Chris on the plane to him singing with Luke mere hours ago.

Normally the one to get right down to it and not mince words, all Gem said was, "Oh," when I finished my story.

"Tell me this is normal," I said again. "To get butterflies from another person. They'll go away, right?"

Laney took the lead. "I think it comes down to who you want to be with. The butterflies may or may not go away, but if you're truly interested in this plane guy, then you shouldn't stay in a relationship you're not happy with."

Sam nodded. "Yeah, the longer you wait, the harder it'll be."

Finally, Gem piped up as Jason appeared behind her to take the baby. "I would take it as a bad sign if you're fantasizing about someone else." Jason's face blanched behind her, and he pivoted away with a comically big step. I would've laughed if I didn't want to cry when my friend continued, "If you're seriously attracted to—like, getting hot about someone else—I think that means it's time to have a conversation about breaking up with Hunter." She seemed excited by the prospect. "Are you fantasizing about plane guy?"

Traffic started moving, a perfect excuse to hang up. "Highway must be cleared. I gotta get driving. I'll text you guys later."

"Hey, don't think I didn't notice the evasion. You—"

I pressed the End Call button, a liar and a coward.

After finally making it to Harrisburg, I yanked my bags from the trunk and hoofed it to Hunter's condo. He only had one parking space, so I always had to find street parking. It was a pain in the ass.

Inside the condominium, I made my way up to the seventh floor, where I knocked a few times on Hunter's door. He opened it with a big smile on his face. "Brontosaurus!"

I gave him a quick kiss, and he grabbed my bags, towing me inside the apartment before slipping his arm around my waist to kiss me again. He tasted like beer, and I frowned, wiggling out of his grasp. "How many drinks have you had?"

"Only two."

I pretended he wasn't lying and headed to the bedroom, taking my bag into the bathroom to line my toiletries on the sink.

"Okay, four," he admitted when I refused to look at him. "I got bored waiting for you." He sagged into the doorframe and ran his index finger down my arm. "Are you hungry? I moved the reservation to eight."

I checked my watch, a thin rose-gold band with small diamonds around the face. It had been a gift from Hunter for my birthday last year, when we'd decided we'd give our relationship another try. "It's almost seven o'clock already, and I'm tired. Can we order in or something?"

He studied me for a moment, then gave in with a soft smile on his face. "Yeah, of course. Whatever you want. How about delivery from Sal's?"

An hour later, I dug into the pizza as Hunter put on a Phillies game, my mind wandering to Chris. I recalled how he bent his head so close to mine to talk on the plane. At my parents' house, when his eyes heated as he confronted me about Hunter. In the coffee shop, his fingers tugging on his lower lip.

Men's lips went wholly unappreciated in today's society, but Chris's mouth, with his full bottom lip and wicked curl on top, could turn anyone into worshippers. And I spent more minutes than I'd care to admit imagining how Chris would kiss. If he'd be slow with soft brushes or dive right in with his hands holding me in place. Soft or hard, languid licks or... I was fantasizing again.

Damn it.

Pushing away those daydreams, I prodded Hunter with my shoulder. "Are you coming for trick-or-treat?"

"When? Friday?"

I nodded.

"No, I have a work thing. A fundraiser."

I pulled off a chunk of my pizza crust. "Can't you skip it? You know Halloween is a big deal for my family."

He huffed quietly. "Everything's a big deal for your family."

"You don't have to sound so condescending," I said, scooting to the other end of the couch.

"I'm not condescending. I'm stating the facts. You guys celebrate every little thing. It's...a lot."

My skin got that tight, prickly sensation. It'd been

happening more and more lately when I was around him. "I feel like you don't care about being with my family."

"I do care, but I don't want to spend every second with them. Whenever I come to visit, we're always with them. If it's not someone's birthday, it's Flag Day, or Earth Day, or Bastille Day. It's a week at the beach or every holiday at your parents' house."

"You're generalizing."

"Okay." The single word dripped with sarcasm, and I snagged another piece of pizza to take into the bedroom. I would rather eat dinner alone than with him, but when I stood up, he held on to my wrist. "I'm sorry. That was... I didn't mean it."

With a heavy sigh, I fell back onto the couch. "I'd appreciate it if you made more of an effort to spend time in Allentown, with or without my family."

He took two deep breaths. "*I'd* appreciate it if you'd seriously consider moving here." His hazel eyes were contrite. "Please? And I'll see what I can do about this weekend." He offered his hand for a shake. "Deal?"

I couldn't stop my smile. He could be charming when he wanted to be, and I accepted his proffered hand. "Deal."

CHAPTER TEN

Chris

Growing up, I'd never been able to dress up as a vampire and knock on doors for candy. We weren't allowed to celebrate Halloween, so now that I had the chance, I wanted to do it right.

I'd bought a couple of plastic spiders to hang on white cotton that I'd spread over the brick to look like a web and stuck some fake tombstones in the yard. I didn't think it looked half-bad. For the candy, Pattie brought me to Costco, which was an adventure all on its own. Besides the bulk candy, I also came home with five pounds of frozen pierogis, mozzarella sticks, and I don't even know how many toilet paper rolls. I was set.

When Friday rolled around, I clicked on my porch light and excitedly greeted every trick-or-treater who came to my door. About an hour in, as I bent down to talk to yet another kid dressed as a dog from a show called *Paw Patrol*, I almost didn't recognize the woman who'd been haunting my dreams.

"Bronte?" I grinned.

She waved, her other hand around Luke's. "Yeah."

I burst out laughing. "That's fantastic! You look great."

She touched her tightly curled hair and ruffled shirt. "I

should. I spent a lot of hours turning into Prince." Making her way toward me, she gestured to my clothes. "And who are you? A Mumford and Son?"

I scratched at my beard, which was growing thicker by the day, and pulled on my red flannel shirt. "I wish. You're out collecting candy?"

She snagged the Snickers I offered to her. "We all go out every year, my brother's and sister's families, but Luke got a little overwhelmed, so I said I'd bring him back to Grammy and Grampy's for some quiet time."

I nodded and knelt down. "Hey, Luke, I really like your costume. I used to love *Where's Waldo*? Do you want some candy?"

He ignored that question, saying instead, "'Nother day, 'nother day."

"You want to play guitar?" I asked, glancing inside at my guitar then back at Bronte. "Can Luke come over?"

"Yeah. Of course."

"'Nother day," Luke repeated.

I held my door open for him, but when Bronte retreated, I narrowed my eyes. "Aren't you coming?"

"I didn't know I was invited."

"Of course. Come on."

She held up one finger. "Let me tell them next door. I'll be back."

By the time I had Luke settled in the living room and my big bowl of candy on the stoop with a paper indicating everyone should TAKE ONE, which I was sure would do jack shit, Bronte reappeared, still in her Purple Rain costume. She sank down to the floor with a smile as I placed my guitar in my lap to sing "Blackbird."

Every time I finished, Luke made the ASL sign for "more" so I gave him more.

It was during the fourth round of "Blackbird" when I noted Bronte's attention diverted to the stack of papers on the coffee table, and I scrambled to shove them under my laptop.

She only smiled blandly at me in response, obviously not offended.

She should've been. I was still hiding the truth from her.

"So, where'd you learn to play?" she asked.

I handed my pick to Luke, who examined it with clumsy fingers. "My parents were big on that saying, the devil makes work for idle hands, and I often found myself at the mercy of the devil." I lifted one shoulder. "They finally gave in and got me a guitar to keep me busy."

"Did it work, keeping you out of trouble?"

"No." I grinned, and so did Bronte.

"Well, clearly, it did *something* for you." She pointedly gazed down at the instrument, my left palm affectionately cradling the body. "You fell in love with it."

I stared off at some faraway point, falling into memories. "It's always kept me company when I was lonely or needed a friend."

She studied me, and I once again felt like she could see everything inside of me, down to the valves in my heart. "So, when you're not playing guitar, what are you doing? You said you're in the entertainment industry, but what does that mean? What's your job that you're able to take this time off?"

I had to tell her. It was the right thing to do. Except I'd never been good at doing the right thing.

Thank god her mom barged in before I had to answer. "Hello, hello, hello!"

I stood and set the guitar against the wall. "Hey, Pattie."

"I brought this over for you." She handed me a pumpkin roll and waved Luke over. "Come on, time to go back to Grammy and Grampy's."

"Is everybody back?" Bronte asked.

"Yeah." Her mother put an arm around Luke as Bronte moved sluggishly, and I hoped that meant she wasn't in a rush to leave. "But why don't you stay here for a while?" Pattie suggested like the saint she was. "You and Chris hang out. The kids are all wound up over there anyway."

She widened her eyes at me, unmistakably urging me on.

"Yeah, Bronte, you're welcome to stay," I said. "If you'd like."

Pattie beamed in satisfaction as if she'd planned the whole thing. Like I said, a saint. "Great. Enjoy the pumpkin roll, kids!"

When the front door closed behind Pattie and Luke, I tamped down the goofy grin crawling across my face. I finally had Bronte all to myself.

And all I could do was gape at her. Like a dope.

After a while, she yanked me back to reality with, "So…"

"So…" I held up the pumpkin roll. "Your mother's really starting to spoil me."

"You seem to be adjusting to it fine." She smiled, her fingers absently tugging at her costume.

"Do you want something to change into? Don't get me wrong, you look good, but you don't have to be Prince all night. I've got sweats you can wear if you want."

I led her upstairs to my bedroom and riffled through some drawers.

"I love what you've done with the place," she said, referring to the mess.

"I don't have much, but what you see is pretty much all of it. How's this?"

She blushed as she took the clothes from me, and there had never been anything I wanted more than being able to read her thoughts as her cheeks pinked my new favorite color.

She always seemed so sure of herself, but I liked that I

could make her stumble, make her nervous. Because she sure as fuck made me lose my mind. Especially standing in the middle of my bedroom, with those huge eyes of hers. If I didn't know better, I'd think she was mentally undressing me with those eyes.

I had to get out of there before I did something stupid. I hightailed it downstairs and to the kitchen, where I tried not to think about her in my bedroom. I didn't imagine what her body looked like. All pale skin, maybe a few freckles here and there, her long arms sliding my shirt over her head. The curve of her collarbone, small breasts, her slim waist. And I certainly didn't go half hard beneath my denim, because that would be awkward to explain.

So, I forced myself to concentrate on cutting up our dessert and definitely not on Bronte's stomach, legs, or ass.

I settled into the couch and found a scary movie to watch as I dug into the pumpkin roll.

"They're a bit big."

I turned over my shoulder to see the gray sweatpants cinched tight at her waist where she tucked in the front of my *Reservoir Dogs* T-shirt, the rest hanging loose off her slight body. I covered my lap with my plate so she couldn't see what I weirdo I was with a stiffy.

"What are you watching?"

"*Nightmare on Elm Street.* You ever see it?"

She helped herself to the second plate of pumpkin roll I set on the coffee table. "I'm not a big movie person."

That was why she hadn't recognized me yet. I thanked the universe she wasn't, because I had this time, however long it was, to get to know her. For her to get to know me. What would happen afterward, I didn't know. All I had right now were these stolen moments with her when I was Chris, not CJ Cunningham.

"Not a movie person? I don't even know what that means."

"It means I'd rather read the book. And," she said, pointing her fork at the screen with a cringe when Freddy Krueger appeared, "I don't like being scared."

With her feet curled up and legs crossed under her, I squeezed her big toe. "It's not that bad. Besides, I'm here."

She let out a mix of a snort and a huff with a stiff shake of her head. "That's what I'm afraid of."

I slanted my gaze toward her, though she only shoved a huge piece of the pumpkin roll into her mouth as if to mute any more conversation. I let it go, and we ate in congenial silence for a while. "I'm going to get another piece. Do you want one?"

"Sure."

She laughed when I returned with the rest of the roll, and I wanted to record that rough-around-the-edges sound so I could play it on repeat whenever I felt like it. Every night.

"To hell with manners, right?" I held the plate between us so we could share, and after we polished off the last bite, I sat back. "I think I love your mom."

"And I think she loves you," Bronte said, putting her bare feet up on the ottoman.

That was when I spotted the tattoo, a trio of four-leaf clovers on the top of her left foot, each one smaller than the next. "I didn't have you pegged for any ink."

When I gestured to her foot, she wiggled her toes. "We all have the same one, Fitz, Shelley, and I."

"Do you have any others?" I asked, like a dog on the hunt for a bone. She was so prim and proper with her glossy, straight hair and demure clothing, and the idea she was hiding tattoos under all that was so hot. A little bit of a bad girl under all that good.

"Yes."

I practically panted. "Show them to me?"

She laughed. "Do you have any?"

I lifted my knee to the couch as I dropped my arm on the back of it, my fingers landing near her shoulder. She jerked her eyes to them, as if to keep track of where my hands were. I was *trying* to keep them to myself, but Jesus, she was killing me.

"Nah. No tattoos. When I was a kid, I wanted one so bad, but my parents would have killed me...your body is a temple and all that. By the time I was on my own, I don't know, it didn't seem as important to piss them off anymore."

She tilted her head. "That's why you wanted a tattoo? To piss your parents off?"

"Yeah. Like I said, idle hands. So? What else do you have?" When she didn't move, I gave her my best smile. "Come on, you know you want to show me." Lowering my mouth near her ear, I added, "Please, Bronte."

She shivered and let out a breath. "Fine."

I barely contained my fist pump, and she playfully rolled her eyes as she lifted her hair, turning her back to me.

"What's this?" I restrained from touching the skin where a small scale was tattooed below her hairline.

"Symbol for libra," she said, circling back around to face me.

"Why on your neck?"

"I get them in places where they aren't really visible."

"Isn't that why you get tattoos? So people will see?"

"No. I get them for me." That cute crinkle between her eyebrows appeared. "If you were going to get a tattoo, what would it be?"

"An old-school pinup, right on my bicep," I tossed out, sitting up taller. I'd gotten a taste of her spirit, a little shy, a little playful, and now I wanted more. Might never be satisfied at this point. "Any others?"

"Wait." She breathed out a laugh, pressing her hand against my chest to force me back against the other end of the sofa. "I want to hear more about why. It sounds like your parents were really strict."

I wiped my hand over my mouth and beard, trusting Bronte enough to tell her about my past but unsure if I trusted myself not to tell her *everything*. I cleared my throat. "You really want to know?"

"Of course."

I never liked to talk about my family, even basic facts about them, and only ever told the whole truth to Wes because he had to know—he had to deal with the aftereffects—so I wasn't sure where exactly to start.

She offered me a jumping-off point. "What was it like growing up for you?"

"Uh..." I shifted, placing my elbows on my knees as I rubbed my hands together. "It was okay." With her dubious noise next to me, I met her gaze. "My parents were very conservative, very involved with their church, and they home-schooled me and my sister."

"Homeschooled," she said, the public school teacher choking on the word.

"Yeah, homeschooled. Me, my sister, and a bunch of other kids of families from the church. It was..." I lifted my hands, searching for an explanation. "We couldn't go trick-or-treating because it was of the devil. We couldn't read any books with witches or wizards. We couldn't watch TV or listen to the radio, and what we did get was Christian and it was awful," I said with a chuckle because I had some humor about it now. Although, back then it was hell. "I didn't even have a door to my bedroom."

"That seems extreme."

I blew out a breath, nodding. "As I got older, I learned real quick that wasn't the life for me, and I hated it. My older sister, though, she seemed to love it. Did the whole white dress, father-daughter promise ring ceremony."

"A *what* ceremony?"

"All the girls had to promise to save their virginity for their husbands and sign a contract. They'd wear white dresses and dance with their dads. It was real creepy."

"What about the boys?"

I sucked air through my teeth. "What do you think?"

She answered with a disgusted sound in the back of her throat.

"Since I knew how to play guitar, I was always playing for those ceremonies and church gatherings. I had bible study three times a week, youth group, all that shit. Every summer, we were sent to bible camp. That's where I first put my hand up a girl's shirt. Maelynn Forrester, behind the girls' bunk."

"Of course you did." She eventually gave in to a reluctant smile. "So, what happened?"

Carefully sidestepping the question, I scratched at the back of my head. "I ended up moving away when I was seventeen. For a while, I kept in touch. But eventually, I made some choices my parents couldn't forgive, and that was that. I was told I wouldn't be able to come home."

Bronte stayed silent, and a few moments passed, where old insecurities telling me I wasn't *good* enough infiltrated my mind, until she said, "I hate your parents."

Her voice held no inflection, and I almost believed her. "You could never hate anyone. It's not in your nature."

"Well, you're their child, and you don't deserve that."

I rolled my head back, staring at the ceiling, the ghosts of a childhood built from fear and self-loathing still haunting me. "Yeah, well, I've done a lot of stupid shit, so..."

"Hey." She wrenched my head up, framing my face with

her hands. "Do not say that. No parent should ever make their child feel like they deserve to be cast out. It doesn't matter what you did in the past. It only matters what you're doing right now, and right now, you are making two people next door very happy. And a kid with autism just so happens to worship you." She paused before continuing, her voice softer. "And me. You make me feel special. You make me feel like I'm extraordinary in this very ordinary life."

"You *are* extraordinary," I said without pause.

She lowered her gaze and hands to the sofa.

"Look at me, Bronte. Please, look at me."

She did, and my mouth instinctively carved into a tiny smile. "I was never able to make it through a flight without getting drunk to pass out. That day, by some stroke of luck, I was seated next to this incredible woman. She helped me through it, and I didn't need pills or drugs to keep my fear in check. And she didn't judge me when I told her what I'd done. She's smart, kind, down-to-earth, and pretty damn amazing."

"Amazing?"

"Yes. Amazing."

Her dimples indented her cheeks, and I pressed my index finger into one before dragging it down her chin.

"Thank you," she said, her voice low and gravelly.

"It's the truth." I dropped my hand to the couch, brushing my fingers against her knee. She took a noticeable breath, and I inclined toward her, wanting to finish what we started the day we met, but as I bent my head, the godforsaken front door opened again.

We both whipped around in the direction of Pattie, who appeared a tad flustered. "You've got a surprise next door, Bronte."

She shot up from the couch, guilt crossing her features before she grabbed her things and met her mom at the door. I curled my lips between my teeth to keep from expelling a litany of curses as I watched Bronte walk away from me. But I'd be damned if I didn't shadow her, curious why this surprise had Pattie so up in arms.

And what a surprise it was.

Hunter.

I entered the Hollingers' living room, my eyes glued to Bronte as she kissed her boyfriend.

Shit.

She was supposed to be kissing me right now, not this guy dressed in a button-down, sweater, khakis, and boat shoes. Fucking boat shoes.

I wanted to knock that shit-eating grin off Hunter's face, but I curled my fingers into my palm as he asked Bronte, "What are you wearing?"

"Oh...I, uh, had nothing to change into from my costume—"

"So I gave her something to wear," I said, loud enough that everyone in the room turned their attention to me.

Hunter's nostrils flared. "Ah, quite the good Samaritan."

The religious reference struck a deep chord in me, not only because of the sarcasm but because of what I'd told Bronte a few minutes before about my childhood. I crossed my arms, leaning against the wall by the door, refusing to break eye contact with the guy. It was obvious Hunter was trying to win some kind of showdown, and even though he was a couple inches taller than me, he looked like an overgrown child with ruddy cheeks and big teeth.

Bronte pulled Hunter's attention back. "What are you doing here?"

"Why do you think? Spending time with you and your family."

She was about to say something else when Luke let out a

frustrated cry, fighting Zoe for a stuffed dog pillow. Fitz broke them up. "And that's our cue to head out."

They left in a flurry of costumes and candy bags, but not before Fitz offered me a stiff clap on the shoulder, in what I assumed might be brotherly support. Guess Fitz didn't like Hunter either. Shelley, Tommy, and Zoe followed, leaving an awkward quiet behind.

Hunter broke it after a while, slapping his thighs as he stood up. "Guess we better get going."

Bronte sat up from her position next to her mother on the couch. "What? I thought we were—"

"I made us reservations at a bed-and-breakfast in New Hope. Surprise." He smirked, seeming pretty pleased with himself, and I rolled my eyes, plopping down on Pattie's recliner.

"What's the occasion?" Steven asked.

"I figured we needed some quality time together, right, Brontosaurus?" Hunter threw an arm around Bronte's shoulders. "You've been saying you wanted to go there for years."

I huffed. "And you're just going now?"

His head snapped toward me, his narrowed eyes unimpressed with me. For someone who never starred in a critically acclaimed film or cashed a check for ten million dollars, I thought he had a pretty big ego.

"Well, I've been busy working with the state legislature, so there wasn't much time for anything else."

I sniffed. "No time for anything else, including Bronte?"

"She understands."

My gaze immediately found the woman in question. Her head was bent down, hiding her eyes, but if I could see them, I would bet they'd show she didn't understand. What *I* couldn't understand was why she'd stay with a guy like that.

CHAPTER ELEVEN

Bronte

In complete shock, I lagged behind Hunter to his car and didn't argue when he rushed me to change and pack a bag back at my apartment. It was already after eight o'clock, there was no reason to hurry, but this was the most romantic thing he'd done in a long time, so I went with it.

The drive was a little over an hour, and he used the time to explain his reasons why I should move to Harrisburg. One through five were about his condo and his future at the lobbying firm. Six through ten were his favorite bars, food, and the fact that we could enjoy naked Sundays together.

Admittedly, it could have been better researched.

New Hope was a quaint town, on the edge of Pennsylvania, with cute antique shops and art galleries I had been dying to check out, but almost everything was closed by the time we arrived.

Hunter tugged me back out the door before I could say no. "There's a brewpub up the street. I heard they've got great burgers." He reached for my hand as we walked. "Did you have fun today?"

Still working through my puzzlement over the night, I only raised my brow.

"Trick-or-treating? Halloween? Your whole family thing?"

There was something off about him. His words jumbled together, and the hand which wasn't holding mine danced all over the place as he spoke.

"Yeah. It was fine."

"Fine? That's all you have to say after you made a big deal over me not being there?"

"It was fun. It always is." I kept my words as brief as possible so my guilt from another almost-kiss with Chris didn't seep into them.

"I was thinking next year for Halloween, we could have a party at our place. I was talking to Jack about it at work today. He used to have one at his house, but now he's got the baby, so he suggested I take over. I didn't think it was a bad idea."

Too confused by his rambling to even bring up the "our place" statement, I didn't give him an answer. Hunter was usually composed and calculated, never one to speak more than he needed to, so his behavior was way out of character. Although once we were seated, he calmed after ordering a beer and chugging it down in a few gulps. He finished with a contented breath and relaxed into his chair. I hated how he'd rather hide in a glass of beer than talk to me about what was bothering him, but I'd had that particular argument with him one too many times already.

The brewery had two floors, with wood and metal furnishings. On the second floor, not far from where we were seated, was a pool table and sliding doors that opened to a deck. The music was kind of new age folk, and the place was packed with flannel and facial hair. I smiled to myself, thinking of Chris.

I hadn't missed the look he'd lobbed at me as I followed Hunter out the door of my parents' house. Basically the equivalent of *WTAF?*

I'd spent the night in Chris's house, in his clothes, talking about his past, and everything was so comfortable between us. Then he touched my cheek, a second away from finally pressing his lips to mine, and my mother walked in.

Like a bucket of ice water over my head.

There was no telling what would have happened if she hadn't arrived, but before I could even imagine it, the waitress reappeared to take our food order. Hunter got another beer, and by the time he'd moved on to his third, he'd made friends with the table next to us: Todd, Mark, and his wife, Kelly. Soon, our tables were pushed together, pints spread among them.

"Loosen up," Hunter said into my ear at some point after midnight.

"I'm ready to go. I want to get up early tomorrow so we can look around."

He placed a sloppy kiss on my jaw. "We have all weekend. There's no need to get up early."

I eyed him. Did he really not know me at all?

"We'll go in a bit." He pointed to the pool table. "Me and Todd have winner."

After downing a gallon of beer and playing a couple rounds, Hunter finally returned to our table, and I had to hold him upright while he said his drunken goodbyes to his new buddies. I kept an arm around his middle once we were outside, and he let his head drop toward mine.

"Are you mad at me?" he slurred.

"Yes, I'm mad. You took me out, got piss drunk, and then ignored me. Might I remind you that *you* planned this getaway."

He broke away from me and walked right into a tree branch. "Did you see that?" He giggled—actually giggled—and said, "Don't be mad."

"Shut up."

"Yes, ma'am." He saluted me and marched back to the B&B, where I poured him into bed.

It was half past five and still dark outside when my phone rang, jostling me from a light sleep. I squinted at the screen, all blurry without my contacts in.

"Bronte!" my sister half cried, half yelled.

I sat up in bed, on high alert. "Shell, are you okay? What's wrong? Is the baby—"

"It's Dad."

My stomach dropped. "What?"

"We're at the hospital. He had a heart attack." I rubbed at my chest as my sister continued, "Mom called me. He got up to go the bathroom and collapsed." Her voice broke on the last word.

"Is he okay? Is Daddy okay?"

"I don't know. Tommy and I just got here. We had to wait until his mom got to our house to take care of Zoe, so we—"

I interrupted Shelley's nervous rambling. "Where's Mom?"

"She's here."

"Is she okay?"

"Yeah, you know, relatively."

"I'm coming home. I only have to wake Hunter up." I shoved at Hunter's shoulder again and again, but he was passed out cold. I cursed and hit him with the pillow before stumbling around for my glasses. Finding them on the dresser, I flipped on the light and dropped to the floor to search for his car keys that I was sure fell out of his pants pocket when we returned. Though they were nowhere to be found.

"Hunter's drunk and won't wake up. I can't find his car keys and don't have a way to get home without him. God, Shelley, I don't know what to do. What should I do?"

While my sister spoke to someone in the background, I took a few deep breaths. My eyes were glassy, chest tight, but I would not cry. I couldn't. Not yet. I needed to focus on getting home.

Hunter didn't move.

"I need a ride," I said more to myself than Shelley. "Are rental car places open all night? Or, um, a cab?" I struggled to think. "How about Fitz? Can Fitz come get me?"

"Hold on." Shelley relayed the message to whomever she was with. Then to me, she said, "I don't think Fitz should leave Mom right now, but Chris is here. He said he'd come get you."

"Chris is there?"

"Yeah, he performed CPR on Dad until the ambulance showed up." I didn't have enough time to process that information because she went on, "He's leaving right now. Text him the address."

I hung up, my trembling fingers tripping over themselves as I texted Chris. After three attempts, I finally sent the right numbers and letters, before trying to wake up Hunter again, but he only rolled over, drool pooling on the side of his mouth. In my panic, I tried once more to search for Hunter's car keys, even ripped open his overnight bag in the process, causing a small square box to fall out. I gasped at the pear-shaped diamond ring, sitting in the middle of the cushion, but his odd behavior earlier suddenly made sense. He was planning on proposing to me.

A thousand thoughts entered my mind, but I forced them all away for now. I needed to concentrate on getting home. I'd deal with the asshole in bed later.

Waiting on the steps outside of the bed-and-breakfast, I lost track of time. It felt like only two minutes later when Chris pulled up to the curb. I ran straight to him as he stepped out of the car. It was then I let my tears fall, burying my head into the crook of his neck. He tightened his arms around me, and it was as if he was the only thing holding me together anymore. If it weren't for him, I might break into a million pieces.

"It's all right. He'll be all right," Chris said repeatedly, his voice low against my ear. He placed one kiss on my temple before shifting to look at me, and I blinked through my tears, my glasses all fogged up. "It will be okay, I promise."

And for some reason, because he promised, I believed it.

He tucked me into the car, helping with the seat belt since my hands were shaking, and drove as fast as he could, accelerating through the yellow lights, hitting the highway as the sky turned a dull gray. Reading the time on the digital clock, I figured he must have been driving a hundred miles an hour to get to me so fast.

"I knew it was probably killing you to not be with your family," he said as if he could read my mind. "I think I broke about fifteen traffic laws to get to you."

My heart thudded at his statement. Chris knew what I needed and did whatever it took to give it to me. It was a stark contrast to what I'd been settling for all these years. "Thank you."

The rest of the drive was quiet, and he dropped me off at the entrance of the hospital to park the car on his own. I made my way to the information desk, where they pointed me to the bank of elevators. When I got off on the floor, my family was in the lobby. Fitz huddled in the corner on his phone, Shelley had her head on Mom's shoulder, and Tommy was stretched out on a few chairs, asleep. My mother, brother, and sister all looked up simultaneously, as if sensing my presence, and enveloped me in a hug.

"How is he?" I asked, holding my brother's hand.

"He's in surgery. They said it would take a couple of hours," Fitz said.

I nodded like a bobblehead as I touched my mother's shoulder. "How are you?"

"Hanging in there. If it weren't for Chris, I don't know what I would have done."

And as if he'd been summoned, he strode toward us, pushing his car keys into his back pocket, his baseball cap following. "How's everybody doing?" He took in the scene in front of him and held up his hands, in an obvious attempt to give us space. "I'm going to go to the cafeteria to get some coffee. I'll be back in a few minutes."

The waiting room was silent, save for Tommy's occasional snore. Shelley eventually woke up her husband, needing to take a walk, probably uncomfortable from being almost nine months pregnant and stuck in hard chairs all morning. Fitz walked away to call Amanda with her hourly update, leaving me and Mom alone.

"When Shelley called, I didn't know what to do," I said. "I was so scared."

"Me too. I heard him get up, and then he fell, and I...I froze. I screamed and, Bronte, I thought I lost him." She dabbed at her eyes. "I don't know what I'd do if..."

I shook my head, tears falling from my cheeks to dot my sweatshirt. "No. We can't think like that."

"I know." She sniffled, worrying a tissue between her fingers. "But he's the love of my life."

I hugged her, both of us crying. I'd never known a greater love than that of my family, and with the unthinkable happening, I wasn't sure I was strong enough to get through it.

A few minutes later, Chris appeared, holding out a cardboard carrier to the newly reassembled group. "Coffee?"

Fitz helped himself, his cell phone still attached to his ear, then Shelley and Tommy, and finally, my mom. There were no cups left by the time it was my turn, but Chris offered his own. I took a grateful sip, and he sat in the seat next to me.

"I want to tell you how much I appreciate you," I said, and he shrugged, accepting the coffee when I handed it back to him.

"If there's one thing I can do, it's drive fast."

I placed my hand on his arm. "No, Chris, I mean it. Mom said you helped her, and Shelley said you did CPR, and I..." His face turned wavy under my watery gaze, and I sniffed back tears. "You came to pick me up. I'm so, so thankful."

"You don't need to thank me. I love your dad—and your whole family. I would do anything for them."

I dug through my purse for a tissue but came up empty-handed. Chris offered me a napkin from his pocket, and I blew my nose before leaning back in my chair, resting my temple against his shoulder. He slipped his arm around me with the slightest kiss against my forehead, and I burrowed into his warm embrace, drifting off to sleep.

"Bronte, baby, wake up."

My eyes fluttered open, abruptly waking to the reality of the hospital waiting room, and not a warm bed.

Chris tipped his chin to my bag on the floor. "Your phone's ringing."

Reluctantly, I moved out of his embrace to find it. When I saw Hunter's name on the screen, I answered with a terse, "Hello."

"Bronte, where are you?" He sounded like he'd recently woken up.

"Allentown."

"What? Why?"

"I'm at the hospital. You'd know if you weren't passed out, completely wasted." I glanced over at Chris, who stared straight ahead with the distinct appearance of someone pretending they weren't eavesdropping.

"Why didn't you wake me up? Why are you in the hospital? Why—"

My temper spiked, and I had trouble keeping my voice down. "I tried to wake you up, but I couldn't. I'm here because my dad had a heart at—"

The line went dead, and I yanked my phone away from my ear to find a blank black screen. Out of battery. I tossed it into my bag with a perturbed huff and sat back in my chair.

"Who was that?" Chris asked, and I turned to him, brow raised. He quickly gave up his pretense. "You deserve so much better."

I deserved someone who had a good relationship with my family, someone who didn't require alcohol to get through a night. I deserved someone who sat next to me in the hospital and put his arm around me without having to ask. I deserved Chris.

When Dr. Mangal appeared some time later, we all gathered around her as she explained the open-heart surgery. Chris rubbed my back as Dr. Mangal used words like stents and arteries and plaque. She informed us Dad was doing well, but it would be a slow recovery.

After an eternity, a nurse led us all down the hall to his room. Mom walked in first, holding Fitz's hand, followed by Shelley and me, then Tommy and Chris.

"Oh, Stevie!" Mom cried, kissing Dad's face.

He was barely awake and attached to a heart monitor, an IV, and a few other wires tangled up from the wall. "Patricia? Pattie, sweetheart, I'm sorry."

"None of that now," she said, gingerly sitting next to his hip on the bed, resting her hand on his.

Fitz patted his shoulder. "You look good, Dad. Real good."

"I feel terrible," he croaked.

"Well, the doctor did basically saw you in half."

Dad managed a smile, and Shelley stepped up, kissing his cheek. Tommy was on her heels. "You had us all nervous for a second there, Steve."

Shelley stood quietly, her hands folded around her belly, and Dad lifted a finger. "Shell's stunned into silence. For the first time ever, I think."

"You had a heart attack, Dad!" She was promptly shushed by Mom, and she lowered her voice to a whisper, her lip quivering. "You could have died."

"But I didn't."

"No, you didn't." Mom smiled. "Thank God. Chris—" she directed a water-logged smile at the man in question "—I'm so glad you were there to help."

He stepped up to the bed. "You guys are there for me all the time. I'm only reciprocating. It's nice to see you with some color in your cheeks, Steve. You look a hell of a lot better than you did this morning."

"I guess I have you to thank for that." Dad reached for Chris's hand and shook it. "Thank you." He then turned to me, grinning as wide as he could on all the medication. "Beanie Baby, don't cry."

I wiped at my cheeks and wrapped my arms around my father's neck, but he coughed.

"Not too tight, Bean."

"I love you, Daddy," I said, pulling away.

"Now, what're you all doing here?" he asked, a sleepy smile on his face. "Isn't it time for brunch? Someone run and get me pancakes."

Mom snorted. "I think it's going to be a long time before you get any of those."

He grumbled but settled farther into his pillow.

Fitz patted the foot of the bed. "I'm going to go get some things for you, clothes and toiletries."

"When you come back, bring my grandkids," Dad said.

Fitz and Shelley agreed before leaving. I followed behind Chris, but my dad called out to him. "Hey, Chris, come here."

I waited and watched as he bent over so my they could speak quietly. After a moment of muffled conversation, Chris rested a hand on my dad's shoulder. "Take care of yourself."

Outside the door, I held on Chris's wrist. "What did he say?"

"Nothing important. You want a ride home?"

I could tell he was lying, but I was too exhausted to argue. "If you don't mind."

He gestured for me to lead the way.

CHAPTER TWELVE

Chris

Bronte's apartment was exactly how I imagined. Neat and tidy. I helped myself to a peek around as she made coffee. The second bedroom seemed to double as a closet, with a sewing machine, desk, and plastic bins filled with craft supplies in the corner. I bypassed the bathroom and poked my head into her bedroom. Surprisingly, her bed was rumpled, her flowery gray comforter barely clinging to the corner of the mattress. I would've thought she made it up every morning, and I smiled at her very slight *mess*.

A collage of picture frames hung on one wall in the shape of a heart, and I studied each one: Bronte tailgating at a football game with three other girls in matching T-shirts, a short one with long, golden-copper hair, a tall, statuesque blonde, and a fire-engine redhead on Bronte's back as if she'd surprised her with a piggyback. These girls were obviously important to Bronte because they popped up in a bunch of other photos, and I had to guess they were the same ones she had been visiting with in Chicago.

Although there were a few photos of her niece and nephews, and a couple more with her parents and siblings, I noted there were none of Hunter. And wasn't that something? But there was one in particular, toward the point at the bottom, that I couldn't stop staring at. It was a black-and-white of Bronte at the beach. She wore a bikini, splashing in the water with one leg up, laughing so her dimples were prominently displayed. A floppy hat covered her head, and she looked an awful lot like Audrey Hepburn there.

"Black with a little sugar, right?"

"What?" I startled at Bronte standing right behind me, holding out a coffee mug with World's Best Teacher in colorful block letters on it.

"Yeah, perfect. Thank you."

Once we were both seated on the couch in her living room, she cleared her throat, holding her cup close to her lips when she spoke. "I can't tell you how grateful I am." Her voice was extra thick, probably from all the crying, making it even huskier than usual. "You drove all that way to pick me up, and you didn't have to."

"I didn't have to. I *wanted* to." I wanted to be the guy she called. Even though I had no right to be since I would be leaving eventually. The attachment I felt to her was too strong to ignore.

And to her family. I was attached to them too.

When Pattie had called me to come over, I'd thought Steven was dead, seeing him unconscious on the floor. Adrenaline must have kicked in, because I assumed control, following instructions from the 9-1-1 operator while keeping Pattie calm. As soon as the ambulance arrived and the paramedics took over, a panic attack had started to take shape. I'd had difficulty filling my lungs with air, my vision closing in, my chest heavy.

I was terrified my neighbor, friend, and pseudo father figure would die right in front of me. Then, to make matters worse, I'd arrived at the hospital to learn Bronte was stuck out of town. I hadn't thought twice as I'd grabbed my car keys.

I hadn't known what to expect when I'd picked up Bronte in New Hope, but I didn't mind when she had launched herself into my arms. I would give her anything—everything—to make her feel better, and the temptation to kiss her, comfort her without words, lose ourselves in each other to forget this terrible day was strong. Now, when she leaned into me, wrapping her arms around my neck, I had no choice but to abandon hope of seducing her at the feel of her hiccupping breaths against my cheek. I held her close, rubbing soft circles against her spine.

"I'm sorry I'm crying so much. I started, and now I can't stop." A strangled giggle escaped, and she lifted her head, the corner of her mouth curling up. She swiped a hand across her nose. "I'm a mess."

I cradled her face between my palms, wiping at her tears with my thumbs. Her cheeks were puffy, lips swollen and chapped, and her eyes rimmed red behind big, dark-framed glasses. Didn't stop the attraction between us from overwhelming me. I figured it'd always be there, no matter what she did or said or looked like. I tucked strands of tangled hair behind her ears. "You're beautiful."

She batted at my shoulder. "I don't want your pity compliments."

I let out a breath, releasing my hold on her to run my hands through my hair. It was long now, past my chin, and I wove my hands into it, keeping them off her. "It's not pity. It's the exact opposite of pity," I said, sharper than I intended. "Bronte, I gotta tell you, I was nervous. I was really nervous your dad wasn't going to make it. I felt…"

I shot up from the couch, needing the physical space from her to get my thoughts together. "When everything went down with my parents, even my sister stopped talking to me. I was out in California by myself, and I didn't think I'd ever get over being lonely. I spent so many years trying to make up for that, surrounded myself with people who didn't give a shit about me, thinking as long as I was the life of the party, they'd care, but they didn't. Then I came here, and your parents have taken me in like one of their own. All I could think was, if he dies, he'll never know how much he means to me." Bronte tried to interrupt, but I stopped her, barreling on with my declaration. "I don't want to live like that. I don't want to live with regrets. So, I'm going to be honest with myself and with you."

Although there were plenty of things I wanted to get off my chest, I hadn't given much consideration to this spur-of-the-moment speech, so I started with what I thought was most important. "I like you, Bronte. I know that sounds juvenile, but I do. And I hate that you're with somebody else who, by the way, I think is a real asshole...but don't let me influence your decision to break up with him."

She fought a smile, and I took that as a good sign, closing the distance between us. I bent over and traced her lips with my finger. "I want to kiss you. Real bad," I said and then straightened, slipping both hands safely into my pockets. "But I won't. Not until you get sorted and tell me it's what you want." I let out a ragged breath. No matter how much I craved her, I wasn't going to kiss her while she was still with someone else. "I didn't realize it'd be so difficult, especially when you look at me the way you do."

She swayed in front of me and reached for the edge of the couch as if to anchor herself. "What way is that?"

"I assume it's the same way I look at you. Like the last piece of your favorite dessert is locked behind a glass door. Like you're trying to hang on to the final shred of restraint you have before losing it all."

Her attention snapped to me, and with her wide eyes and open mouth, I figured I'd either nailed how she felt about me or was dead wrong. Then her features softened, and she gazed up at me with the tiniest lilt to her lips, nodding.

I called it right. She was in this as deep as I was.

Fuck being the good guy.

I wasn't good anyway. Never had been.

I lunged toward the sofa and pulled her to standing. She didn't hesitate to place her hands on my chest, scrunching the material of my shirt in her fingers. I wound my hands into her hair, drawing her close enough to smell the vanilla creamer she put in her coffee, and goddamn, I wanted to taste it. When she leaned into me, every part of her body pressed up against mine, and I fought back a groan.

I'd never worked so hard to kiss someone before.

I'd never worked so hard to *not* kiss someone before.

But as I lowered my lips to hers, her phone rang.

"Every damn time," I muttered with a pathetic chuckle, and she brushed past me to grab her cell phone charging on the coffee table. Skimming a frustrated hand over my mouth and beard, I plopped down on the sofa. I'd waited this long; I could wait another minute.

"Hey, Mom," she said into the phone. She listened for a few seconds then said, "Sure. I'll bring it over when I come back."

I watched as she hung up and tried to smell herself inconspicuously. "I haven't showered in over twenty-four hours. I think I'm starting to ferment."

I grinned. God, she was perfect. "You smell fine. I know, I was up close and personal two minutes ago."

"Yeah. About that..." She fiddled with her glasses.

"We can talk about it later."

After a moment of her looking very unsure of herself, she

moved around the couch to my side and kissed my cheek. "I'll be right back."

Hearing the shower start, I polished off my coffee and helped myself to browse through her bookcase. It was an eclectic mix of hardcovers with the mark of Oprah's Book Club on the corners and paperbacks that appeared as old as she was—and I guessed some were if the *Sweet Valley High* titles were any indication. I skipped over the row of pastel-colored romance covers and found a memoir of a child soldier in Sierra Leone, snatching it from the shelf.

Completely engrossed in the first chapter, I didn't notice the knocking at first, but as it got louder, I realized someone was at the door. Peering into the peephole, I let out a disgusted curse and opened the door to a disheveled Hunter.

"What are you doing here?" the shithead asked.

I placed one hand on the doorframe, taking up as much space as possible. "I should ask you the same question."

"Don't fuck with me. Where's Bronte?"

"In the shower."

He barged past me to scan her place.

"I told you, she's in the shower."

The asshole spun around, stabbing a finger in the air. "And I told you not to fuck with me."

"I don't need to. You're doing it pretty well by yourself." The jaw popping out in anger didn't deter me in the slightest from continuing. "Bronte's father had a heart attack. *You* were comatose, so *I* picked her up and drove her back here to be with her family."

He took two steps forward, puffing out his chest. "I'm her boyfriend. You're just some random douchebag who wants what I have."

I casually scratched at my beard. "That's ironic since I'm

the one who's been with Bronte all morning, and you're the one who's hungover with his shirt on inside out."

He glanced down then shrugged. "Now you think she owes you something, or what?"

"No. I'm not like you." I kept my voice even and nonchalant. The calmer I was, the more agitated it made this jackass.

"What's that supposed to mean?"

"I've met a lot of guys like you. You think you can do whatever you want and people will deal with it because you're arrogant enough to believe they won't find somebody better than you. Like she's got to prove something to *you*." I gestured behind me with my thumb. "But that woman in there? She's way too good for you, and she's been way too kind by staying with you for so long."

"Who the hell do you think you are?"

I smiled politely. "I'm the guy who's gonna steal your girl."

"You son of a bitch." He shoved at my shoulder, pushing me back a few inches, and I automatically set my feet apart, clenching my right fist. I'd had fight training for multiple movies. I could throw a mean right hook, if need be.

"Hunter? What are you doing here?"

Both of us whirled around at Bronte's voice. She was dripping wet, holding a towel around her body, a knot of material between her hands at her chest.

He rushed to wrap his hands around her shoulders. "I'm so sorry, Bronte. I didn't know what happened. You should've woken me up."

"I tried," she said, scowling. "You were dead to the world."

"I'm sorry. I didn't mean to drink so much."

"That's the problem. You never mean for anything to happen." She backed away from him and straightened her posture, tightening the towel in her hands. "I'm tired of being your backup plan."

"You're not my backup plan. Look." He pulled a small box from his pocket. "Would I get this for you if I didn't want to be with you?" He opened it, revealing a diamond ring.

My first instinct was to grab the box and throw it out the window, sending him closely after it. The second was to look to Bronte. Did she want to marry him? Did she want to give up the possibility of what was happening between them for this twat?

She rolled her eyes. "You thought you'd ask me to marry you, and I'd do what you want me to."

I breathed out in relief at her reaction and leaned against the wall. I knew I shouldn't be witness to this particular conversation, but I couldn't find it in myself to leave.

"Hunter, we've been together for so long, we don't even know why anymore. At least, I don't, and I'm tired of coming in second place to your job, your drinking, and your schedule. That's not the kind of life I want to live."

"So, that's it? You don't want to try anymore?"

"We've tried," Bronte said. "We tried in college and broke up. We tried after you graduated and broke up because you moved to Harrisburg. We tried when I graduated and got a job here and broke up. We tried again this year. A relationship needs work, but not this much."

He deflated from her words and stuffed the ring into his pocket. "I'm sorry you feel that way," he said after a while, his gaze on his feet. "Does this have anything to do with *him*?"

Bronte's eyes flickered to me, her mouth twitching. I was about to step in and answer for her, tell this reptile to go back to whatever hole he crawled out of. But I didn't have to.

"Yes."

He raised his head, his voice devoid of almost all emotion as he said, "Well, you and your new boyfriend can go fuck yourselves."

I glared at him, purposely shoulder checking him on his way out. When the door slammed shut, I turned to see Bronte let out a deep breath. "You okay?"

"My dad had a heart attack, and I just broke up with my boyfriend." She let out a hysterical giggle. "Okay is a relative term."

I raked my eyes up from her toes to where her legs disappeared under the yellow-and-white striped towel and pushed a clump of wet hair behind her ear. "You're dripping all over the floor."

She laughed and pressed a hand to her face. "I shouldn't laugh. It's terrible."

"No. Don't do that." I wrapped my fingers over her wrist, tugging her hand down. "Don't cover up your dimples. They're one of my favorite things about you."

"One of your favorite things? Meaning you have more than one?"

"Oh yeah. I've got a list. The dimples are number three."

"Really?"

Her sincerity and humility were ten and eleven, respectively.

"What's your number one?"

"Your heart." Without question, her good, good heart. "I don't want you to feel bad about what you said. You were being honest." And I thought it was about time to finally come clean about who I really was and what I could offer her. Which was not much. I didn't deserve her, and yet I'd make a deal with the devil if it meant I could have her.

"You know how I feel about you," I said, and she nodded in agreement but stepped away. I was desperate to touch her, though I understood her need for space. The last few hours had been harrowing for her. "I don't want to push you into anything, and I promise I won't bring it up again until you're ready."

She blinked up at me, her eyes clear and blue, her teeth nibbling at the corner of her bottom lip.

"I'll wait. It'll kill me," I said with a pathetic laugh, "but I'll wait." I wiped my hands on my pants, anxiety sweating my palms. "And I have to be honest with you. I'm C—"

"Can you hold that thought?" She stuck her index finger up between us. "I..." She waved a hand down her body.

"Well, don't change on my account."

She pursed her lips, playing at indignation and fighting a smile before scampering to her room. A few minutes later, she returned in jeans and a long-sleeved T-shirt. She typed something on her phone, then slipped it into her back pocket. "Everyone is going back to the hospital. Want to come?"

"No, you go. Have some family time."

She balanced herself on one foot at a time to put on her shoes. "What were you going to say before?"

I watched as she tied her still-wet hair up on the top of her head. With the glasses on and no makeup, she looked younger, innocent, and the urgency to tell her my secret left me. I didn't want to add something else to her growing pile of stress. "We can talk about it later."

She accepted my answer and ushered me out the door, locking it behind us. Halfway to my car, her soft voice stopped me. "Chris?"

"Yeah?"

"You're not pushing me to do anything. It seems I'm pretty willing when it comes to you."

And I didn't know what I loved more, the blush of her cheeks when she admitted that, or her self-proclaimed enthusiasm, because my own enthusiasm was still half hard.

CHAPTER THIRTEEN

Bronte

It was almost eight o'clock by the time I left the hospital. My dad had been in good spirits after the visit from his grandkids, plus the second cup of Jell-O the nurse allowed him for dessert. He'd still been pretty drugged up on painkillers, but he had insisted I read to him, and since I happened to have the latest James Patterson on my e-reader, I'd read aloud until his eyes sagged with sleep. My mother had already passed out on the reclined chair with a blanket wrapped tight around her shoulders. So, I had kissed both of them on their cheeks, given my thanks to the nurses, and headed home. Although as I made the left to my apartment complex, I changed my mind and turned around, driving toward my childhood home instead.

I unlocked the front door with my key and automatically flipped on the living room light switch. Evidence of trick-or-treating from the night before was still scattered around, and because I took after my mother, I immediately got to work, cleaning away my anxiety.

I put away the few toys, tossed the candy wrappers, and vacuumed, even though I didn't really need to. Then I attacked the kitchen, unloading the dishwasher and scrubbing at the stovetop. It was already spotless, but it felt good to mindlessly focus on something. I even refolded the dish towels.

My phone buzzed in my back pocket.

CHRIS

Is that your car I see parked outside?

Yes.

CHRIS

Picking something up?

No.

It was another one-word answer, but at the moment, it was difficult to give more. I always had a lot of words in my head, and sometimes it took a while to find the ones I wanted.

CHRIS

What are you doing over there?

Organizing the holiday dish towels.

CHRIS

????

I snapped a picture of the towels all folded up nice and neat, in chronological holiday order, starting with Thanksgiving. I left one of the turkey towels out to use. He replied with a skull and crossbones.

What are you up to?

CHRIS

Eating delivery and working.

Working? Thought you were taking a "break."

Again, his reply came in the form of an emoji. This time the ghost with its tongue out.

You're the only person in the history of texting who has ever used that emoji.

He sent it ten times over.

I was typing, intent on telling him the reason I didn't want to go home was because I didn't want to be alone, when a message popped up.

CHRIS

Want to come over?

How was it possible that someone I'd known for only a few weeks—mere days, even—was able to read me like a book? I wanted to see him but was still uncomfortable with how things were left between us. I'd had the craziest twenty-four hours of my life and wasn't ready to jump into anything else that might make it even crazier.

How about you come here?

Two minutes later, there was a knock at the front door. I hadn't locked it, so I wasn't surprised when it opened.

"You know this isn't some *Leave It to Beaver* town. You need to lock your doors. I tell your parents the same thing all the time."

Chris stood in the entryway of the kitchen with Chinese food containers stacked in one hand and a bunch of DVDs in the other. I was momentarily caught off guard by how good he looked in a plain white T-shirt that clung to his chest. His hair was wet, and it curled a bit in the front, one piece hanging down by his dark eyes.

"Old habits die hard."

He looked me up and down as if checking for bumps and bruises. "How're you doing?"

"All right," I said and meant it. After I'd seen my father was going to be okay and cleaned some of my panic away, I was doing all right.

He held up the movies. "I tried to explain to your dad that he needs to get a smart TV instead of living in the last century with a DVD player like some plebeian, but here we are. Did you know you can buy movies at Walgreens? They have everything at that store."

"You don't say," I deadpanned.

"I needed some Tylenol the other day," he said with an amazed shrug, "and happened to pick these up. *Princess Bride, Bridesmaids, Inception...*"

"I've never seen them."

His eyebrows practically disappeared from his face. "You've never seen any of them? Even *Princess Bride?*"

I shook my head. "I mean, I've heard of them. I know Fitz was obsessed with *Inception* when it came out. That's the dream within a dream one, right?"

"But you've been living under a rock?" he guessed.

"Yep."

"Well, come on, then. Let your education begin. We'll start with *Princess Bride*. It's a classic, and I think you'll really love it," he said and motioned with his arm for me to follow him to the living room, where he set the food boxes on the coffee table and helped himself to turning on the television. He knew his way around like he lived there. "Cary Elwes and Robin Wright are in it. I think Cary is way underrated as an actor. Everyone thinks of him from this movie, and maybe *Robin Hood: Men in Tights,* but he can do smarmy really well. In *Twister,* he plays this—"

"You're really into movies, huh?" I asked as he passed me chopsticks and opened the containers of lo mein and sweet-and-sour pork.

"I, uh, yeah. Yeah, I am."

"If you weren't allowed to watch them when you were a kid, did you sneak them, or…?"

He sat back, munching on an egg roll before finally answering, "When I got my license, I was supposed to go do volunteer work. Instead, I went to the movies. I was caught after a while, and…" He shrugged. "I wasn't the only kid trying to explore, ya know? I wasn't the only one trying to sneak cigarettes or get hold of alcohol to give it a try, but somehow, I was the only one ever caught. I was the troublemaker, the bad kid."

I huffed. "You weren't a *bad* kid—you were a normal kid. Everybody does that stuff."

He snuck a piece of pork from the box I held. "At first, my parents didn't mind when I moved away. They were proud, I was doing it for the Lord." He drew imaginary quotation marks around that last bit, a rueful curl to his lips. "But…"

He didn't need to finish his sentence. He'd already told me how it ended, so I finished my food in thoughtful silence as Chris occasionally let me in on some secrets about the movie or actors. He was incredibly knowledgeable about it all, a real film nerd.

After we finished eating, he slid the leftovers onto the table and brushed his hands before settling into the couch, yanking my legs into his lap. His head fell to the back of the couch, his fingers absently tracing circles on my calves, and if he had any idea of what he was doing to my body, making it tingle and flutter, he didn't show it.

"I do like this movie," I said after a while.

"I knew you would." When he moved his hand higher up my leg, I shivered. "Are you cold?" he asked, grabbing a nearby blanket to drape over both of us.

He towed me to his side to wrap an arm around my shoulders, while he rubbed his other hand along the outside of my thigh. "Better?"

We were close enough that when I nodded, my nose skimmed along his, and I held my breath, waiting for his kiss. But it never came. He backed away, positioning us more comfortably next to each other with a playful smile. "I'm waiting for you to say the word."

I got it. He handed over the controls of this thing to me, but with the speed of everything happening between us, it seemed almost too good to be true. I didn't want to rush any decisions, so I settled against him, trying and failing to keep my eyes open.

I stirred awake the next morning, wrapped up in a blanket burrito with my head on a pillow. I blinked, focusing my eyes to find my glasses, which lay on the coffee table next to my cell phone and the *Princess Bride* box. I put on the glasses and checked the phone. One text from Shelley about going to the hospital today and one from Chris.

CHRIS

Take the DVD so you can watch as many times as you wish.

I understood the reference from the movie and smiled.

Usually, I liked to confront a problem from every angle, analyze the consequences, which was why it took me so long to make a decision. I was even a comparison shopper for toilet paper. Hell, it took a family emergency to get me to finally break it off with Hunter after years of quibbling.

Yet when I woke up to find Chris had clearly taken so much care last night, even down to my glasses, my best intentions to think everything through were blown out of the water. There was no thinking when it came to him. Only action.

CHAPTER FOURTEEN

Chris

I stood patiently, fingers drumming on the kitchen counter as the Keurig brewed my cup of extra bold. I'd showered and changed after I'd gotten back home from spending the night on the couch with Bronte.

She had been soft and warm against me, and I'd reveled in her slow breaths against my chest when she finally fell asleep next to me. Then when I'd moved us both down, stretching out along the length of the couch, she'd curled into me, doing this cute little smacking thing with her lips.

I was more tempted than ever to kiss her. Like some fairy tale, I could've woken the princess with a kiss.

Except I was no prince, and I wanted much more than a simple kiss. I hadn't given in, though, keeping my word of letting her say when, and somehow fell asleep with the stiffest wood known to man.

When I woke, tangled up with Bronte, a pang reverberated in my chest. I'd always been selfish when it came to my sexual partners, never really caring much about what I could give them besides a few minutes of my attention, yet I'd spent the night holding Bronte while she slept because that was what she needed. And it felt good to give it to her.

That was when it hit me.

I thought I was being the good guy, doing the chivalrous thing. But I wasn't. I was still hiding myself from her, keeping my true identity a secret when I *knew* it'd hurt both of us when she found out.

With my coffee mug full, I took it into the living room, but stopped short at the sight outside my window. Bronte was sprinting across the lawn toward my door. I placed my drink down as she frantically knocked and rang the doorbell.

I swung the door open. "What's wrong? Is it your dad?"

She shook her head and brushed messy hair away from her face before fixing her glasses higher on her nose.

"What is it?" I tugged her inside.

"I, um..." Her eyes skirted around the room for a moment before meeting mine. "You were there for me yesterday when I needed you, and I was just thinking it'd be a shame to waste any more time being afraid to make a mistake."

She said that all in one breath, and I had to break her words down to make sense of them.

You were there for me.

I needed you.

Afraid to make a mistake.

I raked my gaze over her face. Those eyes, so clear and yet full of emotion, betraying everything she didn't say with her words. And, of course, her mouth. Her sweet, sweet mouth.

"The only mistake is not kissing you earlier." Then she reached for me, wrapping her arms around my neck, almost knocking me off-balance.

I caught myself, with one hand on the doorframe, while the other held her to me, my fingers thrusting into her hair. I turned and pressed her into the wall, shoving the door closed with my foot.

"I need you," she murmured into the skin of my throat.

"Thank fucking Christ," I said and banded my arms around her middle, lifting her feet off the floor, urging her to wrap her legs around my waist as I coaxed her mouth open. She kissed like she lived, a little reluctant but then dived in with soft whimpers and moans, clawing at me with everything she had.

"You taste like coffee," she whispered, though I didn't let her get another word out as I sat on the couch, guiding her onto my lap, wrapping my hands around her jaw, nipping at her lips. Her hands roamed over my chest and back before resting on my shoulders, fingers pulling me closer, and I wasn't about to refuse her anything. I positioned her knees on either side of my hips, putting her solely in charge, and she tugged at my hair, angling my head back as her lips moved to my throat. Her tongue lashed out against my earlobe.

Fuck, she was perfect in every way.

The pulsing of her hips when she ground down onto me. The soft noises she probably didn't even realize she was making. The nimbleness of her fingers as they unbuttoned my shirt. It was all absolutely perfect.

She had my button-down off in no time, and I bent to kiss and nuzzle her neck, pleasantly surprised when I found she kind of smelled like me from last night. I slid my hand under her shirt, fingertips teasing the skin along her spine and down her rib cage, learning every ridge and curve.

"I think I could kiss you forever," I said into the spot where her neck and shoulder met. She let out a hum of agreement and pulled me back to her mouth, her kisses alternating between wild licks and slow rolls of her tongue over mine.

I had waited so long for this, I had trouble taking my time with her and gave in to the need to have her under me. I gently pushed her back against the cushion, stretching her body out beneath me, and I skimmed one hand down her side, pressing my fingertips into her thigh as she bent her knee toward my hip. I wedged my quickly hardening cock into the pocket of warmth emanating between her legs and skirted my hand over her shirt, squeezing the gentle swell of her breast, her nipple puckering under my palm.

"Oh god," she moaned, her head tilting back. I sucked on her pulse. "I don't want you to stop."

"I won't. I won't," I mumbled, moving to push the edge of her shirt up so I could kiss her stomach.

"But we have to," she told me, halting my mouth halfway to the tiny bow in the middle of her bra.

"What?"

"I have to go back to the hospital."

The mention of the hospital immediately cooled my ardor, and I shifted to run my hand over my face. "Yeah." Undoubtedly, she had a lot of things to do today, and having sex on my couch was probably not one of them. "Okay."

"I was supposed to meet Shelley—" she checked her phone "—twenty minutes ago."

"It's not like you to be late," I said, trying to find humor in my blue balls. I adjusted my hard as steel dick then stood up, offering my hand to her. I hauled her up in front of me. She was slightly out of breath, her glasses crooked, ponytail hanging half off her head. Gorgeous.

After one last kiss, she sauntered to the kitchen, and I slowly put myself back together, agonizing over each button and how uncomfortably hard I was beneath my zipper. When she reappeared in the living room, glass of water in hand, she looked different...relaxed and unworried, as if I had completely taken away all of her anxiety. If I could put that look in her eyes after fooling around on my couch for a few minutes, I wondered what I could do if I had her for hours.

―――――

With Steven recovering in the hospital, the house next door was quiet, and I had to find other things to do to fill up my time besides hang out with my neighbors and daydream of Bronte. Over the last week, we'd spent as much time as we could together, meeting for coffee or for a quick bite to eat before we stopped to see Steven. Twice, I had gone to her apartment to watch a movie, but like we were kids in high school; we never actually watched anything. Instead, we spent most of our time horizontal. We hadn't moved past kissing and some heavy petting, though I was good with that.

I could be slow and steady for her.

Because if there was one thing I'd learned about Bronte, it was that she had to be eased into things. She might've been able to take a big leap with me, but I had to be there to hold her hand. So, we texted and talked. We chatted about everything except my work, which made me feel like a coward. Nevertheless, until she was one-hundred-percent comfortable with everything going on with her family, I wasn't going to lay my world at her feet to create any stumbling blocks.

For a few hours a day, I forced the image of big blue eyes out of my mind and focused on reading scripts. I had it narrowed down to a few I was interested in. The only hang-up was if the directors wanted me. My agent, Tom, had warned me that my behavior the past few years made people nervous. "You're too much of a liability," he'd said, which had led Wes to concoct this scheme, for me to completely remove myself from the spotlight and let the press move on to whoever the next train wreck was.

I was a *good* actor. I'd learned from the best, had a decent list of credits, and, until recently, a respectable reputation on set. I'd always come to work prepared and on time. It was when all the other shit got in the way—the benders, the racing, that foray in Vegas with the dancer, all the scuffles with paparazzi, the DUI—that studio heads said they required proof I hadn't fallen off the deep end. I'd gone from being *offered* roles to now having to beg for scripts, back to auditioning. I only hoped I hadn't screwed it up so bad that I couldn't claw my way back to the top.

One morning, my phone rang, and I placed my laptop on the coffee table, closing the watermarked and numbered script from the screen before answering. "Hey, Pattie."

"Chris, honey, we got good news. Steven is coming home from the rehab center today."

"That's great news."

"Yes, but listen, are you going to be around this afternoon?"

"Yeah, why? What's up?

"He'll be released in a few hours. We're only waiting for the papers, but—"

I stood up, anticipating her next question. "I'll be home all day. I'll help with whatever you need."

"You're wonderful, you know that?"

Opening my front door, I peeked outside over to the Hollingers' house. The yard was full of leaves. "So are you," I said and hung up with, "I'll see you in a bit."

I slipped on a coat and found a rake in the shed in the back-yard then got to work. It took a while, but I got all the leaves from both yards pushed into a few piles next to the curb. As I was about to head back inside, a car parked in front to me.

Bronte stepped out in a dark-gray pea coat, and I couldn't help but want to rip it off her, run my hands over her soft-looking sweater and those tight black pants which ended right above her ankle.

"They paying you?" she asked, her lips curling in a teasing smile.

I tossed the rake down, quoting her from our very first conversation, "I did it for goodwill, karma, and all that."

"My dad's coming home today."

"I know. Your mom called me."

She scanned the yard, then her parents' house. "I came to see if I could do anything before they got home."

"I was thinking about making them something for dinner."

"Since when do you cook?"

"Since your mom hasn't been around to do it, I've mastered a pretty good grilled cheese." Back in LA, I had all my meals delivered, but there was no personal chef here—besides Pattie —to drop off food, so I had to take matters into my own hands, ready to graduate from pancakes and chicken to something more elaborate. "I need to go to the grocery store, though. Want to come with me?"

"Sure. I'll drive."

I ran inside to grab my wallet and phone, then hopped into Bronte's waiting car. I buckled my seat belt, my eyes meeting hers. A guy could get lost in them if he wasn't careful. Holding up my phone in front of her face, I forced them to the recipe I'd saved. "How do you feel about lasagna with turkey and spinach?"

"I hope you're as good at cooking as you are at playing guitar."

"Me too." My laughter died down as my guilt crept up. I resolved to tell her who I was soon. I only hoped, once I did, we could figure out how to stay together, because I wasn't willing or ready to give her up yet.

The drive to the store was only five minutes. Four and a half of those were spent trying to find a radio station we both wanted to listen to, and I was in the middle of my Inigo Montoya impression when Bronte reached out for my hand. I paused only momentarily before weaving my fingers with hers. There was something to be said for taking it slow, all these small moments, like her smiling at me or my thumb caressing her knuckles.

I *liked* slow and steady.

Armed with the shopping list, I steered us through the aisles, picking out items, while Bronte fought with the cart. She kicked at it with the toe of her shoe. "This wheel is wonky."

"Maybe you're the wonky one, not the cart."

When I dropped my arm around her shoulders, she hip checked me out of her way, pushing the cart forward. "What's next?"

"Nutmeg."

"Aisle eight, this way."

"Do you have this store memorized?"

She threw me a look over her shoulder. Of course she had it memorized. I watched her tussle with the wayward cart and let my gaze linger on the back of her coat that draped down almost to her knees. I anticipated getting her alone and naked soon. Before my right hand fell off from overuse.

As she picked up a small jar from the top shelf, I noticed her shirt lifted, revealing the smallest amount of skin. An obscene sight.

Then in the frozen section, my gaze stuck on her breasts, the faint outline of her nipples under the thin cotton of her cream sweater. Utter torture.

The last straw was when she bent down to pick up a loaf of bread she'd accidentally knocked over. When she placed it back, I curled my hand around her neck to kiss her. She sucked in a breath, and I cut off her exhale with my lips. Sliding my tongue into her mouth, I dug my fingers into her hair, messing up the neat bun, learning and *loving* how she liked it a tad rough when she sighed after I nipped at her lip.

A loud throat-clearing broke us apart. It was an older gentleman, frowning. "You're blocking the rolls."

"Oh, excuse us, sir. I'm so sorry," Bronte said, grabbing the cart and nearly sprinting away.

I only chuckled, taking my time before finding her in a checkout line. I pressed my chest against her back, my lips next to her ear. "I couldn't help myself. All the carbs were clouding my judgment."

She glanced at me, adorably scandalized, but my attention snagged on the magazine in her hands. Afraid of what she might see in there, I snatched it from her and let out a relieved whistle when it was only a lifestyle publication. I paged through the ads for perfumes and hair products, a fashion spread with what I thought was rather unattractive clothing, an article about equity at the workplace, until finally, I stumbled on a quiz in the back.

"Should you lay off the apologies?" I quoted and pointedly raised my brow at Bronte. "Number one, a friend borrows a shirt, but when they return it, you notice it's stretched out. You, A, forget about it for now but will bring it up if they borrow something else. B, apologize for giving them a shirt too small. Or, C, ban them from ever borrowing anything again."

"My friends don't borrow my clothes, but I guess A."

I kept a mental score. "How many times a day do you involuntarily say I'm sorry? Once or twice, never, or too many times to count?" Without giving her time to answer, I said, "Too many times to count."

"You aren't with me all day. You don't know."

"Come on, I think I have a pretty good estimation of you, and I'd guess you'd say sorry if someone spilled *their* coffee on *you*."

"No," she said unconvincingly as she started placing the groceries on the belt.

"Three," I said, back to the quiz. "Your boyfriend is supposed to come over to help you paint, but he's missing in action. You, A, send him a text reminding him where he's supposed to be. B, leave him a profanity-laced voice mail. Or, C, skip the blow job the next time you're naked."

"It doesn't say that," she half squeaked, half laughed, stretching over the cart to grab the magazine.

"No, it doesn't." I blocked her hand as I tucked it away in the racks. "But I do have a point. You don't have to apologize for asking for what you want." I pushed the cart forward when the cashier began to ring everything up, and Bronte bagged the groceries, seemingly deep in thought.

As we made our way out of the store, she tilted her head up to me. "Well, if you ever don't show up to paint my house when you're supposed to, you'll be missing out on a lot more than..." She leaned toward me to whisper, "A blow job."

I threw my arm around her shoulders. "So, you're giving me the chance to paint your house?" When she nodded, I pressed my lips against her ear. "I'll be there."

CHAPTER FIFTEEN

Bronte

While I sat at his kitchen table, Chris had found an apron in some drawer and promptly tied it around his waist, but even the pink-and-green frills couldn't hide the masculinity he exuded. With him in dark jeans that fit his legs and butt perfectly, like he was born in them, it was hard not to stare. His black Henley was pushed up to his elbows, displaying tanned forearms I wanted to memorize every inch of.

Although, I couldn't, not with my cell phone continuously buzzing with texts from the girls. I'd told them about my break-up with Hunter and subsequent kisses with Chris, but with everything going on, my updates had been few and far between. Today, though, I would've liked to tell them about my shopping excursion with Chris and how he hot he looked in the kitchen. Except there were more important matters to discuss, like Gem's hair falling out.

At the latest picture of Gem's long hair clogging the shower drain, I sucked in a breath. Hair in the drain always made me gag.

"What's wrong?" Chris asked.

"Remember that friend I went to visit? Gemma, she had the baby?" At his nod, I went on, "Her hair is starting to fall out."

He whirled around with a wooden spoon in his hand, a piece of wilted spinach stuck to it. "Her hair is falling out?"

I held my phone up for him to see. "Yeah, a couple months after you have a baby, you lose some of your hair." When his eyes bugged out, I explained, "It's from the change in hormones."

He shook his head. "What people go through to have babies."

And my heart sank. "You think it's gross? You don't want kids?"

He lifted a shoulder then pivoted back around to the stove, where he put the spoon down in order to pour out the noodles into a strainer in the sink. "I never really thought about it. You know the situation with my family. I've basically spent my whole life resenting them...never really left a lot of time to think about what I wanted."

My phone buzzed in my hand with another picture, this one of Willow, her eyes the same color brown as her mother's but with wisps of dark-blond hair like her father. She wore a onesie with purple and gold letters that spelled out *Wild One*. I leaned on the counter next to Chris. "This is Willow Jane."

He spared a glance then placed a noodle on the bottom of a glass dish. "She's cute."

"She is," I said, refusing to hold back what I wanted. I'd done that with Hunter, and I wasn't about to do it again. "And I want some like her."

He rested his hands on a towel, his elbows locked, his shoulders up by his ears as he pressed his palms against the counter. "You want a bunch of babies named Willow Jane?"

"You know what I mean." I elbowed his side so he'd look at me again. If we were going to be together, I was determined to be honest from the start.

I hadn't transformed into a completely different person,

imagining a life where Chris and I would run off tomorrow, get married, and have a gaggle of kids right away, but I had to acknowledge that what I had with him felt more right than anything I'd ever had with Hunter. We still had so much to learn about each other, so much to talk about. I didn't even know what his plans for the future were and still wasn't sure what his occupation was, and yet, when it came down to it, I was purely following my instincts.

After a few moments, he relented and dropped his arms to his sides, his dark eyes roaming over my face. "You want kids."

It wasn't a question, but I nodded anyway.

He swallowed and gazed down at the floor to where the toes of his bare feet touched the tips of my ballet flats. "I think you'd be a great mom." Then he cleared his throat and focused back on my face. "And I think whoever you choose to have those babies with would be very, very lucky." I was about to ask who he thought that person should be, but he cut me off, pointing to the food, saying, "Gotta finish."

I let the conversation drop as he layered the lasagna then double-checked the directions and put it in the oven. Once finished, he pivoted around with a raised eyebrow as if to ask *How'd I do?*

"Very nice, Chef."

He cleaned his hands and tossed the apron onto the counter.

"You missed a spot." I wiped off a smudge of sauce from his cheek. "How'd you even get it on your face?"

"No idea." He held my thumb to his mouth to lick it off.

It was truly a miracle I could still stand, and the corner of his lips twisted up wickedly. He knew I was putty in his hands.

Gently backing me against the counter, he bracketed his hands on either side of my waist, his feet outside of mine. "What's up? You look like you want to say something."

"How do you know?"

"This." He touched the crease at my eyebrow. "So? Let's have it." When I hesitated, he grimaced. "That bad, huh?"

"Maybe."

He kissed the corner of my mouth. "Maybe you should just say it."

When I had started dating Hunter, we'd been kids in college, and the relationship evolved in the way college relationships did, with parties on the weekends and lunches in the cafeteria between classes. We were together and didn't have to have the weird *What are we?* conversation.

And I didn't know how to bring it up with the man who had his hands inching under my sweater. Especially now that we had to go in reverse, from talking about theoretical children to what was even possible between us. "I, uh, was wondering..."

"Wondering how I feel about you?" He ducked his head, waiting until I met his gaze. "It's pretty simple. I want you. To myself. For the foreseeable future."

I eyed him. "And I want you to tell me if you're some kind of psychic or not."

"Not psychic." He kissed my cheek. "Only able to read you pretty well." Then he kissed my other cheek. "Like you can with me. What do you think I'm thinking right now?"

I pursed my lips, tilting my head side to side. "You're thinking how you should've added a touch more salt to the lasagna."

He nipped at my jaw. "Try again."

"Hmm? Your feet are cold with no socks on."

He leaned in, bending me back over the counter. "Nope. I'm real warm."

I slipped my right hand between us and cupped the hard

outline of him through his jeans. "You're thinking maybe I should stop playing around and kiss you already."

"Bingo."

Gripping him hard, I kissed him, trying to express what I felt for him. I didn't know the word that described this emotion, this innate rightness. Like we were meant to be.

What I did know was how his stomach muscles tensed under my hand when I scratched lightly at his skin. He wrapped his fingers tenderly around my throat, even while his kisses were biting and rough. And when we broke apart, he pressed his palms against my cheek, his thumbs caressing me there. As his gaze bored down on me, I knew from the look in his eyes, this was real. This was *it*.

The timer dinged on the oven, and Chris slowly let go of me before opening the door to retrieve his homemade lasagna.

"Smells delicious," I said as a car honked twice outside.

"Right in time." He carefully moved the dish to the counter, hearing car doors shut out front. "That must be your dad."

We both rushed out to help him out of the car. Trudging up the sidewalk, Chris and I each held my dad up, as Mom opened the front door for us.

"How do you feel?" Chris asked, steadying him on the steps.

"Like I went ten rounds with Hemingway."

"Hemingway?"

"Ernest Hemingway was an amateur boxer," Dad explained with a slight wince as he stepped through the doorframe and took off his coat.

Mom chided him. "You need to slow down. Let Bronte and Chris help you."

He ignored her and waved off Chris's offer to help him sit in his recliner. "He had a ring in his backyard."

Chris cocked his head. "Who?"

"Ernest Hemingway," Mom said, glaring at Dad. "The doctor said you need to take it easy for a few days, build your strength and stamina back up."

"Yes, Patricia."

She dropped a begrudging kiss on the top of his head. "I'm going to clean up a little, and then I'll start dinner."

Chris stopped her. "You don't have to do that. I made something for you already." He darted back to his house and returned with the steaming container held tight between two dish towels. "It's turkey and spinach lasagna."

"Bronte, go grab me oven mitts," Mom told me before saying to Chris, "You're a sweetheart."

"It wasn't all me. Bronte helped too. You guys have been so wonderful to me, I wanted to do something for you."

"I didn't help," I said, returning with two giant Mickey Mouse hand oven mitts. "And I'm not sorry about it at all." I gave him a cheeky smile at our inside joke as I spun around to follow my mother into the kitchen, letting my hand graze his hip with the tiniest of tugs on his belt loop.

"Have a seat," I heard my dad say, and I hugged the wall, eavesdropping on his conversation with Chris.

"You know I really like you, right? I think you fit right in with my family," Dad said. "Remember what I told you in the hospital?"

"You were happy it was me with Bronte and not Hunter," Chris answered.

I smiled to myself, hoping to hear more but Mom interrupted. "Bean, can you find that TV tray? It's downstairs, I think."

I nodded, catching one more bit from Dad about Chris not hurting me, and I had to bite back a laugh. My father wasn't the most intimidating man, but I loved him for trying. Loved him even more for seeing what a good guy Chris was.

After I located the tray, Mom situated a plate of food on it, and we walked it all out to the living room, where Chris was seated next to Dad in the recliners. Though Chris seemed a bit warier than five minutes ago. Must have been quite the talk.

"Look at this hospitality." Dad grinned. "You'd think I had open-heart surgery or something."

I stole a chunk of turkey off his plate, and Chris raised his eyes to me, staring as I stuck my finger in my mouth. Color rose high in his cheeks, and he cleared his throat, dropping his attention to the lasagna. "I hope it tastes all right."

"I'm sure it'll be great," Mom said, and I agreed.

"It's delicious."

He met my gaze again, this time his eyes dark and a little dazed, his tongue poking out to wet his lips.

We couldn't do this. Not in front of my parents.

"I have to go. I have my book club tonight. Chris, call me later," I said to him, essentially letting the world know, AKA my parents, that Chris and I were a *thing*. "Bye, Mom. Daddy, I'll stop by tomorrow with some sugar-free snacks."

I turned with a wave as Chris swiveled his head back and forth between my parents who were grinning.

"Okay!" he called after me.

I hit the road with a big grin, too.

CHAPTER SIXTEEN

Chris

"So, you like that period piece the best?" Wes asked, scratching at his short strawberry-blond hair, his pale eyes blinking back at me over Zoom.

"Yeah." I shuffled some papers around on the dining room table, which had become a catchall for everything. "The writing is really great, and besides the historical aspect, I just really want to play a boxer, you know?"

"Have you talked to Tom about it yet?"

"Not yet. We have a phone call scheduled for tomorrow."

Wes lifted his hand toward the screen. "How's everything else? How are you doing?"

"Everything's good. I've been relaxing, spending a lot of time outside."

"Yeah? Well, you look good. You've got that rugged mountain man thing happening. I think Pennsylvania suits you."

I rubbed at my beard. "Yeah, maybe."

"I got a text from Fitz. He said you're fitting right in."

I snorted at that, but Wes didn't laugh.

"You got something happening with Bean?"

I sucked in air through my teeth. Wes was a good friend, probably my only real friend at this point, and I trusted him implicitly, but I wasn't ready to talk about what I did or did not have going on with Bronte. I barely understood it myself, only that in the short time I'd known her, I'd fallen hard.

I didn't know what my future held, and as much as I wanted to give Bronte the world, all I could give her right now were our moments together.

"She's a sweet girl." When I nodded, Wes raised his dubious single eyebrow, probably only half kidding when he said, "Way too good for you."

"You're telling me," I huffed out, crossing my arms. I would never be good enough for her, even after a lifetime of trying.

"All right," he said, shifting away from the screen. "I gotta get back to work. I've got some calls to make. I'm glad you're doing good over there in PA, and happy birthday, man. Enjoy it. I have a hunch this is going to be a good year for you."

"Yeah. Thanks." I signed off, my mind all over the place. I was happy to talk to my buddy, but it still stung to not hear from my family. Despite the fact that I hadn't talked to them in a few years, the hurt hadn't completely gone away.

And it made me all the more desperate to see Bronte. She had parent-teacher conferences after school today, and even though we'd made plans to be together all weekend, I needed to talk to someone *now*.

Last year for my birthday, I got drunk in Vegas and married a Bally's showgirl named Sadie. Wes and Tom made quick work of the annulment, but still, it hadn't been my best or brightest decision. Especially since it had been splashed all over every magazine, solidifying my position as Hollywood's bad boy.

Since hitting rock bottom with my car accident and subsequent arrest, I'd dropped my bad habits—the drinking and partying, I'd even stopped racing cars—and that left me without a lot of my so-called pals. I didn't miss the big parties and sycophants following me around for any crumb of attention. Those people were never my real friends. They never truly cared for me, only wanted everything that came along with my fame. But being alone on my birthday really sucked.

Needing to get out of the house, I jogged next door. "Hey," I said a little breathlessly when Pattie answered the door. "Can I talk? Do you have time to talk?"

She opened the door wider, concern in her eyes. "Yes, of course I have time. What's wrong?"

"I've been making my own money since I was seventeen, starred in a dozen movies, one of which got me nominated for a bunch of awards, but I haven't spoken to my parents in over three years, and it's my birthday today. Normally I'd get drunk and throw a party, probably do something stupid, but I don't want to do that anymore. I don't want to be that person. I want..."

I want to be loved, I didn't say.

Pattie was momentarily taken aback by my outburst, though she recovered smoothly. "You know, Fitz took Steven to physical therapy, so I'm all by myself tonight. How about we go get frozen yogurt? We've got to celebrate somehow. Come on, I'm buying."

The frozen yogurt place was painted in neon colors, and Top 40 tunes played in the background. Groups of high school kids huddled in corners, and little ones climbed the walls as their parents tried to corral them.

My eyes swept the room, checking for a quiet place to sit. With my long hair and beard, plus the fact that the general public had no idea I was living here, I wasn't worried about being recognized anymore. However, I still wanted a seat away from anyone who might be able to hear our conversation. Pattie pointed out a table next to an elderly couple, and we both enjoyed our yogurt for a while in silence.

When I couldn't put it off any longer, I started from the beginning, describing my parents and my strict upbringing. After being "discovered" at bible camp when I was fourteen, playing in their end-of-summer concert, I booked a Christian teen show where we sang about our love for Jesus and acted out ridiculous scenes, saying no to drugs and sex before marriage. Tom, my now-agent, somehow got hold of one of those stupid tapes and saw something in me, flying out to Indiana to convince me to give Los Angeles a shot. True to his word, Tom made me big with the Disney crowd, but that G-rated stuff only held my attention until the checks were cashed. After that, I wanted to move on, explore, learn. That was why I took the role of James Dean in the biopic, the one which didn't shy away from the rumors and stories about Dean's bisexuality.

When my parents saw it—those sex scenes with my male counterpart, and after I'd come out as bisexual in an interview—they shunned me for good. They'd said they could only take so much. The partying was one thing, but their son being with a man was where they drew the line in the sand. That was when I really let it go. If my parents thought I was a sinner, I was going to prove them right. In as many ways as possible.

Pattie didn't flinch or judge me. Not even when I explained how I went on a weeklong bender after my last conversation with my mother and ended up getting papped completely naked—my bare ass covered magazines for weeks—or how I got into a fight with one of my costars on set.

She listened patiently while I rambled, and after I'd finally revealed every last skeleton in my closet, she smiled. "You're a good person, Chris, worthy of every good thing that's happened to you. I'm glad you've learned from your mistakes." She covered my hand with hers, giving it a small squeeze. "I can't wait to see what you do in the future."

That one sentence was more than my own parents had ever said to me.

When we got back into the car, she stopped me from putting the key in the ignition, wrapping her hand around my wrist. "Chris, I am sorry you're spending your birthday away from your friends and family, but I guess I'm a little selfish because I really love having you around. And I speak for Steven and myself when I say, if you ever feel like you need someone to talk to or a place to stay or anything else, we'll be there for you. You've become part of our family."

"That means a lot to me," I said, my throat clogged, my nose and eyes stinging. "More than you'll ever know."

"Love you, sweetheart."

I buried my face in her neck, feeling more love in that moment than I had in a very long time. "Love you too."

After the solid cry, I pulled myself together and drove back home.

Pattie nodded at a car parked in front of her house. "Shelley's here. Do you want to come in? Steven should be home in a few minutes."

I wasn't quite ready to be alone yet anyway. "Yeah, okay."

"You always know when Shelley's here because she leaves her keys in the door." Pattie clucked her tongue at said keys, although I didn't think she had a leg to stand on since she often left her door wide open. "Shell?"

"I was on my way to the store," Shelley answered, traipsing down the stairs, concentrating on fixing her shirt over her round belly, "but I had to pee so bad, I couldn't hold it." She glanced up and froze, seeing me standing next to her mother.

I waved.

"Oh, hello. That's not embarrassing at all." Then she looked to her mom. "Do you have any Oreos?"

"Do you think I could keep something like that out of your father's hands? Of course we don't have Oreos."

"Do you have any cookies? Of any kind? The baby's hungry."

Pattie led us into the kitchen and dug through a cupboard. Hidden behind boxes of brown rice and Cheerios was a bag of fat-free, sugar-free, chocolate chip cookies. Shelley frowned but opened them anyway.

"So, what's up, Chris?" she asked.

"Not much. Me and your mom just got back from a hot date."

"Oh yeah?"

"Mm-hmm." Pattie started a pot of coffee, waving me over to help. "It was lovely." She smiled at me then turned to her daughter. "I'm making decaf for us, but do you want me to make you some tea?"

Shelley shook her head, and I helped myself by grabbing two mugs, sensing her concentration on me as I busied myself with retrieving the milk and sugar as well. I fixed up Pattie's coffee—half and half with two sugars—then sat down across from Shelley with my own cup.

She eyed me. "So...this date, any particular reason for it?"

"It's my birthday," I said into my cup.

"Oh my gosh, happy birthday!"

I caught the hint of false delight in her voice.

"Scorpio, huh? How old are you today?"

"Twenty-eight."

"Wow, I can't believe it!"

Now, I knew I wasn't imagining it. There was a purpose to her questions.

"That's so funny. You have the same birthday as a famous actor. You know, I'm kind of a student of all things celebrity gossip."

Pattie plunked her mug down, coffee sloshing over the top. "Shelley, what are you—"

"It's okay." I took a breath and met Shelley's challenging glare. "And what did you learn in your studies?"

She looked me dead in the eyes without blinking. It was a bit unnerving. "You're CJ Cunningham."

"I am."

Pattie stomped around the kitchen, cleaning up her spill and other dishes, expressing her opinion with thumps and thuds.

"I must say, your disguise is really working," Shelley said with a laugh.

"That's the point."

I'd always been known for my clean-cut look with a bit of an old-school flair. I usually wore my curly hair styled in a pompadour and had a closet full of skinny ties. With so much competition in the movie industry, especially from those named Chris, Wes and I decided I needed to change my name and focus on more emotional roles. On more than one occasion, my acting had been labeled as "haunting," although only a select few knew the identity of the ghosts that provided me an endless well of inspiration.

"So, CJ—can I call you CJ?" She quirked an eyebrow.

"Enough, Shelley," Pattie snapped. "Leave him alone. He's not here for your personal enjoyment."

"Listen, Shell—can I call you Shell?" I said. "I'll answer any questions you have about my movies or LA or whatever-the-hell, but you can't tell anybody, including Bronte. I'm telling her this weekend."

"Of course," she said. "So, the other Chrises...what are they like?"

CHAPTER SEVENTEEN

Bronte

After I finished up my conferences, I had gotten caught up talking to the principal and by the time I arrived home, it was half past eight. Tossing my things down, I changed into pajamas before rustling up a bowl of cereal. I'd had my phone on silent and missed Chris's call from about an hour ago.

In the short time we'd spent together, our instant connection had grown so that he was the first person I wanted to call when my principal gave me outstanding marks for my observation and the last person I wanted to talk to before bed. I thought about him almost constantly. Whenever I had a free moment, he was there in the forefront of my mind, making a home so deep in my senses I'd sworn I saw him pictured in an ad for watches in a magazine earlier in the day.

It was his birthday today, and I had big plans this weekend, including a home-cooked meal and hours together in bed. But until then, I'd sent him some digital gifts to tide him over. The mere thought of his reaction to them had me smiling, although once I started listening to his message, I lost my light-heartedness.

"Hey, baby. I know you're at school, but I had to call and hear your voice mail message. I needed to hear your voice. I know that sounds silly, but it's true." He took an audible breath. "I'm...struggling a bit today, and you always make me feel better."

My heart skipped at the twinge in his voice.

"I'll talk to you later," he said before the click of the end of the message.

My texts to him that morning started with a picture of my bare hip and leg in bed as soon as I woke up. Then a few hours later, I sent a picture of my stomach. And a few hours after that, the edge of my lace panties. All of his returned messages had been a mixture of crude words and emojis, so I'd had no idea he was struggling.

When I called him back, he picked up on the first ring.

"Bronte."

"Hi, I just got home. I didn't know you'd called, or else I would've—"

"It's okay."

"What's wrong?" I asked.

"I had a tough day today, thinking about things, and I had a tiny meltdown."

Knowing his past, I guessed it was probably a difficult day without his family, but to hear him so troubled, I felt guilty. "I'm so sorry I wasn't with you today. I wish I would've—"

"No, I'm not telling you this to make you feel bad. I'm telling you this because you need to know how important you are to me. You keep me even, you know?"

"I know." I nodded to myself. Curling my knees into my chest, I wrapped my arms around them as I found my words. "I was never really confident growing up. I was skinny and gawky and tripping over myself all the time. I was nerdy and had a few particularly hard years in middle school." I cringed, thinking back to those years of acne and bad haircuts. "I grew out of it, for the most part," I added with a laugh. "But I still never fully felt like myself. When I got to college, it was a whole new world. It was a chance to be a whole new me. And then I met Hunter."

Chris groaned on the other end. "Do I want to hear the rest of this story?"

"Yes. This ends up good for you."

"Does it now?"

"You'll have to show me you can be a good listener and you'll find out."

When silence descended on the other end, I grinned, relieved it wasn't as hard as I thought it was going to be to tell him what I hid away from everyone else.

"When I met Hunter, he was everything a girl could ask for. Other girls were jealous of me for the first time in my life, and I hate to say it, but I liked how that felt. Although it didn't last long. Sure, on paper, Hunter was great, but he made me feel like...like he was doing me a favor by being with me. He was never physically or emotionally abusive, he just had a tendency to forget about me."

Chris grunted. I was sure he had things he wanted to say, yet he only listened. Like I asked.

"I grew up feeling that way—not with my family and my best friends, obviously—but with guys. It never occurred to me that I could feel anything different. Until I met you. You made me feel like I deserved so much more, that I was so much more."

"Because you are," he said, almost as if he'd been holding it in, and he couldn't do it anymore.

"I want you to know how important you are to me," I said. "Because you showed me what was possible."

Three little words entered my mind, but I fought them away, deciding it was much too early to feel them, let alone say them. "So, birthday boy, you've been a very good listener."

"Yes. I have," he agreed, and I could hear the smile in his voice.

"I suppose it's time for your present now."

"I suppose it is."

I held my phone away to press a few buttons, sending him the short video I'd made this morning in bed.

"What's this?" he asked after a few moments.

"You like movies, so I made one of my own."

A few moments passed, and then he blurted a squeaky, "Are you serious?"

"You'll have to watch it to find out, but do it when you're alone. It's definitely not safe for work."

"Wait, wait, wait, wait, wait, don't you dare hang up on me right now, baby."

"Huh?"

"I'm not watching this alone."

"I don't..." My face heated. I assumed I'd send the video to him, and he could have fun on his own. I did *not* expect him to want...whatever it was he wanted me to do.

There was some rustling and a couple of clicks on his end like he was opening a laptop. "This is the best present I've ever received." The sound he made was downright sinful. "Oh god, baby. Why did you make this video for me?"

"Um... I..." I licked my suddenly dry lips. "I wanted to show you how you make me feel."

"Everyone thinks you're so sweet, but you're dirty, aren't you?"

I tugged on the collar of my shirt, overheated.

"Cat got your tongue?" He let out a mixture of a laugh and moan then sucked in a breath that had me throbbing all over. "You wanted me touching myself. You wanted me to watch this video of you touching yourself, and you thought I'd do the same, huh?"

"Mm-hmm." It was all I could manage when he could see right into my brain and pull out every fantasy.

"Well, I want you to touch yourself too." When I didn't answer, he lowered his voice. "Bronte, slip your hand inside your panties. Like I'm watching you do now."

I followed his orders, stuttering an exhale as I brushed my fingers over my clit, so starved for attention, it was almost painful.

"That's it, baby. Tell me how it feels."

"I'm... I'm... I can't..."

"Tell me. Are you wet?"

"Uh huh." I panted, my fingers clumsily slipping over my slick skin.

"Look at you," he whispered, almost reverently. "I see your legs tensing. Are yours tensing now? Are your fingers drenched like they are in my video? Ah, god, Bronte, I'm already so close."

He gasped hard, his hand moving so quick on his end, I could hear it, and I lit on fire. Holding my phone to my ear was becoming more and more difficult with how I was shaking, but I didn't want to give it up even as I struggled to use one hand between my thighs. My heart pounded in my chest, my muscles clenched, and all I could think about was how bad I wanted him.

"I wish I was there with you."

"You don't know," he said. "You don't know how bad I want you, *need* you."

My skin prickled with desire, too much and not enough. Beneath my bra, my nipples rubbed along the cotton as I writhed against the cushions, and I closed my eyes, imagining Chris over me, scraping his teeth over my breasts. I imagined his hand between my legs, urging me on, his fingers pumping in and out of me. With his voice in my ear, every sensation was magnified.

I'd never done anything like this, had never felt so swollen and ready to explode. But, of course, he could read my mind. "It was boring before, wasn't it? You've been waiting for someone to let your dirty girl come out and play. Well, you got him, baby. I want every fantasy you've ever dreamed of. I want all your pleasure."

I could barely move, barely breathe, as light shimmered behind my eyelids.

"You gonna come, Bronte? You gonna come for me?"

My orgasm barreled down on me like a train racing off the tracks, and a half-moan, half-cry escaped my mouth. My back arched against the couch as his voice rasped in my ear. "That's it. So good."

A low moan echoed on his end. The sound of him coming was so delicious, it was enough to send goosebumps trailing down my arms.

I didn't expect *this* when I sent the video, but making it a two-person game was a lot more fun, and I sighed as I relaxed against the couch.

A few moments passed before he laughed, easing the lingering tension of my climax. "You're going to kill me, aren't you?"

I huffed. "If you don't kill me first."

CHAPTER EIGHTEEN

Bronte

It was finally Friday, and I was enjoying my lunch, counting down the minutes until the last bell. It'd been a long week, and I couldn't wait to get home. Since my "date" with Chris last night, I hadn't been able to cool my blood, and once I got my hands on him, I didn't plan on letting him leave my sights for forty-eight hours.

I pulled out my cell phone to text him exactly that when Rachel made a delighted sound.

"What?" I asked distractedly, admiring a selfie Chris had sent. He held a plastic turkey under his arm, one of my mother's Thanksgiving decorations. With a big, cheesy grin on his face, his brown eyes sparkled. How I ever thought I might've been able to ignore him was beyond logical comprehension.

"CJ Cunningham..."

I glanced at my friend reading her celebrity gossip magazine. "Who?"

"CJ Cunningham, the actor."

I shook my head. I could, maybe, pick out a dozen actors by name, and CJ Cunningham wasn't one of them.

"He used to be in the news a lot. He was in *Silence*, that

modern retelling of *Hamlet* a few years ago and got into a physical fight with his costar, Mickey Little."

"I think I remember hearing that, and I actually saw that movie. Not my favorite Shakespeare adaptation." I was able to count the number of movies I'd seen this year on one hand, and Rachel knew it, laughing at the haughty review.

"A source has told us exclusively that Cunningham is in the running to star in a new film, a period piece from the Gilded Age about the daughter of an oil tycoon who falls for a brawler affiliated with the criminal underground," Rachel read. "It sounds promising, although where he is hiding out is still a question. From the new look he's sporting, we're going to guess Portland or Seattle. The source would neither confirm nor deny." She lifted the magazine, pointing at the picture. "That's funny. Doesn't that look like the gas station over on Hamilton?"

My giggle was stifled when I got a glimpse at the photo. "Oh my god."

"What?"

"I know him."

"See, I told you. You—"

I squeezed my eyes shut to block out the printed photo of Chris. "No, I *know* him. He's been living next to my parents." I slowly opened my eyes to see Rachel on the edge of her chair, a grape halfway to her mouth.

"You know CJ Cunningham?"

I swallowed around a thick lump in my throat, suddenly sick to my stomach. "And I may or may not have made out with him. A few times. And done...other stuff."

"What? Holy shit!" Rachel squealed so loud, other teachers in the lunchroom twisted to look at us, and she lowered her voice. "Holy shit. How do you know him?"

"I met him on the plane coming back from Illinois."

"And you didn't know who he was?"

"No. He had the hair and the beard, and I don't really watch—it doesn't matter." I held my head in my hands. "I don't... I thought I might have... I was going to..." My sputtering words broke on a gulp.

Chris had been lying to me this whole time.

"I'm going to run to the bathroom before next period," I said, my vision blurring as I gathered my things and darted to the faculty restroom. Leaning unsteady legs against the counter, I typed out a text to my sister.

Did you know who Chris was?

SHELLEY

Finally figured it out?

I growled in anger. So much for honesty. First Chris, then my sister. Who else knew?

Tears of humiliation stung my eyes as I thought of how I'd acted with him, how I'd *thought* I felt about him. It was all a lie.

With yet another **SOS** text to the girls, I opened the web browser on my phone to find pictures of CJ Cunningham before texting a few of them to the girls. Gem, usually always available with her easy come, easy go work schedule, was the first to appear on the FaceTime call.

"Hey, how's it— Are you crying? What happened? I thought your dad was doing well."

"No, he is. He's—"

Laney appeared next, laughing. "Bronte, why did you send us photos of CJ Cunningham...and why are you crying?"

I could only gurgle a few nonsense words before Sam popped up on the screen. "Hey, I— What's going on?"

I blew my nose and took a deep breath. "Chris is CJ Cunningham."

My best friends said nothing. They went completely mute.

"That's why I sent you those pictures. The guy with the beard and sunglasses and long hair, that's who I met on the plane. That's who's been living next to my parents."

"You're fucking kidding me," Gem said in a hushed tone.

Laney dug her pointer finger into her temple like she was trying to fix a machine. "CJ Cunningham has been living next to your parents? The guy you've been lusting after since the moment you met him is CJ Cunningham? Ho. Ly. Shit."

"Bronte," Sam said seriously. "How did you not know?"

"When he said he was in the entertainment industry, I thought maybe it was something to do with marketing or money...or I don't know." I flailed my arms around my head. "And you see what he looks like. I didn't recognize him. It's not like I'm a movie connoisseur." I recalled sitting next to him on my parents' couch last month, while he went on and on about *Princess Bride*, and how I thought it was so cute he knew so much. Like he was some kind of movie buff. When he was a movie *star*. Embarrassment and betrayal chilled my blood, and I shivered, suddenly cold. "He was so sweet, and-and-and...I thought..."

I thought I was falling for him.

I thought he was falling for me.

When I broke down in tears, Sam stuck out her bottom lip. "Are you upset because he lied to you?"

"Yeah." I wiped at my eyes. "It's not that I care who he is. I don't."

"You care a little bit, though, huh?" Gem said. "Remember we all went to see his movie together when you broke up with Hunter that one time in college." She snapped her fingers. "Oh god, what was it? He was so hot in it...with the girls who were being experimented on. Remember? It was based on that book."

"*Final Girls*," Laney supplied. "There was a sequel too. Didn't he date the girl in it? Layla Mahoney?"

I wanted to wail. This man, who had wormed his way into my heart, whom I thought belonged to me, didn't. He belonged to the world at large. "I don't care about any of that. I don't care he's famous. I care that he lied, and he has this whole other life I won't fit into." I pressed my hand to my heart. "We can't be together. He's a famous actor, and I'm a teacher. It could never work."

"Well," Laney said, her nose scrunching up like she was afraid to say whatever it was she was about to say. "Famous people get together with non-famous people all the time. Look at the couples who've stayed married in Hollywood. It's mostly actors who are married to, like, bartenders and makeup artists."

Gem slapped her hand down on the table, backing up Laney. "Like Matt Damon!"

I wanted to laugh but could only cry.

"Aw, Bron," Laney said. "I'm sorry."

"Do you want us to come down?" Gem asked. "I'll put Willow on a plane or in the car. Say the word and—"

"No, no. It's fine. I'm fine."

"What are you going to do?" Sam asked as the bell rang.

I tipped my head up at the ceiling, like maybe if I stared hard enough, I could reverse time, un-ring the bell, go back to before this day started. Back to when CJ Cunningham was still Chris.

"I don't know."

I spent the rest of the school day in a fog, somehow making it through, mostly due to Rachel's help, then headed right to my car as soon as I could with one goal in mind. To tell Chris off.

I screeched to a halt when I spotted the man in question on

top of a ladder in front of my parents' house. I slammed the car door, and he turned over his shoulder, his face breaking into a grin, proving Gem correct in her observation. He was hot. Stupid-looking hunting cap and all.

"Hey, Bronte."

Even through my anger, I still loved the way he said my name like that. Like it was his favorite word. "What are you doing?"

"Something is stuck in the gutter, so I thought I'd—"

"No!" The word detonated, startling not only Chris but myself too. "I know who you are, CJ."

His mouth dropped open, his jaw flapping like a fish.

"You've been lying to me this whole time."

"No, no. I haven't." He scrambled down the ladder, jumping off the last few rungs. "Everything I told you was the truth."

"How can you say that? You've been lying to me since the moment we met!"

He reached out and wrapped his arms around me.

"I didn't mean to. Not on purpose. My name is Chris. I told you the truth about everything, just—"

I pushed away from him. "Just not that you're some famous actor who's in magazines every other day for hooking up with showgirls or fighting or whatever it is you do."

"Bronte, I told you, that's not who I am anymore."

"I don't care about it. I don't care about what you did or didn't do. I care that all you talk about is being honest, yet you couldn't tell me the one basic truth of who you are. After all the time we spent together, you were really hiding from me." When he tried to get another word in, I held up my hand, silencing him. "And the irony of you being upset with me when I didn't tell you I had a boyfriend—it's laughable."

Then I spied my mother peeking out of her front door, and I

stormed inside the house. "Did you know? Did you know who he was?"

"Wes told me before Chris got here." At least she had the decency to seem guilty over her participation in this mess.

Secrets didn't exist in our family. I couldn't believe my own mother had kept this from me. "And you never told me?"

"I never told anyone. Wes didn't want me to. I promised him and Chris I wouldn't."

"Bronte." Chris was behind me, his hat in his hands, his eyes apologetic. "I never meant for you to find out this way."

"What way did you mean for me to find out? Was I supposed to see you on TV one day? Or maybe you were never going to tell me, and you could keep stringing me along?"

He gripped my shoulders, desperation dripping from his words. "I'm sorry. I wanted to tell you myself. Tonight."

"Why didn't you tell me before? You had so many opportunities."

He cupped his hands around my cheeks, and I hated that I loved the way his fingertips felt on my skin. "I didn't want to overwhelm you. You already had so much going on with Hunter and your dad. It's not like you've had an easy time these last couple of weeks, and I didn't want to make it harder on you."

I wanted to believe him. I knew in my bones he would never intentionally hurt me. Nevertheless, he had. Twisting away from him, I saw my father shuffling out of the kitchen with a glass of water in his hand.

"What's going on?" he asked.

"Daddy, tell me you didn't know too. Tell me I'm not the only one," I said, furiously wiping at my tears.

He frowned. "I'm sorry, Bean."

I touched my breastbone, my heart sinking at the betrayal on so many levels. "I have to go."

I rushed out the door, but Chris was hot on my heels. "Please, Bronte, don't go." He snagged my fingers, stopping me before I could reach the curb. "Talk to me."

I whirled around to face him, barely holding back a shout. "The time for talking is over. You missed it."

He tried to hug me to him, but when I crossed my arms, he held his hands up. "Yeah, you're right. I should have told you. Anytime we were alone, I could have told you. But would it have mattered? Would it have changed how you feel about me?"

"How I felt," I corrected, and he flinched. "But we'll never know, will we? You never gave me the chance to know how I felt about the real you."

"This *is* the real me." He held his arms out at his sides. "What you feel is for me, not some made-up image. I'm so sorry, Bronte, but my feelings for you are still the same. I'm falling in—"

"Don't! Don't say it, Chris. You messed this up." I poked him in the chest as hard as I could. "You lost the chance to hold my hand and tell me..." I stopped. The thought of hearing those words, even by my own lips, was too much to bear. "It's gone. I'm gone."

Before I could say anything else, I hopped in my car and sped away. At home, I threw down my coat and purse and immediately opened a bottle of wine. Being a cheap drunk, I felt tipsy enough after two glasses to boot up my laptop and Google CJ Cunningham.

There were thousands and thousands of pictures. Some from red carpets, alone or with other actors. Some snapped by fans on cell phones. Some from professional shoots with him brooding or glamorous or rugged, all of them utterly handsome. More than any others were the paparazzi photos. There were a lot of pictures of him with various people, some famous, some not. Most were random shots of him walking through the streets of LA, trying to cover his face or driving expensive cars. There were the ones of him in various stages of inebriation: elated and laughing, angry and violent, or passed out. There were even some of his car accident, which looked terrifying. If I hadn't known he was alive and well, I would've guessed anyone inside the car was dead.

Next were the movies. I watched any film I could get my hands on. From the three made-for-TV teen movies, which were cute but didn't make any sense, to *All That Burns*, the HBO family drama miniseries, where he played the son of an addict. Then *Broken Window*, where he played a sniper in Amsterdam during the Second World War. *The Interview* was a thriller I couldn't finish because I still didn't like to be scared, no matter who it starred. So I moved on to *Rebel*, the role that earned him SAG and Golden Globe nominations at only twenty-five years old. It was a beautiful film, and with the right makeup and lighting, Chris really did look like James Dean.

I read some articles in which he said he related to James Dean's estranged family dynamics and was quoted as saying he believed all sexuality was fluid and that working on *Rebel* made him explore his own attractions. In one interview, he said, "I don't feel I owe the public any explanation about my private life, but if it helps to crush the stigma in Hollywood and elsewhere then, yeah, I'm attracted to men as well as women. Sometimes it takes a certain event to realize something about yourself, and this movie did that for me." Connecting the dots from what Chris had told me about his family to the articles describing his downfall since the Dean biopic, I assumed that was when the chasm happened. Because of this movie and his coming out as bisexual.

I also stumbled upon a CJ Cunningham superfan, who had found clips from an old children's television show, which featured him among some other kids talking to a cartoon angel and devil on their shoulders. This superfan had a timeline of his whole career, from that weird *Barney*-like Christian show to his most recent film, *The Heat is On*, a crime drama in which he played the bad guy.

Well after the sun came up, I finally ducked under the covers in my bed, the empty wine bottle next to my head. I wasn't sure if I could ever trust him again. Or if I even *wanted* to.

I closed my eyes, trying to sleep, but it was difficult to shut off what my mind did naturally. I kept coming up with arguments for why I should or shouldn't stay with Chris. If this were any other problem, I would've made a pro/con list. It had always been easier to think in black-and-white.

The trouble was, feelings tended to be every other color of the rainbow except black-and-white.

I threw my phone against the cushions. The sixth time today. I had developed a twitch with every buzz alerting me to a possible message from Bronte, but each time, my irritation got the best of me when it turned out to be a text from Wes or some email with shit I didn't care about.

For as thoughtful and kind as Bronte was, she was also really stubborn. It had been almost a week, and she still hadn't returned any of my messages. She had to acknowledge me at some point, listen to my side.

Not that I had much of a side.

Wes once set me up with a therapist, who told me I had "destructive behavior." It didn't take a genius to figure that out, and I only lasted two sessions—I didn't like the chair I had to sit in; it was too stiff—so that destructive behavior was still alive and well.

I'd barely given my relationship with Bronte a chance to get off the ground, and already, I'd lost her.

When I fucked up, I fucked up good.

Interrupting my bleak mental ramblings, Pattie knocked three times on my front door before opening it. I'd now picked up their habit of not locking my door during the day for such occasions.

"Hey, hon." She smiled. "What are you up to?"

I was in sweatpants and a hoodie, cooking shows keeping me company. "Brushing up on how to bake the perfect apple pie."

"Looks like you're sulking to me."

"I'm not." I sat up taller to prove it.

"Sure you aren't." She took a seat next to me, her eyes on the television. "Hmm, he's adding pear. Now that's interesting." She patted my knee. "I hope you're still coming over tomorrow night."

I wanted to go, my mouth watering merely thinking of turkey, stuffing, and mashed potatoes, and I hated the idea of ordering takeout for Thanksgiving dinner.

"We all want you there," she said.

"Bronte doesn't."

"She's upset with all of us, not only you."

"Yeah, but she'll forgive you. You're her family. There's no reason to forgive me." I thought of her eyes, of how they'd been so cold when she'd confronted me. I'd never cared about a person as much as I did for Bronte, and seeing her hurt tore me in two. Like my own heart was broken.

Pattie offered me a smile. "She will. She loves you. We all do."

She loved me?

Did she?

Sure, she loved everybody because Bronte was like that. A good person.

But did she *love* me? "That's debatable."

"Hey!" She backhanded my arm. "We do love you."

I edged away from her. "I meant it's debatable that Bronte loves me."

Pattie gazed at me with kind eyes, their color a lighter blue than Bronte's. "I know my daughter, and she would only be so worked up over something she really cares about."

I tossed the pillow from behind my head across the room to the other couch to let out some of my frustration. If Bronte was worked up, she had a funny way of showing it. "I don't know. She's gone completely radio silent."

"That's Bean's MO. She picks her words very carefully, and a lot of times when she's upset, she retreats inward."

Yeah, I got that. Bronte said what she meant, and she'd said she was done with me. So…

"Fuck me."

"Hey." Pattie needled my side with her knuckle. "Watch your language. And don't give up. Show her how much you care about her. Give her the truth, and she'll come around."

I nodded, and we both turned our attention to the television until Steven poked his head in the front door a few minutes later. "Knock knock. Shell's on the phone." He held the cordless receiver out to his wife. "Something about a casserole for tomorrow?"

Pattie squeezed my shoulder before leaving with the phone. Steven stayed in the doorway, dressed in his flannel pajamas. "What are we doing over here?"

"Sulking, apparently."

"I hope you have a plan because your last one didn't work out so well," he said, occupying the spot his wife left open. "Did I ever tell you my friend was dating Pattie when I met her?"

Now that was interesting. Steven and Bronte were pretty similar, and if he'd fought through some crappy odds to get what he wanted, maybe Bronte would too. Hopefully. "Really? What did you do?"

Steven made himself at home on the sofa, placing his feet

on the coffee table. "Get me something other than water or tea to drink, and I'll tell you."

"I have pop."

"Perfect. I'll have one while we chat."

"Are you allowed to have it?"

"Come on, Christopher, you made my daughter cry. Do you really want to deprive me of a soda on top of that?"

I caved, shaking my head with a laugh, and brought Steven a tall glass of Diet Coke. We talked until well after midnight, and when Steven finally left, I fell asleep on the couch, listening to the quiet sounds of the television only to be woken up by amused shrieks.

At the window, I watched kids skipping up to a house across the street, followed by their parents carrying towers of Tupperware in their hands. It was after noon on Thanksgiving, and I was alone, still in my clothes from the night before. Not much of an improvement over last year, although this time, I had a place to go for dinner.

After a few hours of practicing my groveling speech while baking, I changed into jeans and a sweater, pulled my hair back with a rubber band I found in the kitchen, then grabbed my apple-and-pear pie and made my way next door. Everyone was already there, except, of course, the one person I really wanted to see.

I still felt guilty about how the truth came out, but as I greeted the Hollinger clan with hardy hugs and kisses, I was shamelessly relieved my secret was finally out. I settled in a seat next to Tommy, who offered me a beer.

"Welcome to the jungle," he said, and I clinked my bottle neck against Tommy's as Zoe and Matty played on the floor at our feet.

"Are you ready for number two?"

Tommy scrubbed his palm down his pant leg. "Physically

ready? Yeah, we have the nursery and everything. But mentally? I don't think you're ever really ready. Zoe was nocturnal for the first six months of her life, and I'm definitely not ready for that again."

"Sounds rough." I remembered the short but mind-fucked conversation I'd had with Bronte about kids. One of her dreams was marriage and family, and I had honestly never thought about it all that much. Though lately, I couldn't help but imagine it, consider how it was possible to be with her.

"Yeah," Tommy said. "But I can work from home if I need to so Shelley isn't by herself with the baby."

"You're a graphic designer, right?"

"Yeah, Shell and I met at the Art Institute in Philly." He was quiet for a while as he sipped his beer then said, "Bronte is pretty left-brained."

"Um...okay?"

"It's why she's having such a hard time with this whole thing. She's afraid."

I plunked my beer bottle down on the coffee table. "Afraid?"

"Yeah, she's used to this." He arched his hand in a wide circle. "This is what she knows. She's got, like, three friends who aren't her family. She dated the same guy for eight years, has lived in the same town she was born in her whole life. Hell, she even eats the same thing for lunch every day. She likes her routine—don't get me wrong, I love her like she's my own sister. That's just how Bronte is, you know?"

I nodded. I didn't want to take her out of her routine—I loved her routine—I wanted to become a part of it. Lord knows I could use some of that in my hectic life. I only had to convince Bronte to let me in, then I could move on to working out how to mesh our lives together. It wasn't impossible. It'd been done before. I'd hung out with Matt Damon and his wife. If they could make a go of it, there was no reason Bronte and I couldn't.

"But what do I know?" Tommy said, as if he were speaking my own thoughts out loud, although he stared at his wife. "I'm only the guy who followed that redhead around until she took me in." He stood to help Shelley when she struggled to sit in her chair and kissed her temple, placing a tender hand on her belly.

Pattie carried a ginormous platter of turkey from the kitchen as the front door opened, and I zipped my attention to the woman stepping through the doorway. Bronte pushed wet strands away from her face, and Zoe ran up, jumping into her arms.

Bronte kissed her niece's cheek. "Sorry I'm late. There was an accident." She placed Zoe down to remove her coat. "It starts raining, and suddenly everyone forgets how to drive."

"You're right on time. Come on," Pattie said, waving her over to the table. "Sit down, everybody."

I didn't move, my attention on Bronte. A light-brown skirt molded to her slight frame, hugging her hips and legs, and her green shirt gaped from her chest when she bent down to fix Zoe's headband. I stood as a hum coasted over my body. It had only been a few days, but I'd missed her, and my fingers practically vibrated with the need to touch her.

When she finally pivoted to me, her eyes betrayed her, exposing a flare of desire before freezing over. Then she fixed her shoulders, walking past me. But the ice queen thing was all a charade, and I was determined to break it.

After everyone was seated, the adults at the expanded dining room table and the kids at smaller tables in the living room, Pattie asked, "Who's saying grace?"

She eyed all her children as they rushed to put a finger on

their noses. All except me. I laughed uncomfortably. "Guess it's me, then."

Pattie shook her head. "You don't have to."

"Hey, nose goes," Fitz said in protest. "You're up, buddy."

Amanda, Shelley, and Tommy all nodded. Even Steven shrugged, clearly aware of the rules. Bronte ignored me from her seat at the other end of the table.

"Uh, okay." I lifted my hands, a habit ingrained from my childhood. "Heavenly Father, uh, we thank you for..." I peeked up from my plate, finding Pattie grinning at me. "I'm thankful for being invited here, into this beautiful home." Then I turned my focus to Steven. "And I know we are all especially grateful everyone sitting here is happy and healthy." Once more, I glanced around the table. "So, let's give thanks to God for not only this delicious food, but also for a wonderful family."

A chorus of Amens sounded from the table.

"Well, now. Let's eat," Steven said, digging into the green beans.

As always, dinner was loud, but it was a distant drone while I studied Bronte. She'd doused her mashed potatoes with a disgusting amount of gravy, and it didn't escape my attention how she cut her eyes to me as she placed the gravy boat back down. I smiled, but she twisted away, talking to Shelley instead.

The house quieted down after dinner, and everyone dispersed to different rooms. Shelley didn't feel well, so Tommy scooted her out the front door with Zoe on his hip. I spent about an hour with Luke before Amanda and Fitz took the boys home. They were going away the following day and needed to get to bed early.

So, with nothing to do, I left a sleeping Steven in the living room and made my way to the kitchen, where Bronte and Pattie were finishing up with the dishes.

"Need any help?" I asked.

Bronte slammed the cutlery drawer shut. "Not anymore."

"It's good to know you still have a voice."

She spun to me, dropping the towel from her shoulder to the counter, narrowing her gaze so I felt like a schoolboy in trouble. "I'll call you tomorrow," she said to her mom, then kissed her cheek and brushed past me with barely an inch of space between us. "Excuse me."

With a glimpse to Pattie, who only slanted her head in Bronte's direction in the universal *Go after her!* sign, I stepped back into the living room in time to see Bronte slip out the front door.

CHAPTER TWENTY

Chris

The rain had slowed to a fine mist, and though the pavement looked slippery, it didn't deter Bronte from marching away from me at a fast clip.

"Watch out!" I called, the heel of her boot precariously close to a crack in the sidewalk.

She turned over her shoulder, and I took the opportunity to hurdle the three steps of her parents' stoop to catch up to her. "Please, Bronte, you have to talk to me."

She started away again. "No, I don't."

"Fine." I jumped in front of her. "Then don't talk. Listen."

She snapped the lapel of her coat and folded her arms like she had somewhere to be. Probably anywhere away from me. When I didn't immediately explain myself, she let out a tiny impatient growl.

"Not out here," I said, pointing to my house "Come inside."

She frowned, her gaze settling over my shoulder.

"Please. Please, Bronte." My voice broke on her name, and even though I knew what I felt for her was bigger and better than anything else in my life, I didn't know exactly how much until this moment. Until I was faced with losing her, and every broken piece of me called in pain.

"Fine," she mumbled and stomped off.

Inside, I tried to take her coat, but she tore away from me. "Okay." So, she wasn't giving up the Ice Queen performance. "How about a seat?"

She sat stiffly and crossed her legs.

"Comfortable?"

"I'm listening, but so far, you haven't said anything."

I scrubbed my hands over my face, willing my brain to get in on the act. She was ready to bolt, and I needed to cut her off at the pass. "First of all," I started, reaching for her hands but thinking better of it. I dropped my arms to my sides. "I'm sorry I got in between you and your family. I would never intentionally do anything to cause a rift between you guys."

She nodded. She knew I loved her family. At least that part, I was confident in.

"And I've been thinking about what I would do if I could do it all over again. If I could sit down next to you on the plane again, would I tell you who I was? But you know what? I wouldn't. I wouldn't because I think if I did, you wouldn't have talked to me. You wouldn't have taken the time to get to know me."

Even though I was putting words in her mouth, she couldn't deny it.

And she didn't try to, only stared off to the corner of the room, her chin set in a stubborn tilt.

"I get that you like having everything in your life planned out, and you'd probably prefer me to be an accountant or someone with a nine-to-five job. I get it. I get why I make you nervous."

At that, she uncrossed her legs and arms, opening up to me. She dragged her eyes to mine, they were rimmed red. She was angry and hurt, and I sunk down to the floor, literally groveling.

"You have to know, I'm nervous too. You're this wonderful, sweet, and good person, who by some chance of fate fell into my life, and I'm scared I'm going to destroy what we have with my...well, by being me. That's why I was afraid to tell you."

She studied me for an eternity, her fingers restless in her lap, like maybe she wanted to touch me, and that gave me hope. She laced her fingers together, and dropped her chin to her chest.

My heart ached.

"You've been acting all along," she said in barely a whisper. "When I thought I was the one person you could be honest with."

"You are, baby, and I'm so sorry. I've told you more about my life than anyone else." I eased a few inches closer. "No one knows me like you."

She nodded, her hair a curtain around her face so I couldn't see her tears, but I heard them in her voice. "I did a lot of research last week. Some movie reviewer called you this generation's Leonardo DiCaprio."

I huffed, but otherwise stayed still and quiet.

"Are you sure you didn't want to tell me because you knew what would happen? You figured you were on this vacation, why not try to hook up with some random chick while you're at it because—"

"Bronte, no. No, no, no," I said, this time clasping her hands between mine. She didn't push me away, and hope fluttered in my belly. I bent my head down and waited until she lifted her eyes to mine. "I never expected to meet you, and I certainly didn't come three thousand miles for a hookup. What I told you on the plane was the truth. I needed to get away, clear my head, and let things settle down. That's all true. I spiraled out of control after everything happened with my parents. I've never been the brightest kid," I said with a laugh, "and I've always been a bit of a menace."

The corner of her mouth threatened to curl, and my hope sprouted wings.

I inched one hand up around her neck. "I'm an actor. I want to work and inspire people, like others have inspired me, but I've let a lot of bullshit get in the way of that. I'm trying to be a better person for my career, but also for my friends, for you."

"For me?"

"Of course, for you. I'm sorry for not being honest with you." I bent my forehead to hers. "It isn't an excuse, but I didn't want to lose what we have. Because whatever it is...it's the best thing that's ever happened to me. So, you can be mad and not talk to me for as long as you'd like, just don't give up on me, Bronte. Please."

She swallowed audibly, her breath mingling with mine as she nodded. "I won't. I promise."

And I think I damn near passed out.

I backed away an inch, sweeping my thumb under her jaw, and she nestled into my palm. This sweet girl.

"I haven't been able to think of anything else but you and your voice and how warm your lips are when you kiss me and how you go all soft in my arms whenever we're together."

Her tongue wet her lower lip, her eyebrows kicking in a teasing invitation. This dirty girl.

"I'm done listening," she said with a jolt from the couch.

I almost couldn't keep up, still a little stunned that she had dropped into my life, allowing me to mess up her plans so thoroughly.

"I'm forgiven?" I asked, from my position on the floor, and she nodded, wrapping her hand around my arm to haul me up.

I could practically feel her shaking next to me. Or maybe it was actually me who was shaking. "Can I finally take you to bed?"

"Please. God, yes." She jerked off her coat and moved to kiss me, but before she could land anywhere near my mouth, I scooped her over my shoulder, taking off upstairs.

I set her down once I reached my room and hastily scanned my mess. I got a quick flash of her dimples as she dropped to the edge of the bed while I tossed laundry into the basket. She'd already taken off her boots but otherwise remained fully dressed. I bent for the briefest of kisses, raking my eyes over her.

"I don't know where to start," I mused, eager to kiss and lick every inch of her body. I wanted to go slow, delight in our first time together, and also fuck her into next week.

She pinched her shirt between her thumb and index finger. "You could start with this."

Taking her advice, I undid the buttons, revealing more perfectly pale skin with each one. With it stripped off, I kissed both of her shoulders, then trailed a finger down her sternum to her black bra.

"What's this?" I poked at the thick cup with a finger, only for it to spring back.

She flushed crimson. "A lie. I need to buy padded bras to make me look as if I have something up top."

I crooked a finger under a strap and lowered it, clicking my tongue. "Tsk, tsk, tsk. Naughty girl. Lying is a sin, don't you know?"

"Like you haven't before." Her words came out rather breathlessly as I unhooked the clasp at her back with an easy flick of my fingers.

I tossed the offending thing over my shoulder and covered a nipple with my mouth, humming. Then I moved to the other, licking and sucking it to a peak. "But you're supposed to be a good girl. And good girls don't lie."

"Do you want me to be good right now?"

I basked in the huskiness of her voice. "No."

She unbuttoned my jeans, and my chest rose and fell in deep breaths when she palmed my cock, squeezing hard. She knew how I wanted her hands on me, hard and fierce and more than a little desperate.

Controlling my greedy urges, I gently pushed her down to the mattress, skimming my hand along her side to find the zipper of her skirt. It was long and tight, and she had to help me get it off, revealing miles of leg. I ran my fingers from her thigh to her knee and back.

"I love your skin." I kissed the inside of her thigh and dragged my nose up her leg. "You smell so good. Fruity." I traced the tattoo at her hip, an anchor with a heart above it formed out of a rope. "And this."

"It was my first one. I got it at the beach during senior week. My parents flipped when they found out."

I smiled, imagining young Bronte getting an illicit tattoo and probably thinking she was so sly, as my hands continued their journey, wanting to discover every inch of her skin like an explorer, mark her as mine. Slowly, I skimmed my fingers up her rib cage, outlining each one, then moved on to circle her breasts.

"I want to tattoo my name on you," I said, giving voice to my deepest desires to claim her.

"Cliché."

I'd give her a cliché. I grabbed her shoulders and secured my mouth to the skin under her collarbone.

She shrieked as I sucked. "Chris!" She giggled and batted at me, but I held tight. "You're gonna leave a mark!"

After a moment, I released her, running a palm over the

hickey. "I claim this body in the name of Christopher Judd Cunningham."

She angled her chin down, trying to view the purple mark I'd left. "Judd?"

"After my mother's father." I threw my shirt to the floor. "What's your middle name?"

"Sophia."

"Bronte Sophia Hollinger. Pretty."

I rid myself of my jeans, leaving only my boxer briefs and her pale pink underwear between us. I dragged my finger over the wet spot marring the silky material. "You've been thinking of this, haven't you? Of me getting you naked?" I rested my weight on top of her, licking and sucking at her neck until she writhed beneath me. "Even when you were angry at me, you knew how good it would be between us." I yanked her panties to the side, gliding my finger down to her opening, parting her flesh. "Tell me, Bronte. Tell me you knew it was going to be good between us."

She nodded, speaking her words against my lips. "So good."

She was wet and ready for me, I groaned. "Do you know how often I think about you? About this?"

She hiccupped her words when I sunk my middle finger into her. "H-how... How often?"

"Every night. Every night I watched that video you sent me," I said, flicking my tongue over her nipple. "I think about being with you like this. I think about your wetness on my fingers and your breath on my neck."

She let out the tiniest sound, her eyes fluttering closed, but I wanted more from her, wanted to see her lose control. When I sucked on her nipple and circled her clit at the same time, she exhaled on a moan, her mouth going slack. And that was more like it. She was so slick, I pushed two and then three fingers into her, curling them up to find the spot that made her legs spasm. Her breathing sped up, and she didn't need to tell me she was close, but she did anyway.

"You're going to make me come." She speared me with eyes so full of yearning, I nearly buckled under my own desire. I would follow her around on all fours, all she had to do was ask. "Chris."

My name was a plea on her lips, and I drank it up, my tongue plunging into her mouth as she orgasmed, her inner muscles clamping down on my fingers, the most gorgeous pink taking over her skin.

I laid open-mouthed kisses across her throat and collarbone until her breathing slowed and her body relaxed. Without leaving the bed, I stretched over to the nightstand and wrenched open the drawer, rooting around for the box of condoms.

I ripped off my underwear and sat back on my heels, but as I fiddled with the plastic square, Bronte wrapped her fingers around my length, stroking me with a perfect mix of hard and slow. "Here," I said, handing the condom to her. "Since you seem so sure of yourself."

Once she had it on, she melted back against the pillows and guided me to her. We let out matching sighs as I slid inside, thrusting experimentally, rocking my hips until she arched up and into me. She reached her hands around to my ass, silently begging for more, and I lifted her leg, pressing it to her chest with my shoulder, hitting a different angle.

Her nail scored down my back, setting all of my nerve-endings on fire.

"Bronte." I lifted off her. "Stop that, or I won't last long."

"So don't." She bit my chest, and I hissed. "I like that you can't control yourself. I don't want you to be gentle. I want you to be rough and throw me down because you can't wait another second."

To further her point, she pulled my hair, and, fuck, she was going to kill me.

"You really are my dirty girl." I sucked another mark into her skin, this one on the underside of her breast and pinched her nipple.

Since this was our first time, I would've liked to take it slow, but I wasn't going to deny her anything. Especially when she wanted it fast and hard. I pitched myself back up to my knees, holding her legs up so they draped over my chest and shoulders, and I thrust into her with a relentless rhythm.

Her fingernails dug into my thighs, and I didn't care. I wanted her to leave evidence that she was here. That she owned me.

Her breathing faltered, a mixture of nonsense words and moans of pleasure rolling off her beautiful tongue. I let my hand venture from her shin, down her leg, to her hip. I needed to see her when she came for the first time with my cock inside her. "Baby, open your eyes. Look at me."

She did, and they were dark and dilated with desire, but only for a moment before she closed them again. I slammed hard into her. "Open, Bronte."

When her eyelids snapped open, she held my stare as she fell apart underneath me, whispering my name. I had done it. I had claimed her, and if I could, I'd press pause on my life and live in the moment forever. Because this right here was what I wanted for the rest of my life. Me and Bronte together.

CHAPTER TWENTY-ONE

Bronte

My cell phone rang, lurching me from a dead sleep. My eyes popped open, then snapped shut from the scratch of my contacts, and I rolled over, blindly reaching for the phone.

"What is that?" Chris grumbled from beside me, and I blinked a few times, fighting my burning eyesight to take in the man next to me. With his arm thrown over his face, all I could make out was his left forearm and full lips nestled in his thick, dark beard. I was held back from kissing him as my phone stopped ringing for a few seconds, then immediately began again.

"Baby, please, pick it up." His voice was all groggy, as if he'd smoked a lifetime of cigarettes or used it too much during the night. Resisting the urge to climb on top of him, I hunted for my phone, hanging my head off the side of the mattress, searching under my clothes. That was when a sharp smack landed on my butt. I yelped, surging back onto the bed.

Chris was up, resting back on his elbows, grinning. "I couldn't resist."

"I left my contacts in. My eyes are like sandpaper." I shoved the heels of my hands into them. "I can't find my phone, can you?" I asked and headed in the direction of the bathroom, bumping into the wall twice. As I blinked under the fluorescent lights, my bloodshot eyes stared back at me. Not to mention the bed head and hickeys on my chest.

Fantastic.

"Found it," Chris called from his room. "It's your mom. Do you want me to answer?"

I heard him pad down the hall as I removed my contacts and set them on the sink before squinting at him. "No." I rubbed at my eyes then squinted again. "I can't see a thing without my glasses."

"Can you see this?" He tugged on his erection, and I frowned.

"Forever thirteen years old, I suppose."

I rolled my eyes as he pushed off the wall and crowded into the bathroom behind me. Wrapping his arms around my waist, he pressed his naked length against my lower back as his lips started on the spot behind my ear.

Even after all the hours we'd spent tangled up in each other last night, I was still so hungry for him and reached my arms up behind his head to hold him in place at my neck. He moved his hands past my hips and between my legs, dipping his fingers inside me, and I purred, letting my head fall against his shoulder.

"You're so sensitive," he rasped against my ear, and I ground into his hand, though a sound downstairs caught my attention.

He bent over, curling me against the sink, spreading my legs open farther, his index finger drawing my wetness lower to gently prod at my behind. "You like this?"

Chris was only the second man I ever slept with, and my experience was vastly different than his, but I couldn't deny that my fantasies often strayed outside of what I knew. "I don't know," I confessed quietly. "I never tried."

He hummed into a kiss against my neck. "I like it." His teeth sank into my neck, and I shivered. "You can touch me there whenever you want."

I wiggled back against him, that new knowledge sending goosebumps over my skin at all the possibilities, and I felt him smile against me. "My naughty schoolteacher."

Just as he brought his finger back to my clit, the doorbell rang.

"Chris."

He stopped, peering at my reflection in the mirror.

"Someone's at your door."

"I didn't hear." He shook his head like he was in a daze. With a reluctant graze of my hip, he stepped away from me and snatched a pair of sweats from the floor then tossed me a pointed look. "Don't move."

I combed my hands through my hair, straightening it out as best I could, then ransacked the medicine cabinet. I hastily finger-brushed my teeth, rinsed with a bit of mouthwash, then tried out a few poses in the bathroom, contorting myself into something sensual but quickly gave up the ridiculous idea of being sexy in a green-tiled bathroom. Instead, I ambled back to the bedroom, my legs still a little wobbly from last night, and plopped onto the bed, swiping my cell phone on. I had three missed calls and one voice mail, but before I could listen to them, Chris stormed up the steps.

"Your sister's having the baby." He held his hand right in front of my face as if testing my vision. "Also, your mom knows you're here," he added, almost as an afterthought.

I gaped at him. "She knows?"

"Your car's out front." He shrugged.

"She knows I'm *here*?" I paced the length of his room. "Oh god. She knows we had sex."

"What?"

"My car's out front, you answered the door like that—" I flailed my hand at his bare chest, a few marks of sex left there "—and she figured out we're doing it."

He snorted a laugh. "Doing it?"

"Yes! My parents can't know I have—" I lowered my voice on the last word as if they could hear me saying it "—sex." This was worse than the time they walked in on me making out with Anthony Rudnick in the eleventh grade—the ultimate embarrassment.

He only laughed harder. "Bronte, you're a grown woman. Of course you have sex."

"Yes, but they don't have to *know*. And right next door!"

He gathered me in his arms and kissed my forehead. "You do realize your parents have sex too, right?"

"No, no, they don't. And as far as my parents are concerned, we don't either."

He kissed me again. "Okay, whatever you say." He tossed me the crumpled skirt from last night. "I told your mom we'd be at the hospital shortly."

I held up the wrinkled clothes. "I can't wear this. It screams walk of shame. I have to go home."

He appraised me from the top of my head to my toes and back. Usually, I'd feel gawky and self-conscious, maybe cover up, but not under his stare. He made me feel beautiful with the way he looked at me. "You're gorgeous." He approached me like a hunter stalking his prey and raised his hand to my cheek. "I'll take you home, but can I have a few more minutes first?"

I slipped my arms around his neck. "A few minutes won't hurt, right?"

Two hours later, I raced into the hospital with Chris trailing behind. I hoped no one would notice how long it took us to arrive, but the waiting room was empty, save for my dad and Zoe, who was busy coloring.

"Aunt Bean!" Zoe hooked on to my legs. "Mommy is giving me a brother!"

"I know. Are you excited?"

"Yeah! Yeah! Yeah!" She hopped over to Chris. "Hi, are you here to see my brother, too?"

"Yep." He took her outstretched hand and followed her to the table where a coloring book and crayons were spread out. He greeted Dad with a handshake. "Congratulations, Grandpa. This family has a thing for spending holidays in the hospital."

He grinned. "This time, it's for a great reason."

I leaned over to kiss his cheek, a warning in my eyes. He had a knack for letting embarrassing things drop at the most inopportune times.

"I didn't say anything." He held up his hands. "Though, I couldn't help but notice your car was parked outside of our house today, yet you weren't visiting your dear old dad. Curious."

"Daddy." My cheeks heated as I slouched into a chair next to him.

"Imagine my surprise. My Beanie Baby has a life of her own."

Chris covered his laugh with a cough. Why wasn't he as mortified as I was? He had been caught with his pants down, so to speak.

"Zoe, what are you coloring?" he asked. "Princesses? Can I color too?"

"Yeah, here." She clumsily ripped out a page for him. "You color Snow White. I color Ariel."

He sat down next to her and diligently went to work on the birds flying around Snow White's head.

"How's it going?" I asked when my dad checked his watch.

"Good, I guess. Your mom's in there with your sister. Tommy keeps coming out to give updates."

"Yeah? He's nervous?"

"It never gets easier. Each time your wife is in labor, it's as nerve-racking as the first time. With you, I barely got your mother out of the car before you were poking your head out. I thought I was going to have to pull over on the side of the road and deliver you myself."

I laughed, picturing how frazzled he must've been.

"Oh, sure, it's funny now, but I was losing my mind. Your mother was screaming at me, and I was stuck behind a car going twenty miles an hour."

"Is that the reason Bronte drives so slow now? Because it was her first experience on the road?" Chris asked, smirking at us over his shoulder.

I nudged the toe of my shoe into his lower back. "I do not drive slow. I follow the rules of the road. You, on the other hand…"

He pursed his lips, and my gaze automatically dropped to them. His tongue poked out, wetting them, the corner of his mouth kicking up, and I raised my eyes back up to his. They crinkled in a wicked smile.

Twenty-four hours ago, I was so mad at him, I look him in the eyes. Now, all I wanted to do was stare. This man was mine. To stare at, to touch and kiss, to hold his hand as he drove way over the speed limit, to celebrate holidays and births.

He belonged to me.

And to the world. But I couldn't think about that. Not yet, not after our amazing night together. Maybe once we had more time, I'd be able to understand the full picture of what it meant to be with CJ Cunningham, but for now, Chris was here.

Mine.

From the flare of his nose and the chest-expanding breath he took, I could guess what he was thinking right then too.

Mine.

Abruptly, Tommy burst through the doors, beaming. "He's here. Mason Henry Daneker. Eight pounds, seven ounces, nineteen inches, and a full head of red hair."

I leaped up to hug my brother-in-law. "When can we see him?"

"In a little bit." Tommy hugged everyone, including Chris, twice. Picking up Zoe, he said, "You want to see Mommy?" When she bobbed her head, he waved to us. "Give us a few minutes?"

"Guess I should call your brother," Dad said, tugging out his cell phone.

"I'm going to go down to the gift shop, see what they have." I gestured to Chris. "We'll be back in a bit."

Walking hand in hand to the elevator, he towed me into his side. "Your family never wants for excitement, huh?"

"Too much?"

"Nah. I love it. All the energy, how everybody is in everybody else's business. I feel really lucky to be included with the Hollinger crew."

If I weren't already smitten with him, that would have sealed the deal. I planted a swift kiss to his cheek, and the elevator arrived, the doors opening with a soft ping. A pair of nurses strolled in, settling into the corner opposite us.

Chris kept his attention on the red numbers above, counting down to the lobby, but I could have sworn the nurses did a double take toward him as they exited. He either didn't notice or care, so I tried not to either.

At the gift shop, we perused the merchandise, deciding on flowers for Shelley, a monkey balloon for Mason, and a chocolate bar for Zoe. As the old man behind the counter pecked at the cash register with his index fingers, slow to ring everything up, I browsed the magazines. A picture of Chris graced the cover of one, the same one Rachel had shown me a few days before. The caption read, *"CJ Cunningham Bearded and Beautiful."*

He snagged it out of my hands. "Don't read that."

"It's kind of hard not to."

He wrapped a hand around my elbow, tugging me close so no one else could hear. "Promise me you won't read that kind of stuff. They'll print anything for money."

Celebrity gossip magazines and sites had never held much interest for me, but now that Chris was on the covers, it was kind of impossible not to pick them up out of curiosity. "I promise." I glanced at the gossip rag once more. "Who even took that picture anyway?"

He shrugged. "Could have been anyone with a cell phone. It paid for somebody's college tuition."

That didn't make sense to me. "Why haven't people flooded here to see you if they know where you are?"

"They don't. Wes made a deal. If the magazine didn't print my location, they'll get first rights on my next photos."

"But...what? I don't understand." It was obvious where he was. The picture showed him walking out of a gas station down the street from my parents' house.

"It was a close-up, no street signs or landmarks to designate where I am. The only people who know where the photo was taken are the person who took it and the magazine, and they were both paid handsomely to keep their mouths shut. The next time I'm out and ready to be seen, Wes will call their photographers, and they'll get their exclusive. This Hollywood thing is all about making money. It's a big scam." He described the whole ordeal with a sneer as he paid the old man, who didn't put two and two together even though he got a good peek at Chris and the magazine.

Although it didn't escape my notice how he kept his head

down as we walked, his shoulders raised until we were back in the elevator. It was empty this time.

"Do you want to borrow my glasses?" I held them out to him. "It might help as a disguise."

"I like them better on you. Like a sexy librarian." He kissed my neck, towing me in front of him, the proof of his librarian kink against my backside, but I shoved him away, hopping out of the elevator when it opened back up on the maternity floor. "You better return those overdue library books, or you'll have to pay a fine."

I tossed him a lascivious, over-the-top wink that had him laughing until I bumped into the table, not watching where I walked. "Son of a..."

He caught up to me, his hand on the small of my back as I bent to rub the side of my knee. "You okay?"

"Hard corners and I don't mix."

He shook his head, bemused. "Will I have to get those plastic things for all the furniture, then?"

"Only if you're planning on keeping me."

"Oh, I'm keeping you." He wrapped me up in a bear hug.

"Good." I grinned into a kiss until Tommy called us back.

We followed him to the room where my mother, father, and Zoe were seated on either side of Shelley, all three staring at the baby in Shelley's arms. Congratulations were given, and Chris passed out their gifts. Zoe tore right into the chocolate, the candy evidently better than her baby brother.

Shelley held Mason out to me. "Want to hold him?"

I cradled my new nephew in the crook of my arm, touching his copper-colored peach fuzz. "Happy birthday," I whispered, soaking him up, his nose and the twitch of his lip. "He looks like you, Dad," I said, angling my arms so Chris could confirm. "Doesn't he?"

"Yeah, he does."

I held out my arms. "Want to take him for a bit?"

"No, that's okay. Someone else could hold him."

"Go ahead, Chris," Dad said.

"I've..." He cleared his throat with a cringe. "I've never held a baby before."

I gently positioned Mason in his arms. "Now you have. Not so bad, right?"

Shelley snatched up her cell phone. "I have to get a picture of this. It'll sell for millions."

I was ready to pounce on her, seeing how we'd just talked about such pictures, but Chris only held Mason closer, swaying instinctively in the way people did when they held babies, his face exuding wonder as he stared down at the newborn. "It might. Or maybe it'll make this handsome guy a star."

CHAPTER TWENTY-TWO

Chris

"Seriously, Bronte?" I bit out, rattling the colored twinkle lights in my hand. "You asked me to pick up lights for you. I did. I'm not returning them."

She sat cross-legged on her living room floor, meticulously organized decorations scattered around her. "I didn't think you'd come home with those big, atrocious bulbs."

"I like them. They're retro, like the ones in *A Christmas Story*."

"And your taste is as bad as the dad in that movie. Do you want me to put a leg lamp in my window, too?"

"I'm surprised you got that reference," I said with a sniff and threw my hands up. "They're tree lights, for Christ's sake, not..." I glanced around the room, struggling for an argument. "Kitchen appliances or something."

She motioned to her red, gold, and white decorations, then meaningfully raised her brow at the neon orange, blue, and green lights I'd purchased.

With another huff, I stuffed them back into the box. "Then you return them."

"Fine. I will."

I tossed the box on her kitchen table and grabbed a can of

my favorite pop from her fridge. She'd been stocking up on it since we'd gotten together, and I couldn't actually be mad at her.

After a quiet minute with only Bing Crosby singing in the background, I dropped down next to her. "Sorry I snapped at you."

"Me too."

I propped my chin on her shoulder as she carefully unwrapped glittery ornaments. "I'm really stressed out. I didn't mean to take it out on you."

"What are you stressed about?"

"*The Gilded Cage.* I have to go to New York City for a few days. I've got a meeting with the director. They want to do some screen tests."

She stopped fiddling with the baubles, smiling at me. I had given her the script to read for her opinion on it, and we had talked about me eventually going back to work. Although what we hadn't talked about was how our relationship would continue when we lived on opposite ends of the country. Neither one of us seemed ready to burst our bubble with reality. I certainly wasn't.

"Screen tests are good?" she asked, climbing into my lap.

I nuzzled into her neck. "Really good. They signed Ruthie Van Acker as the lead, so they want to see how our chemistry is."

She nodded as if she was an old pro at this. In the last few weeks, I'd given her a crash course on my career, and last weekend we had watched my rom-com *Pretty Little Thing.* Or, more accurately, she watched it. I put on headphones to listen to an audiobook. She had loved the movie.

"I'm sure you could have chemistry with a two-by-four," she said, and I gathered her hair in my fist, tugging on it until she met my gaze.

"Why do I feel like that wasn't a compliment?"

She scratched her finger along my beard. "When I watched your movies, it wasn't you. It was like, I don't know, some other person on-screen, but thinking about how you'll be kissing another woman—"

"It's not real."

"No, I know. I know." Her throat worked on a swallow, and I kissed her there. "But I also know you have love scenes, and it's weird to think about you doing that." Her hands crept up my shirt, the material bunching under her fingers at my shoulders. "Someone is being paid to put their hands on you."

"And you feel like you're missing out?" I joked, grabbing a handful of her ass. "You're touching me for free."

She ignored my attempt to sidetrack her. "I know it's your job, and you'll be excellent as Roy, but wouldn't you feel the least bit jealous or uncomfortable if it were me? What if it were part of my job to make out with the parents of my students?"

I wrapped my hands around her jaw, her point clear. "I'm really glad you don't have to."

"So, you agree? It would be weird for you?"

I pressed one soft kiss to her lips. "I get it. I do. The only thing I can say is when I would have to prepare for those scenes, I need motivation. I would need to draw on inspiration for that big monologue at the end when he's trying to prove his love, and where do you think I'd get it from?" When her eyes dropped to my throat, I tipped her chin up, forcing her focus back to my eyes. "You. It might be someone else's story, I might be dressed as a different person, saying the words written by someone else, but I will always be thinking about you."

She wrapped her arms around my neck, kissing her words into my skin. "When are you going?"

"The twenty-seventh. I'll be back for New Year's."

"Okay." She back away and ran her hands over my beard, her fingers digging into it. "I'm really proud of you."

My chest ballooned. Nothing could make me feel more like a god than her pride in me.

Then she had to go and pop it.

"And I say this with all the affection and encouragement in my heart, but I think it's time to get rid of the beard."

"You think so?"

"I really do. It's grown past hot mountain man and now borders on Old Testament proportions."

"Harsh, baby." I huffed out a laugh. "It'll be harder to hide if I get rid of it."

She pitched her lips to the side and shrugged, like *oh well*. "Guess you'll have to stay here where no one can find you."

I closed my eyes and took a deep breath, considering the outcome of this decision. It was ridiculous to be afraid to shave, and yet, it would change everything. I would step back into my role as CJ Cunningham.

"I wish." I heaved myself up off the floor, taking her with me. "Let's do it."

Inside the bathroom, I swiveled my head right and left in the mirror. "I need to trim it down."

She opened the cabinet but only came up with small nail scissors. "I assume these won't do?"

"Don't you have some with all your craft stuff?"

"Oh yeah. Hold on." She skipped out to the guest room and returned with a pair of scissors, stopping short in the door.

I had taken off my shirt, and she apparently liked the physique I'd gained from my new two-hours-a-day workout regimen in hopes of attaining the role of Roy in *The Gilded Cage*. I'd lost the belly I'd grown from months of doing noth-ing. It felt good to see her pupils expand with desire, even though she said she didn't mind my soft stomach, just like I didn't mind all her bony, hard edges.

"You about finished ogling me yet?"

She darted her attention up to my face. "It's not fair you're so tan in the middle of winter."

I pulled her close, licking the blush rising up from her neck. "I like you exactly the way you are, pasty white and all."

"Talk to me when we go to the beach, and you have to help me juggle all the umbrellas and bottles of SPF 5,000."

With my hand on her ass, I laughed. "Baby, I will buy you your own beach house with a completely covered porch so you don't have to worry about it."

Her jaw dropped, but she recovered quickly. "Momentarily forgot you can do things like that. Buy a house—" she snapped her fingers "—just like that."

"Does it freak you out?"

She laid her hands on my chest, her fingers tangling in the hair there. "A little, yeah."

"I only really started making a lot of money after *Rebel*."

"What do you mean by a lot of money?"

I didn't want to freak her out further, but she had to know the truth. "Before *Rebel*, my biggest role was in the *Final Girl* franchise, and I made ten million from that total, but since *Rebel* was low budget, I only got three million for it."

"Only three..." She blew out a breath.

"Wes is really good with money and invested some of it for me, so even without my pay raise for my last two films, I still have a pretty big chunk of change in the bank."

She seemed almost afraid to ask. "And what did you make on the last two?"

"Twelve each."

"Twelve million dollars each." She slapped her hand to her forehead. I understood these numbers were not "normal" person numbers, although if we were going to really do this, we were going to do it. Get it all out in the open.

"But that's when everything started going downhill, which is why every producer is pretty hands-off right now. They don't want to pay me to fuck up their films. I need to show them I've changed. That I'm worth those paychecks."

She blinked a few times. "Right. Yeah. Of course."

I kissed her temple. "You all right?"

"It's a lot to digest, you know? I make a little over fifty thousand, and I'm taking grad courses to get a bump in pay, but I still have to buy a lot of my own classroom supplies, and I'll never ever be able to..." She snapped her fingers. "Buy a house or a car or..."

It's a good thing I can, I didn't say, and instead kissed her palm.

"I get it." I brushed my hand over her head. "Let's go back to the easy stuff. Let's get rid of my Moses beard."

That elicited a smile, and she handed me the scissors before taking a seat on the closed toilet lid, legs crossed with her chin propped in her hand.

I got to work, clipping off chunks of hair, and when it was close enough to my jawline, I grabbed her shaving cream and razor from the shower.

"Flirty mango. This is what makes your legs smell so good?" I didn't wait for her answer. "Guess it'll have to do." I carelessly smeared it all over the lower half of my face and neck, the scent delivering a visceral reaction straight to my dick. I shifted closer to the sink in an effort to hide how turned on I was from simply coming into contact with the thing that rendered her legs edible.

Once finished, I rinsed off, and she handed me a towel. "So that's what your face looks like."

"You like it?"

"Yeah." She stood up and examined me with narrowed brows. "You'll have to stay here forever." Then she sucked my bottom lip between her own, tracing her fingers over the skin of my newly exposed face.

I let out a satisfied hum and pressed her back against the sink, dropping my mouth down to her throat, sucking and licking from her ear to her collarbone.

"You're so smooth," she said. "It feels so good."

"Should we see where else it feels good?" I lifted her up and sat her on the edge of the sink, tugging her jeans and under-wear off. I held up the red and green Christmas tree panties. "Festive."

"Bought them on sale," she said, all pleased with herself, once again forgetting I could buy her an entire store of holiday underwear if she wanted. For now, I pocketed them and sank to my knees to prop her legs over my shoulders.

I rubbed my chin along her thigh and tickled her knee with my nose. "How does it feel?"

She gripped my hair, groaning. "Like you're purposely trying to kill me."

I teased the tip of my tongue along her slit. "Death by oral sex."

Her laugh was cut off when I parted her open with my thumbs and sucked on her clit. "Oh god, Chris."

I hummed against her. "I love hearing you say my name like that. Like you're praying."

"Chris," she repeated on a breath, and I rewarded her with a flick of my tongue. "Oh god, oh god."

"No, baby, it's me doing this to you," I murmured against her, and like I had to prove I was the god she made me believe I was, I slid one finger into her, strumming the spot inside of her until her legs tensed. "You're so sweet, everything about you, from the top of your head to your toes. Everything." I added a second finger, and she squirmed on the sink, edging herself closer to me. "But you're sweetest here. Sweetest thing I've ever tasted."

She threw her head back when I licked and sucked at her, drawing out every bit of pleasure. I was relentless in my pursuit of her climax as a weary shadow crept up in the back of my mind that I had to make up for our future now. I had to prove myself in this moment, prove I was the one who knew her best, who untangled every thought and fantasy from her overactive brain. I was the only one who could pull her wants free and offer them up on a platter.

With one hand on the sink and the other in my hair, she jerked her hips. "I want you inside me."

"Give me this first. Come on my tongue, soak my fingers, and then I'll give you what you want."

She let go, and I lapped up her orgasm before digging into one of her drawers for a condom. I had her turned around and was thrusting inside of her seconds later. I met her gaze in the mirror, holding her throat with one hand, and dragged my wet fingers over her lips with the other.

"See how sweet you are?" I asked, nipping at her earlobe. She sucked my fingers into her mouth so hard, my balls ached to release. "My dirty girl."

"Chris," she whimpered.

"I know. I know." I dropped my hand to her clit, and after a few swipes, she and I were both exploding. I let my forehead drop between her shoulder blades, offering her my whole truth. "I will give you whatever you want, just don't leave me."

"I won't," she said, meeting my eyes in the mirror.

But I knew it wouldn't be that easy.

———

Two days after spending Christmas with Bronte and her family, I packed up my new suitcase, a gift from Pattie and Steve to replace my duffel bag. It was filled with newly acquired button-downs from Bronte. Naturally, she'd gone practical for Christmas and had given me clothes. Though, she did surprise me with a nice photo shoot, where she wore nothing except one of those new shirts. In return, I also had a two-part gift for her. The first, a new e-reader to replace the one she'd had that was on its last legs, and I went old-school for the second present, spending hours putting together a playlist for her.

I had thought I was being all slick and romantic, waiting until we were alone in her apartment to send her the link to the music. She grinned in delight. "Aw, like in seventh grade."

"Middle school gift for the middle school teacher."

Lying on her bed, she had flipped through the list on her phone, all songs that reminded me of her and of our time together. I had always loved to play guitar, and if I was a more talented musician—despite Bronte thinking I was *phenomenal*—I would have tried to write her a song. Instead, I let others do the talking for me.

I included her favorites, like Hozier, Elton John, and Prince, and I'd sung each song into her skin as I removed her clothing, touching and teasing her until she was completely naked and panting under me. And then I'd done exactly what Bronte suggested. I'd hid in her bed until I had to reluctantly disentangle myself from her when the alarm went off, signaling I absolutely had to leave. No more "only fifteen more minutes."

"Good luck," she said when I leaned down for a kiss. She was still wrapped up in the sheets, but the tattoo on her hip peeked out, and I was tempted to sink back to the mattress to lick it. With a knowing smile, she pushed me away. "Get out. Go. Go get your close-up. I'll still be here when you get back."

I arrived in New York City over three hours later when it should have taken only two, thanks to rush-hour traffic and a driver slower than Bronte behind the wheel. I checked in to the Bowery Hotel and was met by name by the concierge, who swiftly led me up to my room, a suite with soaring ceilings, industrial furniture, and dark hardwood floors.

The hotel had sent a basket of fruit and champagne, but I let it sit on the living room table in exchange for a shower and change of clothes. I still smelled like Bronte, and even though I didn't mind, I thought I should look a bit rested for my dinner meeting.

Wearing one of my new shirts, I headed out into the cold with my beanie pulled down low over my hair to walk the few blocks to the Mexican place on Second. Wes was already there, seated at a table in the corner.

He waved me over. "What's up, buddy? How've you been?" We gave each other a hug and quickly caught up before Dante Salvo, the director of *The Gilded Cage,* strolled in a few minutes later. In his late forties, Dante had cut his teeth as a young indie filmmaker, known for impactful yet low-budget hits. Ever since one of his films had premiered at Sundance over a decade ago, his budgets had steadily increased. This historical drama would be his biggest film to date.

Dante and I had already had a few phone conversations about the script and our ideas for Roy. However, he'd informed me he was still considering another actor. These next few days would make or break the decision to cast me.

After a three-hour dinner, I was pretty sure I'd won him over. As long as the reading with Ruthie—who was the actual star of the film; this was her character's story, after all—went well, I'd have it in the bag. To celebrate, Wes treated me to a round of drinks at a blues club in Harlem, but when we left the bar after midnight, a paparazzo showed up. Wes had warned me someone would be outside to meet our end of the bargain, and it wasn't bad until two women showed up out of nowhere, drunk and in my face, asking for pictures. I struggled to break free of what felt like tentacles around my neck and escaped into a waiting car.

As soon as the door to my suite closed, I had my phone out, dialing Bronte. It rang a few times before she picked up. "Hello?"

"Hey, baby. You sound tired. Did I wake you up?" I toed off my shoes and flung them toward my luggage, then finagled my shirt and pants off with one hand, keeping the phone connected to my ear with the other.

"Yes, but it's okay," she said through a yawn.

"Big night out?"

"Oh yeah. Leftovers and a *Downton Abbey* marathon."

"I can't believe out of all the content there is in the world, you watch the same show on repeat."

"It's my self-care, but I don't want to talk about that. Tell me about your night. How'd it go?"

I flopped on the bed in my underwear and T-shirt. "Really good. Dante and I get along really well, and he agreed with almost everything I said about Roy's character and his back-story. I ended up telling Dante about my parents since, you know, Roy doesn't have his family either."

"Really?" She let out a surprised hum. "Wow."

"I love the way he talks about using physical space, and he said he's not big on marks and relies heavily on his DP to—"

She yawned again. "DP?"

"Director of photography," I said with a laugh. "Why don't you go back to sleep? I'll talk to you tomorrow."

"No, no. I'm awake."

I pictured her all snuggled up in bed with the comforter pulled up to her chin and her cell phone at her ear. "Barely. I bet your eyes are closed, and you're lying on your side in the fetal position with the pink-stripe pajamas on."

"The green plaid." The covers rustled on her end. "How is it?"

"How is what?"

"How is it you're one hundred miles away, but it feels as if you're right next to me."

That was exactly what it felt like. Like we were two sides of the same coin. I knew her better than I knew myself. "I don't know. Maybe we were just meant to be."

CHAPTER TWENTY-THREE

Chris

I had signed the contract for *The Gilded Cage* with a thin black clicky pen. And I'd taken it. Stuffed it into my pocket as a memento of the day. Dante had asked me to stay another night and celebrate New Year's with him and some film execs, but my agent had only come to Manhattan for the length of time it took to sign the contracts, and Wes had already flown down to Florida to visit his parents. There was no point in staying. I needed to get home to Bronte. She was who I wanted to celebrate with.

Still amped-up, I knocked on her door like an overly enthusiastic woodpecker. She opened it, wearing a long sweater dress and super-sexy knee-high boots, but she didn't look nearly as excited as I thought she'd be to see me. "What are you doing here?"

"I came home early."

She studied me for a beat. "Oh."

Her reaction caught me off guard. "Are you going somewhere?"

She spun around, leaving the door open for me to come in. "No, I just got home. I went out to dinner with some friends from work." She held on to the couch as she peeled off each boot. "How'd it go?"

"I got it." I held up the pen, needing something concrete to hold to remind myself it was real. "I'm Roy."

"Congratulations."

"I'm going to take a wild guess and say you're upset about something."

She stalked around the couch to the coffee table for her laptop and showed it to me.

"What's this?"

"Scroll down."

I did, and in bold letters, the headline read, *CJ Cunningham Back at It Again*. There were four pictures from outside the bar in Harlem. I was smiling and laughing in two and had my arms around the girls in the other two.

"You were hanging out with girls at a bar?"

I closed the laptop, irritated at the accusation. "Yes, I went to a bar. No, I wasn't hanging out with girls. We were leaving, and they wanted a picture. I was with them for, like, thirty seconds. It's a bad angle. Why are you even reading this? You promised you wouldn't."

"I didn't read it. But a picture paints a thousand words, doesn't it?"

I scrubbed a frustrated hand over my face, a habit I hadn't lost since I'd shaved off my beard. "I told you how this stuff works. I was with Dante for dinner for a long time and then went out with Wes for one drink. That's it. I even told you about it. It was my first night there. I can't believe you think something else happened."

Her arms unfolded from their stiff hold, and she shook her head, stepping backward. She looked as lost as I felt and panic welled in my chest. "I don't know, Chris. I...I don't know what you're like when you're out doing the CJ Cunningham thing."

I reached for her arms, circling my fingers around her biceps. "I would never, *never* be unfaithful to you. Wes and I went to the bar to hang out, we listened to music, and those girls happened to pop up when the photographer showed up."

"No, I know you wouldn't be unfaithful. It's just that…" She pressed her hands to her face. "I'm trying to be logical about all this, but your life is so different from mine, and it's hard to get used to the idea of you as a famous person."

"Hey, I get it." I slipped one hand around her neck, closing the gap between us, and tilted her head up. "But you know me, Bronte. You know exactly who I am. You know that I always forget to add softener to the laundry and that I'd rather eat breakfast food all day than anything else. You know I need to fall asleep to some kind of sound but hate the beep of your alarm. You know me. I'm Chris from Fort Wayne, Indiana, and I am in love with you."

Barely even registering what I'd confessed in my haste to get it out, it took a second for me to process that she'd responded. "What?"

"I said, I love you too."

My heart stopped. I forgot to breathe. Even when Bronte smoothed her palm over my cheek, my lungs still didn't remember how to work.

I couldn't believe this woman *loved* me. This pure and good woman loved *me*. Despite everything she knew about me, all the shitty stuff, all the demons, she still chose me.

"Did you hear me, Chris?"

With a blink, I came back, her blue eyes anchoring me to earth. "Yeah, yeah. I heard you."

I slipped an arm around her waist and gripped her hair with my other hand, angling her head to kiss her, sweeping my tongue into her mouth, rediscovering the little gasps of sounds I'd missed for the last three days. Bunching my fist in the soft material of her dress at her hips, I said, "You look really good in this, but I'm sorry to say, it's going to have to come off."

She bit into her bottom lip and held up her arms so I could pull it over her head. With my hands wrapped around her middle, I easily lifted her off the floor and eased her legs around my hips as I sat her on the kitchen counter. She leaned back, guiding my lips to her neck, where I nibbled and sucked at her throat. I removed her bra and teased her nipples to stiff peaks as she tightened her hold around my waist with her legs. "Hurry, I need you."

If her words weren't enough to bring me to my knees, she shoved her hands down my pants, giving me a rough squeeze. With more control than I thought I could muster, I removed her fingers from around me and kissed the center of her palms.

"Please," she said, wrenching me closer.

"I know, I know. Let me go grab a condom from the bathroom." I took one step back, but she clung to my arm, shaking her head.

"No."

"No?"

"I'm sorry. I trust you, I do. I only needed some time to wrap my head around everything." She wiggled her hips to push her underwear down her legs. "I'm on birth control, and I've always used condoms anyway, but I don't want to with you."

I understood the implied meaning and heaved my gaze up her naked body, resting briefly on her flat stomach, her breasts, and neck marked red from my kisses, then finally her eyes, wild with want. They were my undoing. "I had a full physical before I left LA, and I haven't had sex since with anyone but you." My words were rushed and desperate. "I will never give you reason not to trust me. With your heart or your body."

A sweet smile grew from one side of her mouth to the other. "I know. I love you."

My heart ached at how much I felt for this woman. I'd do anything to have her. Anything to *keep* her.

She leaned back on her hands, and I gripped her hips as I glided inside, groaning with relief. This, right here, was heaven, and I lowered my mouth once again to her breasts for another taste. I alternated between licking and biting the tender flesh there until her breaths came out in short spurts.

"Touch yourself," I said against her neck. "I need you to come first."

With a sigh, she slowly inched her hand down between our bodies and did as I said, working her fingers to get herself off. When the orgasm finally racked her body, I lifted her from the counter and pinned her to the wall with one thigh around my hips, opening her up for me. I was still fully clothed, but my pants had dropped low enough that my belt buckle clanged against the wainscoting with every movement. I bit the juncture of her shoulder and neck, unable to find any of the filthy words I knew she loved. I couldn't right now, not when I was still stunned by our mutual confession.

"I love you," I murmured, and she sucked in a breath before kissing and biting my ear. It was savage and sloppy and amazing.

My own climax climbed up my spine, heat filling my veins as I released inside her, and I pressed my lips to her neck, holding her against me while my breathing slowed. She soothingly patted the back of my neck. "I missed you."

The word didn't encompass how I felt being away from Bronte—like a piece of me was missing, even if it had been only a few days and one hundred miles away. Unless a new word was invented, it was the only one I had to use. "I missed you too."

Tugging on my hair so I would lift my head, she kissed me once. "You're coming to bed and not leaving until tomorrow."

I was happy to agree to her terms. "Yes, ma'am."

She led me down the hall and ducked into the bathroom to clean up while I crawled into bed, where I promptly fell asleep.

I woke up sometime later from a movement next to me. Bronte's head was on my shoulder, but her right arm was stretched up toward the ceiling, index finger extended. I watched her draw what looked like invisible letters.

"What are you doing?"

She startled and immediately dropped her hand, folding it into herself. "You're awake. You must've been really exhausted. You were out in less than a minute."

"Don't change the subject," I said with a laugh. "What were you doing?"

"Nothing."

I rolled onto my side, resting my head on my hand. "Tell me."

She hid behind her fingers, but I pulled them away, and shrugged. "It's...I don't know. I don't even realize I'm doing it most of the time."

It wasn't much of an answer, so I waited for more. She stared at the ceiling and gave in with an embarrassed exhalation. "I write things I remember from books. Whatever's on my mind, I write it."

I added it to my growing list of Favorite Things About Bronte. Number fifteen: she writes invisible quotes on the ceiling. "What were you writing?"

"Did you, by any chance, get to read anything by my namesakes yet?"

I shook my head. Lately, I was having a hell of a time getting through Chaucer's *Canterbury Tales*. Maybe it was time to move on.

"Well, I was thinking about *Wuthering Heights*. Emily wrote that one. It was kind of out there for its time because Heathcliff was so violent and ungentlemanly, and Catherine would go into these fits of rage, driven crazy with sexual desires. It was very unladylike, you know." She tossed a tiny smile my way. "See, Catherine had to choose between Heathcliff, who was her soul mate, and Edgar, who was the better, safer choice."

"Sounds familiar," I grumbled.

"Mm-hmm." She wrapped her arm around my torso. "The Brontë sisters are interesting writers, but Emily's my favorite, and I was remembering some of her words."

"Like what?" If I could, I'd shrink down and crawl inside Bronte's brain to learn what made her tick, though I'd settle for this.

"Um." She hesitated for a moment then cleared her throat. "'If you ever looked at me once with what I know is in you, I would be your slave.'"

"Oh yeah. I get that one."

She angled her head back to meet my eyes. "Are you saying you'd be my slave?"

Without a doubt. Yes. "Absolutely."

She raised a challenging eyebrow, and I played along, moving to sit at her feet. Her guileless blue eyes flickered to her sparkly red toenails, instructing me without words. I cradled one foot in my hands, massaging the insole with my thumbs before pressing a kiss to it.

She made a sound that let me know I should keep going, and I did, tracing a line with my lips from her ankle, up her calf, to the inside of her knee, and finally her thigh. She moaned again, her eyelids closing in pleasure, and I nearly lost it as her hands moved to her own breasts, kneading them.

Yes, I was most definitely her slave.

She moved her fingers down her stomach to dig into my

hair, pulling my mouth where she wanted. My lips found her pussy swollen and needy, and I kissed her there until she called out my name, deep and uninhibited.

I hauled myself up, planting my palms on the mattress, to rake my eyes over her skin, damp and flushed red. She smoothed her hands over my chest as I entered her, and I watched her gaze travel down my body, her fingers blazing a trail over my shoulders, arms, and hips. She worshipped me with whispered words, blessed me with light kisses, and sanctified me with her body. I may have been a sinner, but she made me holy.

Sated and exhausted with pleasure, I lay down, coming to rest between Bronte's thighs, my head against her chest. "I can't get enough of you. You are…" I kissed her breastbone before settling my chin there to look up at her. "Everything."

She closed her eyes, saying quietly, "'He's more myself than I am. Whatever our souls are made of, his and mine are the same.'"

Stretching up to take in her face, I stroked the length of her nose until she opened her eyes. "That's beautiful."

She ran her fingers through my hair and down my cheek, quoting again, "'Whatever our souls are made of, his and mine are the same.'"

CHAPTER TWENTY-FOUR

Bronte

It was the Sunday before I had to go back to school, leaving behind winter vacation and my time with Chris. I wasn't sure what our future together looked like, but I was resolved to figure it out. We were snuggled up on my couch, watching the Eagles game, when I tapped my fluffy bunny slipper against his foot to get his attention.

He dipped his chin down. "What's up, Bunny?"

"Bunny? Really?"

Even though he had shaved two weeks ago, sometimes it still struck me how different he looked. He was ruggedly handsome before, but without all the hair covering him up, he was...well, he was beautiful. High cheekbones stood out against the hollow below them, and without his beard, his mouth seemed even bigger, dark pink with a permanently pouty bottom lip. A shallow cleft in his chin and slightly bumpy nose gave him a classic sort of look that belonged in black-and-white movies.

He smiled his movie star smile at me. "Yeah. I like it. Bronte Beanie Baby Bunny. Rolls right off the tongue."

"What will I call you?"

He tilted his head back and forth, listing off the choices

with his fingers. "Bae, boo boo, honey bear, stud muffin, love bug, sugar lips, sex god..."

I curled into him, tracing his lips with my index finger. "Interesting choices."

He bit the tip of my finger. "But fitting, huh?"

"Sex god? I'm not so sure."

He wasted no time in hauling me into his lap. With my hands in his hair, he ghosted his fingertips across my back as his lips, as usual, found a home on my neck.

Somewhere in the back of my mind, I remembered I wanted to actually use my mouth to speak and tried to hold on to the idea as his lips roamed up my throat and chin. "What's... uh, what's...um, your idea for us?"

"My idea?" His hands inched up my back. "I thought we'd start by removing this incredibly thick and kind of impenetrable sweater."

It was cable-knit and one of my favorites, but I'd burn it if it was an obstacle between his fingers and my skin.

"Then I was thinking I could lay you down and slide these jeans off to feel the smooth skin of your legs." He traced my jaw with his thumb. "What do you think?"

"I think that's a great idea, but first I want to talk."

When I tried to move, he clamped his hands down on my hips, keeping me in place. "Okay. About what?"

"I go back to school tomorrow, back to the real world, and I was wondering what your real world is. What does it mean for us?"

His dark, thoughtful eyes focused on something across the room, though his fingers dug into my skin. "Filming starts next month."

"How long does it take to make a movie?"

"It depends." His gaze met mine again. "There's usually a few weeks of preproduction, costume fittings, and rehearsals for the actors. Then depending on the script, actual filming could take a couple weeks or a couple months."

I swallowed down the pebble in my throat. "How long is yours going to take?"

"It's scheduled for ten weeks."

"Two and a half months."

He nodded, his fingers tracing along the waistband of my jeans. "The set pieces they're building are incredible, according to Dante. He had wanted to try to film in New York, but it was too expensive so they're recreating the city on a studio lot."

"So, you'll be in LA for three months?"

"It's not like it's forever, right?" His hands drifted down, rubbing the outside of my thighs. "I'll have days off. You'll have days off. We'll make it work."

Although, I didn't feel as confident as he sounded. Long-distance hadn't worked with Hunter, and he was in the same state. But maybe it wasn't the distance so much as the person. I'd been indifferent to Hunter for so long, I had given up. This time, I *wanted* to make it work with Chris.

"Hey." He brought my attention back to him with his fingers on my chin. "We can do this. It's only three months. Besides," he said, rubbing his thumb along my lower lip, "I have a while before I have to be out there. We have all the time in the world right now."

I nodded woodenly like a bobblehead. "Right. Sounds like a plan."

He laughed and nestled against my neck. "Always with the plans. As far as my plans are concerned, I'm going to take you out to dinner and a movie tonight. A real date."

That perked me up. See? Already, we were making a real go of it. Bronte Hollinger and CJ Cunningham. We could do it.

We arrived at the restaurant to discover it hopping, even on a Sunday night. Bright mosaics in rainbows of color depicted life in Mexico on the walls while the floor was jam-packed with wooden tables and chairs, and a tequila bar sat right in the center.

"Table for two, please," Chris said.

The hostess didn't raise her gaze up from the seating chart on her iPad. "It'll be about twenty-five minutes, but you can have a seat at the bar to wait if you'd like."

"Okay."

"What's the name?" she asked.

"Chris."

The woman glanced up as she began to type then did a double take. "Chris?"

I caught the anxious look he sent me, and I grabbed his hand as he cleared his throat.

The whites of the hostess's eyes widened. "CJ Cunningham. That's you, isn't it?"

"Yes," he answered quietly.

Her posture changed, and she rolled her shoulders back, flicking her long hair over her shoulder, undoubtedly attempting to call interest to her huge boobs. Even when I stood *right there*. As if I was invisible.

"It's very nice to meet you, CJ. My name's Gina." She held up a finger, winking. "Let me see what I can do for you."

When Gina flitted away, he puffed up his cheeks and blew out a long breath, scratching at his chin. "I should have worn a hat or something."

I placed a reassuring hand on his arm, having no words at all to offer. It was incredibly strange to witness other people's reactions to him, so it must have been even more unnerving to be the subject of it all.

Gina returned a minute later, waving us forward to a table in the back next to the kitchen. A few people took notice as we walked, and when Gina pointed to our seats, her eyes flickered back and forth between us before finally settling on Chris, ignoring me completely. "What brings you here tonight, CJ?"

"I've been spending some time in town, and I heard you guys have great food." He smiled at me. Gina didn't care.

"Wonderful. Ricky will be over to take your order shortly." She pivoted away slowly, but her swaying hips went completely ignored by Chris, who hid behind his menu.

"You all right?" I asked.

"Everyone is staring. Last year, I wouldn't have cared, but now..."

I skirted my gaze around the restaurant, lots of heads turned backward, necks craning up, big owl eyes blinking, and I suddenly wished we'd stayed home. I had convinced myself I was okay with the other half of Chris's life, but it was a difficult 180 to make. To go from dating the guy only I knew to one the whole world knew.

"We don't have to stay if you don't want to," I said, hoping I didn't sound too anxious.

"No. No." He put the menu down and twined his fingers with mine on top of the table. "I want to have a nice night with you, a regular date."

I nodded. If he could stand the curious stares in his everyday life, I supposed I could handle it for an hour or so.

"It won't always be like this, right?" I asked hopefully, and even though he smiled, it didn't reach his eyes as usual.

Ricky arrived and thankfully wasn't as starstruck as Gina. He was professional and understanding when Chris asked if he could make sure we were afforded as much privacy as possible. We finished our meals quicker than normal and, after leaving a large tip, made our way out of the restaurant with a few whispers trailing behind.

Chris waited until we were outside to take my hand in his,

pulling me close. "After all this time out of the public eye, it feels like I was hibernating or something."

"You were." I rubbed his days-old stubble. "I can't decide which I like better, this pretty-boy version of you or the other, hairier version." When he dragged his jaw along my palm, it scratched like sandpaper, and I smiled. "I know I like the feel of this."

"Yeah?" he rasped.

"Mm-hmm. I like the feel of it against my thighs, seeing the red marks the next day."

He groaned, grabbing my hips. "Jesus Christ, Bronte. You need to stop. Now."

"Why?" I laughed, breaking away from his grasp to face him, walking backward. "Is someone getting a little tight in his jeans?"

When he lunged for me, I hopped back, but my heel caught on the sidewalk and I tripped, almost hitting the pavement if it weren't for his grip on my arm.

"See." He righted me. "That's what you get for teasing me."

"Like you don't love it."

He opened the door to the movie theater and lightly smacked my ass on the way in. "Behave."

I playfully glowered at him over my shoulder. *He* was telling *me* to behave?

Once inside the dark theater, Chris led me to the last row. The movie was some action flick that'd been out for a while, so only a handful of other people were there, and they all sat toward the front, leaving us alone in the back to make out like high school kids. Which we did. With vigor.

I had to slap his hand away when he went for the button of my jeans.

We snuck out before the credits rolled and hightailed it to

his car, but he abruptly stopped with a curse, his eyes on his cell phone.

"What?"

He didn't answer, and my nerves got the best of me.

"What is it?"

He ran his hand through his hair and rocked back on his heels before finally meeting my gaze, his face a mixture of irritation and distress.

"What?" I asked again.

"A couple texts from Wes." He held up the screen so I could read them.

I squinted at the picture. It was a screenshot from Wes's phone, but I couldn't tell what I was looking at. "What is that?"

"Twitter."

"Okay?"

Chris handed me his phone with the text still up. "You know what trending means?

"I'm not *that* behind the times."

"Okay, well, I'm apparently what people are talking about on Twitter."

My eyes scanned the screenshot again, and there it was: **I found CJ Cunningham**. Right below **Worst New Year's Resolutions** and **Sherlock** but above **POTUS**.

"You're more popular than the president, but not as much as a PBS show."

He growled something unintelligible and started making his way to the car again. I followed while reading through Wes's texts explaining people from the restaurant tonight were tweeting about him, some with pictures. Others blatantly lied, saying they spotted him in other cities and states, like he was the Loch Ness Monster come up to sunbathe for a while.

"This is bizarre." I handed his phone back.

"Yeah, and terrifying. These people are able to send out details of where I am to the entire world." As we reached his car, his phone dinged with another text. He shook his head in disgust. "Wes says it shows people are still interested in me after all this time out of the spotlight. It's a good thing."

Intellectually, I could understand Wes's point. The old adage, *There is no such thing as bad publicity*. Yet, I couldn't help but feel outrage at Chris's invasion of privacy—and hell, mine as well. To them, he was CJ Cunningham, the public figure, bad boy, movie star. He was something to point at and watch, a sideshow act in the circus of show business. But I took solace in the fact that I knew the truth about him.

That Christopher Judd Cunningham was a man who was afraid to fly. That he was rather soft-spoken and thoughtful. That his lips moved when he read to himself, and he hated when his food touched. His social media fans would never see him interact with Luke, or hear his voice shake when he talked about his family, or ever have to deal with his annoying habit of leaving the toilet seat up. No, they would never know the real Chris.

He was my secret.

Chris walked me to my door and kissed my cheek.

I paused with my hand on the doorknob. "Aren't you coming in?"

"I wanted this to be a real date, and I think since it's technically our first, proper etiquette says I should kiss you good night and go home."

"Yeah, right." I laughed. "Come on." I opened the door, but he didn't move. "Really? You're not coming in?"

"Not tonight."

I studied his somber face, guessing the whole Twitter debacle had really shaken him up, and I leaned into his chest, trying to cheer him up. "Hashtag please? Hashtag yolo."

A slow smile unfurled across his mouth, and he moved his hands from his pockets to hug me close. "Hashtag you make me happy. Hashtag blessed."

"Hashtag kiss me."

He bent his head down, his lips meeting mine softly, barely there, but I corded my arms around his neck and pressed up onto my toes, bringing my head level with his. I did my damnedest to convince him to spend the night by licking at his lips, coaxing him to do the same, and eventually, he gave in, pushing my back against the front door as I kissed along his jaw, whispering pleas for him to stay.

He rested his forehead against mine, breathing through his nose a few times. "It's late, and I don't want you to be tired for your first day back at work tomorrow."

My hands found their way inside his coat and around his waist. "I won't."

"I'm sorry, baby. I have a lot on my mind." He gently uncoiled me from around him, kissing both of my cheeks and nose as consolation. "Tomorrow. I promise."

He waited to leave until I gave a small wave from inside, and I closed my door with a sigh. Our whole relationship was based on the fact that we could always talk so easily with each other, our words flowing effortlessly about any subject, but he'd gone quiet now. If he wanted to block the world from coming in, I couldn't help but worry I might get shut out along with everyone else.

Chris

I had been up all night thinking, worrying, *planning*.

My date with Bronte was supposed to be a nice little outing, but it had turned sour real quick. I hadn't been away from Los Angeles that long, but I'd almost forgotten what it was like to be in the spotlight. Sure, it was part of my job to expose at least some of myself to the public, but I had no responsibility to them when it came to my love life or Bronte.

It was obvious she was uncomfortable last night, and the shitty part of it was, I couldn't do anything about it. Unless Bronte and I wanted to stay hidden away, which didn't sound so bad if it meant I could keep her locked away, naked, forever and ever. But that wasn't going to happen anytime soon, and I was tired of hiding.

If she was going to be with me, she was going to be made a part of my spectacle by proxy. It was clear from all the online articles and posts with questions about the mystery brunette I was with that I was dragging Bronte into all my bullshit. She was smart and kind and deserved to be so much more than CJ Cunningham's mystery brunette.

After a lot of consideration, I decided it would be better to go back to LA early to prepare for the movie, give us both time to adjust to what our new life would be like, and then figure out what to do when filming ended. The longer I stayed in Allentown, the more curious the world would be about her. Yes, I loved Bronte. Yes, it would suck to be away from her. But we had to let the storm blow over. Once I had a feel for the future of my career and the media moved on to someone else, I'd be able to focus on her.

It was better this way.

I only needed to explain it to Bronte...and her parents.

I knocked on my neighbors' door. It felt odd, like a formal greeting.

Pattie answered. "Hey, Chris, why'd you knock?"

I stepped into the house, not bothering to answer her question. "Is Steven around?"

"Steven?" she yelled out toward the steps before stepping away, but I gently held her arm.

"Wait. I need to talk to you too. Both of you." I cleared my throat of the uncertainty in my voice.

"Okay?"

"Well, hello," Steven boomed as he walked into the living room.

Pattie patted the seat next to her on the couch. "Chris needs to speak to us."

He smiled and sat down. "What's up?"

I flinched inwardly, knowing I was about to disappoint them. "I came over to tell you guys I'm leaving."

"Oh. Okay." Pattie shrugged like it was no big deal.

"I mean I'm going back to California."

Steven's smile dropped. "When do you leave?"

"In a few hours." Pattie and Steven exchanged a look before facing me again, and I hurried to explain myself as best I could. "I haven't told Bronte yet, but I wanted you to hear it from me because I don't want you to think this is a spur-of-the-moment decision."

Steven made a motion like I should continue, and I felt marginally better. They weren't angry or were, at least, letting me speak before they let me have it.

"You both know I love your daughter. I love her more than anything else in my life, which is why I need to go home for a while. I don't want Bronte or you, for that matter, to get involved with all this media bull—" I backtracked at Pattie's eyebrow "—stuff. It won't be long before someone discovers who she is, and I know how relentless the press can be. There's no way I'm going to sacrifice Bronte's life or livelihood for my own."

Pattie nodded, and Steven scratched his head. They both appeared a bit stunned, yet neither said anything.

"I want to protect Bronte, and until I know how my career is going to play out in the next couple of months, I think it's best to keep her away from my spotlight. I wanted to let you know I appreciate everything you've done for me. You taught me what family means, and I thank you for that."

Pattie stood up then and hugged me tight. "Thank you for coming over here. It's very brave of you."

Steven followed suit. "It's an admirable thing to do what you think is best and even more admirable that you're looking out for our daughter, but as Bronte's dad, you know what I'm going to say."

"Don't make her cry," I guessed.

He clapped my shoulder. "Not even a famous movie star is good enough if he makes my Bean cry."

Insecurity wrapped its claws around my throat. I wasn't good enough for Bronte, period. Not if I couldn't protect her from the possible hell I was dragging her into.

Pattie kissed my cheek. "Stay in touch."

"I will." I saw myself out and got right into my car, already filled with my bags, and texted Bronte.

Can I come over?

BUNNY
I thought you'd never ask.

Minutes later, she swung her door open in a sweatshirt and leggings. "Did you teleport here or something? I didn't even have time to make myself look presentable. I'm so exhausted. I came home and—"

I didn't care what she looked like. She could've been in a burlap sack for all I cared. I only needed what was underneath. I wrapped my arms around her waist and pushed inside, holding her up when she stumbled back. Kicking the door closed, I crept my hands up into her hair, my lips hasty, my tongue unrestrained, and by the time I had kissed my fill, she was limp in my arms.

I stepped away, putting a few inches of space between us. "Hi. How was your day?"

She swiped her palm over her forehead like she had a fever. "Oh, the usual, math, Levi meltdown, spelling, Levi meltdown, reading, Levi meltdown."

"Good, then?"

She sat on the couch, and I followed, shrugging out of my coat on the way. As soon as my body hit the cushions, she moved to my lap, wrapping an arm around my shoulders. "Better now."

I smoothed my hands over her calves and up her outer thighs, stopping at the curve of her hips. I dug my fingers into her, and she rocked into my growing length, swiping her lips across mine. "I want to come home from work every day to this."

My stomach churned with guilt, but I needed to feel her one more time before I explained myself. "Best way to de-stress is you in my lap."

I guided her hips up so she hovered over me, and I bunched the leggings in my hands, yanking them down to the tops of her legs, my blunt fingernails scratching her skin through the thin material. She rested her hands on the back of the couch to steady herself as she balanced on one knee at a time to pull the spandex off but toppled forward onto me. I chuckled and helped her drag them off, then motioned that I wanted her arms up. I pulled off her sweatshirt, revealing the white cotton bra on top.

When she covered herself with her arms, I yanked them away. "Why are you hiding from me?"

"This is basically a training bra. I feel like a thirteen-year-old."

My gaze roved over her, hungry. "You look like a woman I can't get enough of, but I'm not sure about this matching white set. So virginal. And we both know you like it dirty."

Her skin flushed as she nodded, and I slid down, positioning my head toward the end of the couch, and tugged her hips over my mouth. "Come here. Come give me a taste."

With my lips mere inches away from her center, I gripped her hips harder, burying my nose and mouth between her legs, and she let out a low mewl. I sucked on the cotton material of her underwear, dampening it before letting it settle back against her skin. I took a deep breath through my nose, my eyes connecting with hers. I could smell her desire.

A smile crawled across her face, her eyes brightening with a wildness I'd come to expect. Whenever we were together like this, she turned into this wanton creature, totally free of her inhibitions. I traced the seam of her over the cotton, and she pleaded my name, but I took my time torturing her. My nose tickled her hip while my finger sometimes dipped inside the edge of her panties, barely touching where she needed it. I teased her again and again like that until she grabbed at the roots of my hair, forcing my eyes up. I grinned. "Goddamn, I love when you do that."

Playing coy, she untangled her hands from my hair and traced her index finger across my jaw to my lower lip. "Do what?"

I bit the pad of her finger, and she squeaked out a surprised gasp. Drawing the tip into my mouth, I sucked the sting away as she wound her other hand back into my hair, tugging hard on it. With one swift pull, I had her panties out of the way and my mouth on her pussy. My tongue worked a few long and flat licks before pushing inside.

"You taste so fucking good. I'll never forget it as long as I live." I landed a sharp smack against the back of her thigh when she backed away slightly and tightened my grip, forcing her harder down on my mouth. She moaned and circled her hips, rubbing wetness all over my lips and chin. I devoured her, sucking and licking and biting. She was so close to going over the edge, it took merely one press of an invading finger for her to crumple in my arms. I kissed up her belly and pushed her down to the couch, aligning her along the length of it. I stripped off my shirt and wiped my mouth before tossing it behind my head, in a hurry to remove her underwear.

I was barely in control of myself as I pulled at my jeans, and she batted my fingers out of the way, quickly undoing the button and zipper, then grabbed my dick with a confident hand. Without saying a word, she lifted her knees to her waist, guiding me inside, and I blew out a thick breath in relief, letting my weight sink against her for a few long seconds.

I buried my face in her neck. Of all the things I'd miss, this was at the top of my list. "I just need..."

"I know," she said and lightly ran her nails down my back so my hair stood on end. "It never feels like enough."

I murmured my agreement against her breast. I had a sudden urge to scratch her open and bury under her ribs to get to her heart. Take it with me.

Maybe then it would be enough.

I surged up off of her and pressed my palm to her sternum, holding her still as I drove into her with long strokes.

She stretched her arms above her head, holding onto the arm of the couch, elongating every part of her, and I wrapped my hand around her jaw, sticking my thumb in her mouth. She sucked on it, and I swear my soul tried to leave my body. "You've ruined me. You know that?"

"Good. You're mine." She locked her legs around my waist, baring her teeth like she was feral.

I fucking loved it. "I fucking love you."

She scored her nails down my sides, and my breath whistled through my teeth. I was hanging on by a thread, completely undone, and I barely managed to brush my thumb over the swollen bud of her clit before I lost all of my senses and came, crying out her name.

She arched her neck, and I bent sucking on her hammering pulse, and I emptied myself into her, feeling the echo of her own orgasm gripping my cock.

After a minute, she lazily combed her fingers through my hair as she breathed out a drunken giggle. "Now *that* was enough."

I pushed myself up to a sitting position, towing her into my lap, and she laid her head on my shoulder. Her skin had broken out in goose bumps, so I grabbed a throw from the back of the couch, wrapping it around us both.

"No, I'll never get enough of you." I gently forced her head back up. "But I need to talk to you."

CHAPTER TWENTY-SIX

Bronte

"I think maybe we should get dressed," Chris said, and I frowned, confused by his sudden change in demeanor but slipped away to use the bathroom and put on my leggings and sweatshirt, forgoing my bra and underwear. By the time, I padded back into the living room, he'd dressed completely. Taking my hands between his, he pulled me down next to him on the couch, taking forever to spit it out.

"What is it?"

He didn't answer, and I wiggled my fingers in his palms. When he finally looked up, his eyebrows were drawn together. "I was on the phone all day with Wes and Tom."

"Tom, your agent?"

"Yeah. I'm going back to LA."

"Okay." I knew he had to at some point. "When?"

"Today."

But not that soon. "Oh." I blew out a breath from my bottom lip, and a few wisps of hair flew away from my face. "Okay. Do you have meetings or something?"

"Yeah, and preproduction stuff."

"I thought...I thought you said you weren't needed for most of that."

"I'm not, but I've got a special trainer to help me out, and I need to get my head back into my work. I can't be distracted."

My stomach churned. "I'm a distraction?"

He shifted closer. "No. What? No. Bronte—"

"You just said—"

"*You* are not a distraction." He let go of my hands to run his fingers through his hair and over his neck. "But you know what people think about me. I need to prove to the studio heads I'm a safe bet again."

I appreciated that but still didn't know what it had to do with me. "You told me you wanted to be with me for the foreseeable future."

"I do." He curled his hand around the back of my head.

"I thought that you wanted to be with me for as long as possible before you had to leave."

"I did. I do." His use of the past tense didn't escape me, and it was like a punch in the gut. "I do want to be with you, but I think it would be best if I go back now. There are pictures of us all over the internet."

"I don't get it." I shook my head, so lost with all of this.

"It's out. Who I am, and where I am."

"I don't care about that."

"This isn't coming out right." He stopped to take a deep breath then hugged me close. "I know you don't care, and that's why I love you, but it's only a matter of time before they start coming after you. Your life won't be yours anymore, and I won't let that happen. If I go back to California, it won't. "

I pushed against him. "Am I missing something? You say you love me, but you *have* to leave. You told me filming doesn't start until next month." When he nodded, I stood up, pointing to the sofa. "You just... We just..." My voice wavered, and I spun away from him, hurt by this sudden news and embarrassed to be so panicked about it. I'd known all along he would have to leave; he had a job to do. I only assumed we would have more time. I wasn't prepared for the shock of it. "So, what was that? Goodbye and good luck?"

Chris stood, turning me around by my shoulders. "That's not what that was, and you know it. I don't *want* to leave, but you get why I should, right? I have to think about what's best for you, your job—"

"How about *us*? What's good for us?"

"What'd happen when random people start calling you, asking for interviews? When photographers start showing up across the street from your school for pictures, hanging around your parents' house? I know how this goes, Bronte, and I don't want that for you."

The last month had been a whirlwind, and I specifically avoided thinking about all the negative consequences of dating someone famous, but there was no reason why we shouldn't have been able to talk about this now. To work it out. "You aren't even giving me a choice in this. We should have talked about this. You should have told me what you were thinking." My heart rate spiked. "But you left me out of the decision. You're leaving, and that's it."

"That's not it." He wrapped his palm around the nape of my neck, and I closed my eyes, calming down under his touch. "It's not like I'm going to outer space. People do long-distance relationships all the time. I know what you went through before with Hunter, but I promise I will do whatever I have to do to make this work." He pressed our foreheads together. "We'll work out times to talk and FaceTime, and—" he broke away from me with a gasp like he had a sudden bright idea "— let's share a calendar. You'll be able to see what I'm doing every day, and we can pick out some days you can visit. Or, I can probably find some time to come back here."

I didn't miss the word *probably* in that sentence.

"We can do it," he said. "I'll buy a private jet if I have to."

I let out a pitiful laugh. I didn't know how he could be so cavalier about all this, and the faint remembrance of my time with Hunter rose to the surface. How he assumed it would all work out, if I acquiesced enough. Chris was not Hunter, and this was not the same situation, but I wasn't so naive to think this would be easy.

"Don't be ridiculous," I said.

"It's not ridiculous."

"You're afraid of flying." I lifted my head, eyes brimming with tears. "And it's three thousand miles."

"It's nothing."

"It's everything. You're going to go back and forget about me."

"*That* is the most ridiculous thing I've ever heard." He cradled my wet cheeks in his palms, kissing me once, twice, three times as I hiccupped a breath. "Could you forget about me?"

I didn't answer, and he loosened his grip so I could ease away from him. I tugged the sleeves of my sweatshirt over my hands to wipe my face dry then tied my hair back in a ponytail. I needed to focus on something to clear my head and straightened up the mess we'd made. I folded up the blanket, tossed the pillows onto the couch, and pushed the cushions back into place.

"Bronte."

I picked up my bra and underwear and marched to my room to throw them in the laundry basket. When I came back into the living room, I could feel Chris's eyes on me as I rearranged the magazines on my coffee table, but before I could finish, he stole them from my hands. "Bronte, come on."

I refused to look at him, and he curled his hand around my chin, forcing me to. He either truly believed we would get through this together, or he was much less heartbroken over this than I was because he stared at me with sure and steady eyes. "Bronte, please, talk to me. Say something. You're breaking my heart."

I swiped some loose strands of hair behind my ears and stared up at the ceiling. I couldn't find words of my own, but a few from someone else filtered into my mind.

"Please," he said again, almost a whisper.

"'I have not broken your heart—you have broken it; and in breaking it, you have broken mine.'"

Chris considered this with questions in his eyes, but I wouldn't say any more. I *couldn't* say any more.

He kissed my forehead, cheek, and mouth. "I'm sorry, Bronte. I didn't mean to surprise you like this. I've thought about it all night, and I don't know what else to do...how else to keep you safe from this life until I can get my career on track. Right now, people only care about my personal life, assuming I'm another car wreck in the making, but I won't let you get caught up in that." He stroked my cheek. "I promise I won't give up on us. I don't want you to either."

I didn't want to give up on Chris, but my brain was fighting my heart on this one.

He swiftly put on his shoes and coat and gave me a kiss. "I'll call you later." He stalked to the door before spinning around for another kiss. "Last one," he said with his lips on mine, then left without a spared glance behind.

I wasn't sure if I wanted him to look back or not. To know whether he battled with this as much as I did.

CHAPTER TWENTY-SEVEN

Chris

I got into my car, drove straight to the airport, where I returned the rental and made my way to the terminal. A male flight attendant with platinum blond hair and a thick South Carolina accent addressed me by name. "Mr. Cunningham, we're happy to have you on our flight today. Can I get you anything before takeoff?"

From my seat in the front row of first class, I shook my head, and the man retreated toward the galley to begin his spiel about safety. Regretting not driving back to California, I closed my eyes. Not only did I have to try to ignore my fear, but now I had to contend with the memories of the last time I was on a plane. There was no comforting blue-eyed stranger next to me, and my only hope was that the double dose of melatonin I took before boarding would take effect soon.

It was almost midnight in Los Angeles when I shuffled out of the airline gate. I yawned, exhausted from the flight and change in time zones, and yanked my baseball hat out of my back pocket to cover my head. The airport was relatively quiet, and I had an easy time finding my luggage, although there were always one or two paparazzi hanging around outside.

Wes was waiting at the curb to pick me up, and as soon as the sliding doors opened, the camera lights turned on.

"Hey! CJ! Hey, how was your vacation?"

"Rumor has it you were in rehab?"

"Where's your girlfriend? You meet her in rehab?"

"CJ, over here! You look a little rough, man!"

"She break up with you?"

"Nice hair!"

"Come here, come talk to me for *Hollywood Magazine*!"

I ignored them and kept my head down as I hopped into Wes's car.

"Nice to have you back."

"Yeah," I said rather apathetically.

We were quiet for a few minutes until Wes maneuvered us away from LAX and back onto the highway. "You're booked with Yanni on Thursday, and Sandra tomorrow."

Yanni was a personal trainer who specialized in boxing, and Sandra was one of my first acting coaches, whom I still kept in touch with. She helped to prep me for every new project. "Great."

"Are you excited to get to work again?"

"Yeah."

"Should be good. Did you enjoy your time away?"

I had found family and love there, and this time, I answered with more than one word. "It was exactly what I needed."

"I knew it'd be good for you. Get a new routine, remember what life outside of LA is like."

I nodded. My new routine was Bronte. Life outside of Los Angeles was Bronte.

Wes turned on the radio. Some slow country song played, and I dropped my head back, too exhausted to talk.

"You're home."

I woke up with an elbow into my side and swiveled my head to the window. It was pitch black, except for the single porch light waiting for me. Wes popped the trunk and held out my bags, but before they could change hands, he deposited them on the ground and hugged me. I reluctantly gave in when he said, "I'm glad you're back."

"Me too."

He slapped me on the back a few times. "Didn't sound very convincing."

I picked up my stuff. "I had to come back eventually, right?"

"I guess that's one way of putting it."

"I'm just really tired."

"Okay, I'll talk to you tomorrow." He gave me one more slap on my shoulder, then got back behind the wheel.

I made my way inside my house and leaned against the closed door, taking in the once-familiar surroundings. My home was nestled in the Hollywood Hills, encircled by lush greenery I could see through the windows. It wasn't too huge of a place comparatively, although it was a perfect party house with a big pool you could step right into from the sliding door. It had a wide-open first floor that I could crowd as many people into as I wanted. Also, there was a stripper pole.

Yet looking at it now, I hated it.

Upstairs, I flopped on the bed and opened the photos app on my phone, scrolling to my favorite picture.

It was from Luke's birthday party back in October. Seemed like ages ago but still only yesterday. Bronte's face lit up by the yellow reflections of the candle made my chest ache. I typed a short message to her, even though I knew she wouldn't respond because it was the middle of the night there.

I'm home. Miss you. Love you.

Thinking back on Bronte's words from earlier, I Googled them.

"I have not broken your heart—you have broken it; and in breaking it, you have broken mine."

Wuthering Heights by Emily Brontë. I should have known.

CHAPTER TWENTY-EIGHT

Bronte

Chris had been gone for three days, and my life had never felt so boring. Or maybe it always was, and I just didn't realize until he showed up. Now that he left, it was back to bland and boring again.

True to his word, Chris created a shared calendar so we could see each other's schedules. We'd only been able to speak on the phone twice since he'd landed in California, but we texted enough to ease the sting a tiny bit. I was still at work when I received another message from him.

CHRIS

What are you up to?

Finishing up some emails.

CHRIS

You're still at work?

With you not here anymore I have no reason to rush home.

CHRIS

If you rush home now we could have a FaceTime date. Naked.

He included a ton of emojis including a rabbit, lips, multiple hearts, a few flowers, and an eggplant.

An eggplant? Is that your idea of dirty talk?

CHRIS

You know it.

CHRIS

How about it? You, me, and our screens?

I have class at the gym at five.

The calendar was your idea. Have you even looked at it? How about 8? My time?

CHRIS

I'm going to dinner with some of the cast tonight. I've got to leave my place by 6, sooo

So no naked date?

FILL OUT THE CALENDAR.

CHRIS

Don't yell at me. I'm doing it right now.

Might I remind you this was your idea.

CHRIS

I know. I know.

CHRIS

I could call you when I get home but it'll definitely be after 11 your time.

After briefly considering sending him the plane emoji to remind him of his offer to buy a jet—I was ready and willing to get on it—I typed **OK** and put my phone away. I had work to do and didn't have time to wait around for his next flirty message to appear.

Chris said he was determined to make our relationship work, and I had to have faith we could. Although seventy-two hours in, I already hated it.

CHAPTER TWENTY-NINE
Chris

My days blurred together with table reads, training, and traffic, yet I trudged along in silence, detachment, and loneliness. When I wasn't throwing myself into learning the script, I was at the gym or in meetings. That didn't leave much downtime, but when I did have it, the ache resurfaced. Chronic and bone-deep.

I had assumed three thousand miles wouldn't be a big deal. Not when we had cell phones and text messages and Facetime. Yet those three thousand miles might as well have been three continents. Three hours didn't seem like that much of a difference until it came time to talk. By the time I woke up in the morning, Bronte was already halfway through her day, and when I got home, she was already asleep. We had scheduled a date every Sunday night to watch a movie together, but a few hours each week wasn't enough.

I missed her voice and her dimples, the way she slurped her coffee in the morning, and how her body felt wrapped up in mine. I missed the piece of myself I'd left with her, and the only place I found comfort was work, where I could channel someone else for a while.

It was after rehearsal, on Wednesday at the end of January,

when Wes showed up to the make-up and hair trailer in the backlot. Production was set to start the following week, and he came to check in. I slumped in a director's chair with Jericho, the film's head hairstylist, behind me, and Wes off to the side.

"I've been waiting to get my hands on this man-bun," Jericho said with a menacing snip of his fingers.

I rubbed my palms together. "Do you worst."

"Which will be the best." Jericho smiled at my reflection in the mirror, a diamond stud winking, his teeth bright white next to his dark skin.

"How's it going today? You feel ready?" Wes asked, lifting his ankle over his knee, his ever-present cell phone in hand. I had met Wes at a party when we were both practically babies. He had graduated college, interned with a few production companies, and was working his way up the Hollywood chain. Since things had slowly been unraveling with my family after I'd hit it big with the *Travellers* trilogy, I needed guidance and business advice, which Wes had in spades. Over the years, he had become business partner second, friend first.

"After Jericho takes care of me, that'll be the last step to Roy."

And that was when me made the first snip. Jericho held up the small bun as evidence then dropped it in my lap. "Goodbye and good riddance."

Wes gestured to the side of his own face, referring to my reflection. "The sideburns are coming in nice."

"I'll shape those up too," Jericho said, spritzing my hair with water, a few droplets landing on the book in my lap. I wiped them off the cover with the sleeve of my hoodie, wondering what Bronte might be doing at the moment.

She was scheduled to have a faculty meeting after school and was probably sitting there now. Maybe in her dark-blue hip-hugging skirt and the white shirt with the big buttons.

Maybe her legs were bare, and maybe she was wearing her glasses with her hair pulled back in a sleek ponytail. Maybe she had her lips wrapped around the end of her pen, biting it...

Jesus fucking Christ, maybe I needed to fly to her tonight just to—

"What happened to the mustache you wanted?" Wes asked, skimming his finger along his own clean-shaven upper lip.

"I fought for it," I said.

"And I vetoed it." Jericho pointed to a few photos taped up along the mirror, some of real-life people, some of sketches or art from the period, all of them inspiration for the look Dante, Jericho, and I had decided on together. "When was the last time you saw a love interest with a mustache?"

Wes shot his arm out. "Tom Selleck!"

Jericho rolled his eyes, and I chuckled. "I was doing research and—"

"I did too, and Roy Callaghan would not be able to afford the styling products to keep his mustache groomed." Jericho pressed one hand into his hip, directing his scissors at me in the mirror. "You might be the one with their face on the screen, but I'm the one who's supposed to make this face look pretty, huh? Don't argue with the master."

I held my hands up in surrender. "You're right. You're right. Make me look pretty."

"Is that even possible?" Wes joked, his eyes on his phone as he scrolled. "Listen. One of the producers of the Oscars called me. She asked if you'd consider presenting." He barreled on before I could say anything. "I told her you would be in production, and she was very interested to hear that. She reminded me the television audience would love to hear from you."

I ran a hand over my face. "The Oscars? Seriously? They

haven't invited me since…"

"Since you made a scene at the Governors Ball."

I grimaced. After I'd played Hamlet in *Silence*, I hadn't been nominated even though I'd been highly speculated to be since I'd had such a great run with *Rebel* the year before. Although my costar, Mickey Little, had been nominated for Best Supporting Actor for his Polonius.

The thing was Mickey was a pompous ass, and I didn't ignore the flirtations from Mickey's "assistant," who everyone in Hollywood knew was really Mickey's longtime boyfriend. Bad blood had been brewing before that, but when the story broke out about Mickey's "assistant" and me, so did a small fight on set. It was one of my worst performances to date, though at the time, I wasn't willing to admit it was my fault. I had blamed everyone and everything else, even if that meant doing so publicly after Mickey's Oscar win, with a drunken tirade at the ball.

Wasn't my best moment.

"It's your big comeback," Wes said, and since Jericho was a true professional, he didn't even acknowledge the conversation.

"I'll think about it."

"How are you doing otherwise? How're the paps?"

I folded my arms over my chest and stretched out my legs, crossing them at the ankles. "I don't go anywhere now, so they don't bother with me. I'm boring these days."

"That's good." He tipped his chin to the book sliding down my lap. "What's that?"

I held up *Wuthering Heights*.

"You've been reading a lot lately. What's that about?"

What was it about? Trying to expand my horizons? New hobby? Or just Bronte? "Inspiration."

Wes smiled, a little too perceptively. "So studious of you."

CHAPTER THIRTY

Bronte

I was stretched out on my bed, propped up on my elbows with my feet in the air behind me. It was the most flattering position to lie on my stomach so Chris could see the curve of my butt if I angled the laptop exactly right. I was in a matching black lace bra and panties since we'd dropped the formality of clothes last week.

I checked my hair one last time before Chris's face popped up.

"There you are. I thought maybe you were going to stand me up for a second."

"Never," he said, scooting closer to the screen. His hair was shorter now, only a few inches on top but even curlier, except for the sideburns, grown out long for his role. He scratched at the one on his left side. "I was...uh, caught up."

"With what?"

He ran his hand through his hair a few times before giving me a weird, fake smile.

"What?" I braced myself.

"I got a dog."

That was the last thing I expected to hear. "You what?"

He left the screen and returned a few seconds later with a

mangy-looking thing in his arms. It had wiry brown and gray hair that stood out in every direction, and its huge tongue lapped out, licking anything it could, including the computer.

"I was at the vet with him," he said, rubbing the dog's belly. "His name's Taco."

"You named him Taco?"

Chris shook his head. "He was already named. I adopted him. They found him on the side of the road chewing on a paper plate."

I didn't want to say it, but I thought the dog looked as if he'd chewed on a lot more than a paper plate. Maybe an electrical wire.

"What kind of dog is it?"

Chris shrugged. "The vet thinks part greyhound, though, because of his body. And he's a fast little shit. I took him for a walk this morning, and he was running all over the place."

The dog faced the screen then, and I finally noticed his big, droopy caramel-colored eyes. "He is kind of cute, I guess."

"You guess? No. He's the handsomest dog ever."

"Most handsome," I corrected, and Chris rolled his eyes before leaning in to the screen.

"I miss you. I miss you in my bed. That's why I got Taco. I need a warm body next to me."

I laughed. "And Taco is going to sleep next to you every night?"

"He's not a very good kisser, but he'll do. Besides, he's got abandonment issues. I feel bad for the guy." He glanced down at the dog, and Taco gave him sloppy licks across his chin. "Right? You don't like to sleep alone, do you? Me either."

I pulled my T-shirt over my head. We weren't going to have a naked date after all. Not that I minded. Any time with Chris was precious, especially when we could *see* each other, which was becoming increasingly harder and harder since he had started filming. I wasn't going to take it for granted.

Instead, I put on a happy face and tried my best not to sound too frustrated with our situation when I said, "I hope Taco doesn't mind sharing you because the next time I see you, I plan on chaining myself to your body."

He grinned. "I'm looking forward to it."

CHAPTER THIRTY-ONE

Bronte

I held Mason in my arms, his tiny lips pursing in sleep. He was almost three months old now, yet still so tiny and fragile. I leaned down to kiss the top of his head. "I'm going to make you love me."

"I think he already does," Shelley said, strolling out from the kitchen carrying a mug of tea for me and a glass of water for herself. "I think the only time he doesn't cry is when you're holding him."

"He knows who his godmother is. Don't you, Masey?"

Even though Zoe was upstairs with Tommy getting ready for bed, I still idly watched cartoons. Shelley grabbed the remote and turned it off.

"Hey!" I whisper-shouted. "Mickey just called Toodles."

She stretched out her legs on the sofa. "Spoiler alert, they solve the mystery. We already missed most of the red carpet."

The Oscars were on tonight, and although I never paid much attention to the award show, I was excited to watch this time. Chris was presenting, and he called me earlier in the day to get my opinion on his tie, but I knew he wasn't really calling about his clothes.

He needed a distraction, reassurance, and I was glad to give it to him. I only wished I could be there to do it in person.

I kissed Mason again, then repositioned him to my shoulder so I could reach for my tea. Before I could grab it, my phone rang, and I diverted to pick it up instead. It was Chris.

"Hey, wha—"

"Bunny, you'll never believe who I just met," he said without any preliminaries. "Robert Redford. Robert motherfucking Redford."

"Is that his full name?"

"Who is that?" Shelley asked, popping a pretzel into her mouth.

I mouthed "Chris" as his outburst continued.

"I totally fangirled. I told him, for an entire year of my life, all I did was study his films." He chuckled to himself like he couldn't believe it. "I don't think he knows who I am, but why would he, right? I mean, he's too busy being Robert motherfucking Redford to watch my movies. And then, oh my god..."

"What?"

"I quoted one of his lines back to him." He moaned out a laugh. "I said, 'Don't you get sick of being right all the time?'"

"What's that—"

"From *Butch Cassidy and the Sundance Kid.*"

"I've never—"

"When I get home, we're going to have another lesson. All on Robert Redford."

If my brain hadn't stumbled over the word *home*, maybe I would have laughed too.

Then he added fleetingly, "I gotta go do the media lineup. Talk to you later."

"Good luck. Have—" The line went dead before I could finish the sentence, and I was left staring at my phone.

My sister pulled my attention away from the screen. "What did he say?"

"Uh…he met Robert Redford."

"What's that face for?"

"No face. Just miss him, that's all."

After almost two months apart, our relationship was more or less me pretending I was comfortable with our situation. It was acting as if conversations in twenty-minute spurts were perfectly normal. It was controlling my tone of voice so he wouldn't hear the doubt in it.

I snapped a picture of Mason's tiny butt covered in a onesie with a stitched pig's tail, happy to concentrate on something that wasn't the gnawing uncertainty in the back of my mind. I sent it to my best friends.

Gem responded with her own picture of Willow lying on Jason's bare chest.

Then everyone, including me, sent all kinds of thirsty GIFs.

"Ooh. There he is." Shelley turned up the volume.

On television, the hostess, a white woman with sleek blond hair, greeted him. "CJ Cunningham, so nice to see you."

He was gorgeous in a dark charcoal tux with a maroon bow tie. His face was clean-shaven, save for those long sideburns, and his dark hair was brushed back off his face. It was the ultimate pain to know that millions of others were watching too. I wasn't special, merely another one of his fans. I went from being able to touch and kiss him whenever I wanted to resorting to a nationally televised event to see him.

"He looks really good," Shelley said in a squeaky voice, like she didn't want to admit it.

"Who are you wearing tonight?" the woman asked Chris.

"Tom Ford."

"I love this new look. You're really working it."

I rolled my eyes.

"Thanks," Chris said, not frowning but not really smiling either as he smoothed down his suit jacket. "I'm in the middle of filming."

I knew he hated these kinds of interviews. He hated talking about inane things like hair and clothing. He wanted to talk about what was important to him—the work.

"We have great weather here today," the hostess said, leaning in close to him. "How are you enjoying yourself so far?"

He grinned and lifted his right arm, running his hand over his hair then chin, and I remembered the last time that arm was wrapped around me.

I'd gotten pretty good at ignoring those memories, diving into assignments for my online master's classes. I'd tire myself out enough so that when I laid my head down at night, I wouldn't relive those vivid memories of his body around mine, his voice at my ear, his hands on my skin.

The first time seeing him on something other than my laptop screen, and I *had* to be at my sister's, holding my nephew. Terrible planning on my part.

"Well, I met my idol, Robert Redford, tonight, and he didn't run away screaming when I told him I was his biggest fan, so..."

The woman giggled, pressing her hand into his biceps, and if I could I'd crawl through the television to kick her.

"You mentioned you were in the middle of filming. Can you tell me anything about the new project?"

"Yeah, sure." Chris scrubbed his hands together. "It's a historical drama that takes place during the Gilded Age in New York City. My character has a bit of a sketchy past, and he runs into the daughter of a big business tycoon and falls in love. The story is really about her. Ruthie Van Acker has been so great, and Winston Charles, who plays her father, has been really welcoming. It's awesome to be able to play opposite such wonderful actors and people."

The interviewer nodded. "Well, I think it's safe to say there are a lot of people out there excited to see you back on the big screen." On cue, the camera panned to the fans in the stands and back as the hostess looked past him. "You didn't bring a date with you tonight?"

Chris's smile dropped. "No, not tonight."

She gripped his arm. "Well, you look wonderful. I'm so glad you're doing well and happy to know you're back. When can we expect your movie to premiere?"

"Early next spring, I think."

"Looking forward to it." She smiled brightly. "Thanks for chatting with us, and good luck tonight."

"Thank you." He nodded and waved at the camera.

Shelley slowly faced me, lowering the volume of the television. "You okay?"

I sniffed, my nose and eyes stinging.

"Do you want me to turn it off?"

"No. Really, I'm fine."

"In that case, you're going to need something stronger than tea." My sister, an angel, opened up a bottle of wine. She poured herself a few ounces before filling my glass almost to the top.

As the show officially started, Tommy plodded down the steps. "What's going on down here?"

"The Oscars are on," Shelley said, her gaze never leaving the television.

Tommy took his son from me and patted my shoulder. "Bean, you look like you're being tortured."

"You'd look like that too if you hadn't seen your boyfriend in a while, and he was appearing on national TV and looking really, really great."

"Thanks, Shell," I mumbled into my wineglass.

Tommy went back upstairs to give Mason a bottle and put him to bed, leaving the Shelley and me to our own devices. And as if they knew, my best friends assembled.

The FaceTime alert popped up, and there were Laney, Sam, and Gem.

"You guys planned this?"

"We're worried about you," Laney said.

Sam lifted a spoonful of yogurt to her mouth. "We didn't want you to watch alone."

"I'm not alone. I'm at my sister's house." I rotated my phone screen so Shelley could wave. "And there's nothing to watch. He's only presenting an award. He's going to talk for, like, a minute."

"But we know how hard it's been for you," Laney said, her chin in her hand. "Him there and you home."

Home. There was that word again.

"When are you seeing him?" Sam asked. "In person, I mean."

I shook my head. With Chris on set all day, we barely got to speak more than a few words to each other, let alone plan when we could see each other. And according to his calendar, he never had more than two days off a week. Not enough time to make any real visit by him or me worthwhile.

"You did a lot of waiting around for Hunter," Gem noted in that way she could, always cutting straight to the core. "I know you said you love CJ...or, Chris, whatever, but just because he's rich and famous doesn't mean you need to wait around for him. He's still a regular dude."

Sam nodded. "Regular dude with a weird job."

"Regular dude with a weird job who you said isn't even good at doing his own laundry," Gem added. "Is he worth it? Is all this—" she gestured to the screen "—worth it?"

Shelley stole my cell phone to chime in. "I wish you guys could've seen him while he was here. He really does love her."

"Can you not talk about me like I'm not here?" I snipped, snatching my phone back to find my three friends all with thoughtful faces.

"Do you think you could have a future with him?" Laney asked.

"Bronte," Sam said seriously, "you've wanted marriage and babies and the whole lot since I've known you. You think you're going to get that with him?"

I rubbed at my forehead, suddenly hating my best friends. "Is this some kind of intervention?"

Shelley grumbled next to me. "She doesn't need an intervention. She needs to take a chance!"

Gem laughed. "I knew your sister and I were kindred spirits. When are we hanging out, Shell?"

I spun my cell phone so Gem could see Shelley, who raised her wineglass. "Whenever you want. Kids can have a playdate, and moms can drink."

Gem whooped, but Sam interrupted, "Can we get back to the intervention?"

Laney snorted a laugh.

I whined. "I thought it wasn't an intervention."

"You remember how afraid I was when Jason asked me to move in with him?" Gem said, and I recalled how their relationship progressed so fast Gem had tried to torpedo the whole thing because she was so afraid, especially when she got pregnant. "But at some point, you have to make a decision. It's the indecision that kills you."

I nodded. She did have a good point. All this in-between, missed calls, text-only communication wasn't helping the matter any.

"You have to shit or get off the pot," Laney said helpfully

with a big grin, and Sam only shook her head, hiding her smile behind another bite of yogurt.

"Hey, when's your spring break?" Shelley asked.

I tipped my head back to my sister. "End of March, why?"

"Did you know you can get a nonstop flight to Los Angeles for, like, four hundred bucks?"

Laney gasped at Shelley's suggestion. "Yes, you should go to LA!"

"What? No."

Gem nodded as Sam said, "It would get you your answer."

"I think you should go," Laney told me. "You need to go see him in person."

"But no pressure," Sam said.

"Yeah, no pressure," Laney agreed.

"Although I did just buy you a ticket."

"You *what?*" I sat up, my wine sloshing over the rim of my glass.

Shelley showed me the receipt of purchase on her travel app. "You should be getting the email with the ticket momentarily."

I grabbed my sister's phone in disbelief. "You didn't."

Gem cackled. "I love it!"

CHAPTER THIRTY-TWO

Chris

Hey baby

I got caught up with everything going on last night and had to be on set early this morning. But I'm glad you got to watch the show.

I wanted you there on the red carpet with me. It would've been so much easier if I could've held your hand.

I guess I'll call you later. Love you.

———

BUNNY

OMG you'll never believe this.

BUNNY

We're all at Mom and Dad's for dinner and Luke started singing Blackbird with no prompting. NO PROMPTING.

BUNNY

He obviously misses you. But he's not the only one.

BUNNY

BTW everyone says hi. Call me if you have
time. I'll put you on speaker.

Hey, sorry. Just saw this. I'm so sad I missed
it. Did you get a video?

————

I was taking Taco for a walk today and I'm
pretty positive he ate goose poop. A. no big
deal. B. call the vet C. I'm the worst father
ever?

BUNNY

Since you haven't called me, I'm going to
assume Taco's still alive. I don't think dogs
should eat goose poop, but I'm sure dogs
have eaten worse. Especially Taco.

BUNNY

And you're not a terrible father. It's a learning
curve. Speaking of…

BUNNY

I had an idea for our next FaceTime date. Me,
you, and some student-teacher role-play. Let
me know what you think.

————

I've been missing you like crazy today. I had a
production meeting and couldn't concentrate
at all cause I was thinking about last night.

I've had a fucking hard-on all day, and it's all
your fault. Maybe you should be punished,
and next time, I'll be the teacher. I love you. I
miss you.

————

BUNNY

I swear I didn't do it on purpose but I was waiting in this really long line at the store and saw a picture of you on the cover of some magazine. You were wearing the blue shirt I got you for Christmas. You should probably get your clothes dry-cleaned. Just saying.

Harsh but fair.

Also I need to reschedule our Facetime.

BUNNY

Again?

Sorry. How about Tuesday?

BUNNY

I have a Best Buddies meeting, remember?

No. I can barely keep up with my schedule let alone yours.

———

I'm sorry. I didn't mean to snap at you. My mind is all over the place today. I'm upset that we can't connect lately. But I did appreciate the creativity of how many ways you can tell someone to fuck off in emojis.

———

BUNNY

I had a terrible day today. Please call me.

BUNNY

Ian came in talking about blow jobs because his older brother told him what it was, so he decided to explain it to the class, and suddenly I had to take over sex ed. I'm not trained to do that, so I babbled on and on. I think I might have said something about puberty and urges, but I can't be positive. My brain had a complete breakdown.

BUNNY

It might be the worst day I've ever had at school. Please call me. I don't care how late it is. I'm not going to sleep until you call.

I'm so sorry, baby. It's almost 3 in the morning your time. It was a late night on set today.

I feel so bad you had such a horrible day, but it sounds like you handled it well. I'm proud of you. You're a great teacher, and those kids are so lucky to have you.

I love you.

I hope you had a good night and tomorrow is a better day for you.

CHAPTER THIRTY-THREE

Bronte

"I can't believe I'm going." My stomach flip-flopped as I lifted my suitcase from Tommy's hatchback. Chris and I hadn't had the best track record lately, yet here I was on my way to surprise him. I must've been on another planet when I'd agreed to my sister's plan.

And I still hated my best friends. Even if they had stayed up with me on FaceTime last night as I packed.

"This is the worst idea you've ever had," I said, meeting Shelley at the drop-off curb.

"It's romantic!" She wrapped her arms around me. "And you're going along with it, so it can't be all that bad. Maybe not the worst idea ever?"

"Hey, have fun, okay?" Tommy said.

"I'll try." I leaned in through the open back window to stroke Mason's cheek and lay a big kiss on Zoe's head.

"He's going to flip out when he sees you," Shelley said.

That was what I was afraid of. This was going to be a complete shock to him. He still had a few weeks left of filming, and I didn't know if Chris would hate or love having me there.

I hoisted my carry-on over my shoulder. "See you guys when I get back."

After an agonizing six-hour flight with a screaming kid two rows back and, even worse, my own screaming nerves, I grabbed a Lyft to check in to a posh Westwood hotel room. I messaged my family's text thread as well as the girls to let them know I was safe and sound in California then, as instructed, texted Wes. I changed into fresh clothes and redid my hair no fewer than fifteen times before Wes showed up.

"Bronte?"

I squinted up at the man I hadn't seen in years, although his big smile and peach-colored hair were still the same. "Wes?"

"How the hell are you?" He picked me up from the floor and hugged me tight.

When he finally put me down, I slugged his arm. "I can't believe you're going along with this. It's ridiculous."

He feigned hurt, grabbing his bicep. "This isn't ridiculous. It's sweet."

I pivoted, flailing my arms, with my nervous energy having nowhere to go. "I flew three thousand miles to surprise CJ Cunningham on set, and what? I'll show up there and be like, 'Hey, Chris, what's up? Remember me, your girlfriend?'"

Wes shoved his hands in the pockets of his jeans, his shoulders up by his ears. "Yeah."

I bent over, my hands on my knees. "I think I might puke."

"You need a doctor?" he asked when I stood up, breathing deep.

"Maybe a Xanax?"

He patted himself down. "Fresh out. I'll need to make a run to the pharmacy."

"This is nuts. Am I nuts?" I looped my purse across my body before trailing him out of the room and into the elevator.

"It's Los Angeles. We're all a little nuts."

"That's not very reassuring."

"Don't worry. He's going to love seeing you. He's filming until about seven tonight. He's been doing good work. Really good work."

Inside the garage, the valet brought around Wes's car, and I hopped into the passenger side. "So, how are you? How've you been?"

"I'm great." He ran his finger along his nose, a spray of freckles making him appear younger than his thirty-four years. "Working hard. I've been trying to convince Chris to go into production with me."

"Go into production?"

"Yeah." He tapped his fingers along the steering wheel to the beat of the Sam Smith song. "I think it would be smart if we opened up our own house. You know? Make our own films. He's got the talent. I've got the business sense."

I covered my frown with my hand. It was the first I'd heard about this, and if they opened their own production company, I couldn't imagine what that meant for Chris. Or for me.

"The backlot isn't far from here," Wes informed me as he pulled onto a highway. The drive was only about fifteen minutes, and even though he told me stories the whole time, I didn't hear a thing. At the security gate, Wes checked in and handed me a guest pass. The bright pink lanyard was like a neon sign around my neck. *I'm not from here!*

Waving to someone he knew, Wes introduced me to Logan, Chris's production assistant, who led us to set. Inside the studio, walls had been erected to look like an ornate basement of sorts with a boxing ring in the middle. A few dozen people scurried back and forth, while some men, including Chris, stood inside the ring chatting.

Chris's costume consisted of plain brown pants and a loose white shirt with the sleeves rolled up to his elbows. The right side of his face had been made up to appear like he'd been in a fight. I assumed this was a scene toward the end of the movie, when his character tries to make a deal with his criminal boss, to whom Roy is indebted, so he can go after Lillian, the upper-class woman he loves.

"Ooh, they got Twizzlers at craft." Wes tossed his index finger up at me then jogged to tables set up with snacks.

A few feet behind me, I heard distinctly feminine voices.

"I can't believe your dad got us on set."

"I know, right? He's good for something... Look, CJ's right there."

Chancing a glance over my shoulder, I regarded the two women chatting and fluffing their hair, pink lanyards around their necks too. They were guests, and apparently one of them was related to someone important.

"I bet his dick is huge. Did you see his pants?"

I snapped my teeth together so hard, I feared for lock jaw, and focused back on the set. It had been cleared of everyone except Chris, an older man wearing a long coat, and a young woman with a headset and clapboard.

"Okay, quiet on set!" someone yelled through what sounded like a stereo system. Everyone stopped moving. I held my breath.

From somewhere else, someone said, "Camera rolling."

Then from another corner, "Sound rolling."

The woman called out the scene number and closed the clapboard with a smack before the person I assumed was Dante called out, "Ready CJ and Winston...action!"

From my spot, I stood on my toes to see over the heads of the people in front of me to where Chris, in character, exchanged words with his co-star, which ratcheted up until Chris threw a punch. It looked so real, I startled, pressing my hand to my chest.

"Cut!"

Movement everywhere resumed, and Wes strolled back over, grinning. "Good, right?"

"Yeah." Although I wasn't sure what exactly I'd just witnessed.

Then the two behind me started up again.

"Sweet baby Jesus, he's so hot. You know which trailer is his?"

"No, but I could find out. My dad told me to talk to Helen. She's the second AD."

The other one hissed out what she probably thought was a seductive sound. "God, I want to fuck him so hard."

Wes's eyes went wide, and I crossed my arms, digging my fingers into my biceps.

"You want to go to his trailer?" he asked, elbowing my side. When I turned my attention to him, he offered me a piece of licorice.

I bit into it as opposed to those women.

Pointing out big wires to avoid, Wes led me back outside toward a row of trailers. He opened the door to the one labeled CJ Cunningham. It was a small but nice space. "Have a seat," he said, gesturing to the couch. "You want anything to eat or drink?" When I shook my head, he closed the refrigerator door. "Bathroom's back there. Help yourself to whatever. I'll be back in a bit."

I nodded.

"Lost your voice?"

I nodded again, this time smiling at my old friend.

"Okay." He laughed. "Be back in a few."

Though it was more than a few. It was almost an hour.

An hour of pacing. Of texting the girls. Of hanging up clothes Chris had left in a pile on the floor. Of sorting through the stack of paperbacks next to the couch.

Then suddenly, the door swayed open, and there he was,

trying and failing to brush off those two women from set. Wes shoved his shoulder in between the platinum blonde and one of her tentacles. "Look who's here!"

Chris literally shook the redhead off his arm as his dark eyes darted up inside the trailer. "Bronte?"

I waved, unsure what to do when those women wouldn't let go of my boyfriend.

"Can you...please..." He hopped up onto the step, shaking his leg as if an amorous dog were attached, and reached for the door handle to close it.

"We have free time," the redhead said, trying to sneak in.

"Ladies, if you'll follow me, I can give you a tour of the lot," Wes suggested, waving his arm behind him. "CJ needs time to prepare for tomorrow."

When it was obvious their mission was a lost cause, they gave up. The blonde winked at Chris. "Maybe another time."

He shut the door on them and huffed. "I don't think so." With a visible breath and shudder, he closed the distance between us, tangling his fingers with mine. "Hi."

"Hey."

"I can't believe you're here." He swept his gaze over the length of me. "I'm so happy."

I peered at him through my heavy lashes. "Are you?"

"Of course." He plucked at my slinky black tank top. "You look different."

I blinked, running a single finger underneath one eye, feeling silly. "I..." I shook my head slightly. "They're fake eyelashes."

His eyes turned soft, his mouth easing into a smile, then combed his hands through my hair. "You got it cut. I like it." His fingertips grazed my collarbone, below the new blunt slant of my hair. He ghosted his lips across my cheekbone and skimmed his nose along my neck. "You smell so good."

"Chris."

His name came out all breathy and not at all like I meant it.

"God, I missed your voice." He placed a soft, wet kiss on my pulse and wrapped a hand around the nape of my neck, licking and nipping at my throat.

"Chris," I said again, this time finding the wherewithal to move away from him.

CHAPTER THIRTY-FOUR

Chris

I lifted my head, not realizing I had pressed Bronte into the cushions of the couch. I smiled sheepishly and sat up, leaving just enough space between us to still breathe in each other's air. I searched her eyes, swirling with desire and apprehension.

And not for the first time—not even for the millionth time—I regretted leaving her. Although in this moment, with her in my grasp, it was worse. Seeing doubt in her gaze cut me in half.

"Bronte," I whispered, reaching for her hand, but she pulled away from me and blew out a slow breath. I knew—was absolutely aware—it was really important to talk now, yet all I wanted to do was touch her. I needed that reassurance. That she was here. That she was real.

I had dreamed about her almost every night since I'd left Pennsylvania. About the smooth skin below her ear, the gentle curve of her back under my hands, the slight swell of her breasts as they pressed against me. It was as if I had dreamed her here into reality, and my lips were greedy. She allowed me one taste of her neck.

"Is this how it always is?" she asked after a while, and I jerked away from the slope of her shoulder.

"What?"

She lifted a delicately guarded eyebrow. "Women throwing themselves at you."

"No. It's never like that. That was a total fluke. Random strangers aren't allowed on set. One of their dads is an executive producer, so he got them a pass."

"They're quite determined," she said evenly, as if I couldn't see the jealous tick of her jaw.

Truly, stuff like that never happened. Security was tight around here, but even if it weren't, it wasn't like I was looking for someone else. I didn't care about anyone else but Bronte.

"I kinda love that you're so jealous."

She let out an adorable growl. "Well, I'm so glad you like it because I hate it. Do you know what it's like for me to come here?"

I shook my head even though it was a rhetorical question.

"For me to come all this way and surprise you, and—" she pointed toward the window, to the world outside "—be here with all these people and this stuff? It's really intimidating." She flicked at the lanyard around her neck. "I'm a guest here, and it's so weird and cool and, yeah, super hot to see you work, but it makes me feel like..." She lifted one shoulder, the corner of her mouth drooping down. "Like an outsider. Then there are those girls with huge fake boobs and big lips, and I had to stand there listening to them talk about how much they want to have sex with you."

She dropped her chin toward her chest, and for one moment, I thought she might cry. But instead, she said, "I hate them. I hate that they think they stand a chance. That they might be able to come back here and put their hands on you, try to claim you."

With two fingers under her jaw, I tipped her face up. "They can't. You're the one who's here. You're the one I want." When she shifted the slightest bit away, I held her steady with my hand on the back of her neck. "You came all the way across the country to give me the silent treatment?"

She ducked out of my hold.

"Talk to me, Bronte. Tell me what you're thinking about."

Her chest and shoulders expanded on a big breath, her cheeks puffing up before she let it out. Her arms flopped at her sides as if she was exhausted. I was too. "What do you want to talk about, Chris?"

"Anything. Everything."

"You want to do this here?" She gestured around the trailer then to my face. "Like that?"

"Yeah." I didn't care if I had to sit with this paint on my face all day, all week. She was here now, and I needed to hear what she had to say. "Why didn't you tell me you were coming?"

She refused to meet my eyes. "It was Shelley's idea. She bought me the ticket."

"Does that mean you don't want to be here?"

She turned her back to me. "Of course I want to be here. I just didn't know what your reaction would be."

"What did you think? That I'd be pissed?" I huffed. "Bronte, this is the best surprise you could have given me."

"Well." She circled back around, lifting one shoulder. "I didn't know."

"You didn't know?" I cradled her jaw in the palms of my hands. "How could you thi—"

"Because I'm mad, Chris!" She batted me away, her brows narrowing. "I've *been* mad."

"You've been mad at me? This whole time? Why didn't you say anything?" There was no way we'd ever be able to make this work if she refused to let me know what was going on in her head.

"How could I? You had already left, so it's not like it would've changed anything."

I deflated against the counter. There was a very distinct, acute pain in the middle of my chest, and I rubbed at the spot.

"I'm mad I didn't get a say. I'm mad we hardly ever get to talk. I'm mad I have to wait for everyone else to be done with you before it's my turn," she said, pointedly tipping her chin toward the door, where those two women had fought for my attention only minutes ago. "And, in my weakest moments, I wonder if you're ashamed of me, if you think I'm not good enough or strong enough to be with you."

"No." I pulled her against my chest. "God, no. I don't think that at all. You are *everything* to me."

She tilted her head to finally meet my gaze, and her eyes were rimmed with tears. "Then why? Why did you leave without including me?"

With Bronte back in my arms, I could breathe again, think clearly again. "I thought by leaving early I was doing what was best."

"What you thought, huh?"

"Yeah, but that was stupid. We both know you're the brains in this relationship." I kissed her temple and crossed my arms around her back, wishing I could go back in time. Maybe kidnap her and steal her away to some deserted island to live out the rest of our days naked under the sun.

"I know this was a self-inflicted wound, but you have to believe me when I say I didn't want to hurt you. I was only trying to protect you. Protect us."

She buried her face in my neck. "I felt...I feel so far away from you. I was starting to think what we had wasn't real."

"It was real. It *is* real." I kissed her head, her ear, her temple, until she lifted her face to me again.

"But how do you know?" she asked in a whisper. "We barely had a chance to see what it was like. Texts and phone calls don't make for much of a relationship."

"Can I show you now what it would be like? Chris and Bronte take on Los Angeles."

That earned me a tiny smile, and I held her at arm's length, my heart racing like I was at the starting line, ready to take off in a sprint. "How long are you staying?"

"For a few days. I have a hotel reservation through Sunday. My flight leaves early that morning."

"Screw your reservation. I've been away from you for too long. Come home with me."

She pushed away from me with a casual shrug and a flirty smile. "If you insist."

"All right. Give me five minutes." I held up my hand, repeating, "Five."

I cleaned off my make-up, tossed my costume on a hanger, and took the quickest shower known to man. When I grabbed my towel, stumbling out into the tiny hallway, Bronte giggled, and it was the sweetest sound I'd heard in a long time. I yanked on jeans and a T-shirt then towed her out of the trailer.

The head of the costume department was headed my way.

"Hey," I called out to her. "I left all my stuff in the trailer. Sorry, it's a mess in there, but it's all hung up for you." When she made a move to stop me, I kept walking, calling over my shoulder, "I gotta run, Deb. Thanks so much!" I dipped my mouth to Bronte's ear. "Once she starts talking, she doesn't stop. Sweet lady, though."

I waved to a few more people on the lot, including Logan, my PA.

"Wait," they said, handing me a few papers. "Your new sides. And Trevor wanted to talk to you."

I rolled my head back to my shoulders. When I needed to leave, suddenly everyone wanted to chat. *Now.* "About what?"

They adjusted the headphones hanging around their neck. "Fight choreography."

Tugging Bronte in closer to me, I shook my head. "I can't. We've been over it already. If he wants to change it, we can do it another day. It's after seven. I'm done for the day." Then tipped my chin to Wes, who jogged over. "We're out of here."

His eyes toggled between me and Bronte before he nodded with a smile. "Yeah, sure. I'll talk to you later?"

"I'll call you," I said slowly, sending a message. No interruptions.

"See you later, Bean."

I barely let her get out a reply before I was practically sprinting toward my car.

"Chris. Chris, wait. Slow down."

I did, finally noticing she had trouble keeping up in her wedge sandals. "Why'd you even wear those? They're not very you." She blanched, and I backtracked. "Not that I don't like them. I love them. You look so sexy. The whole—" I waved from her head to her toes "—everything. I'm not..." I closed my eyes and shook my head once to clear it. "It's just that you surprised me tonight, and you look so gorgeous, and my brain can't take it all."

I curled my arm around her waist, aiming for a kiss, but someone called out, "Hey! CJ! What's up, bro!"

I didn't wait to see who it was, only opened the passenger side door of my car and all but threw Bronte inside. "Let's go."

I wasn't dumb enough to waste even a second of this visit by not having her in my bed. While she went up to her room to grab her stuff, I stayed in the lobby of the Westwood hotel, checking her out and paying the cancellation fee.

When the elevator doors opened, I took hold of her suitcase in one hand and laced my fingers with hers in the other. "Ready?" I guided her outside only to stop abruptly. "Son of a bitch."

She poked her head around my shoulder. "What are you—"

The first flash went off.

She shifted away from the cameras. "We were only here for fifteen minutes."

"Enough time for someone to let them know where I was," I snarled quietly, blocking her with my body as we marched back to my car.

She let out a painful sound, and I glanced over my shoulder. "What?"

"They're taking my picture, and I look like the woman from *Mary Poppins* who feeds the birds."

I reeled around, laughing, and wrapped my arms around her. While she was upstairs, she had changed out of her super-sexy black tank top, jeans, and heels into an oversized cardigan and leggings. "Well, I think you make an adorable bird lady."

I was giving the paps exactly what they wanted, but if I could make Bronte feel at all better about the situation, I didn't care about the assholes taking my picture. That was until they started whistling and catcalling.

"Ignore them," I said, ushering her into my car.

"I'm trying." She sank down low in the passenger seat as I got in the driver's side, resisting the urge to throw the vultures the middle finger.

I sped away with screeching tires, checking my rearview mirror a few times. "You can sit up now."

She did, reluctantly, seeming a bit shaken. It was her first real run-in with the paparazzi, and I was being rather blasé about it.

"I'm sorry." I brought her hand to my mouth, kissing her knuckles. I forgot for a second that she wasn't used to all this. I tried again. "Are you hungry?"

"No, I just want a bed."

"That I can do." I gunned it toward the highway.

Half an hour later, I pulled into my private neighborhood in The Hills and clicked a button on my visor to open the iron-rod gate that led to my house.

Bronte gasped, leaning forward to get a better look. It was dark, but enough light illuminated the property to see the beautiful landscaping with flowering bushes, ivy, and tall trees, all a contrast to the white house. I put it on my mental to-do list to give the landscapers a raise for making her smile.

I parked in the garage, then took her suitcase from the trunk, escorting her into the house. When I hit the lights, her jaw hung open for a while.

"It's like *The Jetsons*."

"Yeah, the guy who designed it studied with Frank Lloyd Wright. It was built in the '60s."

She walked in a slow, exploratory circle. "Wow."

Each room bled into the next, and she ran straight to the back of the house, pressing her nose up against the sliding glass doors, revealing the pool and sparkling lights of the city below.

"That's the canyon," I said, pointing. "And look, the Hollywood sign."

"Wow," she murmured in awe.

"You like it?"

"Yes." She turned, eyes tracing the chrome and black furniture and Warhol-esque art on the walls. "It doesn't seem very you, though."

A decorator had put all of it together. I couldn't have cared less back when I first bought it. Now? I wanted to decorate all over again with Bronte. "I guess not."

I gave her a smile before crossing to the kitchen. "Taco!" I snagged two bottles of water from the refrigerator as my boy poked his head around the corner. "There you are." I kneeled down, signaling him forward. "What were you doin', buddy?"

He sniffed at the air between me and Bronte and dared to take two slow steps toward me, his tail between his legs.

"Don't be shy."

"Hi, Taco," Bronte cooed, reaching for his gray and brown fur.

Taco leaned against my shins. "The vet says he has self-esteem issues."

"Self-esteem issues?" She took a cautious step to him, but he made no move to make friends.

"Come here. It's Bronte. We like Bronte," I stage-whispered, leading him to her hand. After a minute, he warmed up, letting her pet him for a while, and I stood, leaning back against the counter. "You want a tour of the rest of the house?"

She shook her head, seeming as if she was about to fall over. "I'm really tired."

Of course she was. It was after midnight her time. "Come on. Let's go to bed."

I led her upstairs, to the back of the house where my bedroom was situated, looking out over the hills. Taco jumped right up onto the bed, settling in between the pillows, and Bronte laughed.

"Self-esteem issues, but clearly spoiled," I joked, setting her suitcase next to the bed. "I'll be right back," I said and scooted down the hall to dial Jillian, my publicist. I needed to change my schedule around, because with the day off filming tomorrow, there was no way I was leaving the house in the next twenty-four hours if I had any say.

CHAPTER THIRTY-FIVE

Bronte

"Hey, sleepyhead, you finally awake?"

I begrudgingly cracked one eye to find Chris sitting next to me. Even through the fog of sleep, my body automatically responded to him, with my heart kicking up and my skin warming. "Hmm?" He was dressed in a sweaty T-shirt with the sleeves cut off, and I gave him my full attention with a smile. "Morning."

"Since when do you sleep in?" he asked, leading my gaze away from his arm, tanned and veined.

"Since now." I yawned, my fingers roving over the comfiest sheets I had ever slept in.

"Well, wake up. Me and Taco went for a walk and worked out already."

"Taco works out?"

"Yeah, part of his confidence-building." He jostled the covers. "Come on. It's ten o'clock." Leaning down so he was nose-to-nose, he added, "And I want to play."

I sat up, reaching for my glasses on the nightstand out of habit. Obviously, my nightstand was not there, and Chris retrieved them from the top of his dresser for me.

"You fell asleep with them on last night."

"I was exhausted."

"I know. You didn't even snore."

"I don't snore." I smacked at his leg, but he caught my hand, hauling me up out of the bed to kiss my jaw. "I thought you wanted to play."

"Later." His eyes went dark, and I knew that look.

I wiggled away. "I didn't even brush my teeth yet."

"I wasn't planning on kissing you on your mouth."

"Oh."

His mouth drifted lower, skimming down my throat, and he lifted my T-shirt over my head. After guiding me back down to the bed, he pressed open-mouthed kisses against my collarbone and sternum, and I let out another, "Ooh."

I'd waited my whole life to meet the one person I loved like this, and after being apart from him, it was like coming back home. I couldn't contain myself, every moan and groan reflexively communicating what I wanted, my brain too overloaded with sensation and infatuation to function properly.

"I missed all your sounds," he said, taking one nipple into his mouth, sucking and licking before blowing a stream of cool air across it. I squirmed under him, and he held my wrists down when I tried to clutch his hair as he kissed down my belly. "And the way you taste."

He had my leggings and panties off in one long pull, and he lowered his head, breathing over my naked skin. It had been so long, I pulsed with need, my heart beat thumping between my legs.

"I need to apologize."

"You did last night."

"Not enough." He licked up my center, prompting a gasp from me. "My sweet girl."

"I thought I was…" I licked my dry lips, my breath coming out in pants as he flicked his tongue repeatedly against me. "I thought I was your dirty girl."

He hummed, vibrating my nerve endings until I was twitching uncontrollably, and when he twisted two fingers inside of me, I cried out, an orgasm unexpectedly crashing over me like a tidal wave.

With his mouth still on me, his eyes peered up, over my chest, heaving with tortured breaths. "You soaked my hand, baby."

"I want more. I want to do more with you," I rasped, combing my fingers through his hair.

Even though I couldn't see him smile, I felt it. "My sweet, dirty girl."

He shifted over top of me and shucked off his shirt then reached into a hidden drawer at the base of the bed frame. He tossed something next to my elbow, though I was too light-headed with desire to care what it was, all of my awareness fixated on every glorious inch of him above me. He was slightly bigger and stronger with the thick muscle at his shoulders that he hadn't had when he left Pennsylvania. Not to mention the abs. But what really got me was the tattoo on the left side of his chest above his heart.

He'd never mentioned it before, the three lines written in small script.

Be with me always

Take any form

Drive me mad

I read the words out loud, remembering what book they were from. "You read *Wuthering Heights*?"

"Yeah." His gaze dropped to the tattoo then lifted back to me. "You're with me always. Even on days when we played phone tag or days when we argued or days we didn't talk at all. You were with me."

I grabbed the back of his head, pulling him toward me for a biting kiss, one that let him know how much I missed him and how much it meant to hear how he missed me. I wrapped my fingers around his erection. "I missed the way you feel."

He let out a throaty groan, holding himself up so he could watch as I guided him into my wet sex. He dragged his eyes back up my body and when he was fully buried inside me, he dropped his chin, exhaling harshly. "Yes. So good. It's so good." He moved his hand to my breast, strumming his thumb back and forth over my nipple until my back arched, playing me like he would his guitar. "You really want to try more?"

When I nodded, he rolled to his back, so I was on top, though he held me to his chest, scraping his teeth along my throat. "You're going to touch me. Don't be afraid, just go slow and easy."

I barely had time to respond before he pinched my nipple and sucked a mark into my shoulder. He held my palm up and placed a small tube of lube in it, saying, "Turn around, let me see this beautiful back of yours." He held me steady as I followed his directions, sinking back down onto him. "That's it. Now make your fingers wet like you make mine."

The lube was cool, and I rubbed it along the pads of my index and middle fingers. When I bent forward, the angle of his thrusts changed, and I saw stars, enough to make me pause my movements. He held my waist with a bruising grip. "Come on, baby, don't be shy now."

His words nudged me on, and I glided my fingers along the soft skin of the weights under his shaft at the same time I circled my hips. He sucked in a sharp breath behind me and that emboldened me enough to sink my fingers lower, along the seam of his backside, until I reached the ring of muscle. I hesitantly pressed my middle finger into it, and I felt him tense underneath.

"Sweet fuck, you're gonna make me go off quick."

"Feels good?"

"So fucking good."

I loved being able to give him so much pleasure, and I rocked back into him at the same time as I inserted my finger in deeper. He was hot and tight, the same words he used to describe me, and we learned a rhythm of give and take.

Everything was awareness and color, heat and sweat, moans and sparks of hedonism so sweet it bordered on agony. I wanted to reach the peak and yet stay here forever, clawing with desire.

I curled my finger inside Chris, and he gasped. "Shit, fuck, I'm coming. I'm coming."

He surged up behind me, pulling my back against his chest, his fingers flying to my clit as his teeth sunk into the crook of my neck, and I was coming too.

Once we caught our breath, he towed me back to the mattress, leaving a line of quick kisses along my shoulder blade. "You like that?"

I sighed, completely boneless. "Yeah. I'd say so. It was quite a wake-up call."

"Mm-hmm."

"And since you're behind me, I'm going to assume that's not you licking my foot."

He whipped his head up. "Taco!"

The dog scampered away.

"Self-esteem issues?" I asked, laughing. "Seems more like a pervert."

"What can I say?" He stood up, holding out his hand. "Takes after his dad." He pressed a kiss to my shoulder when I stood. "Shower?"

He tugged me to the bathroom, where he had spread out my toiletries exactly how I liked. After we showered together, he escorted me through the four bedrooms, three bathrooms, and game room—stripper pole included—before circling back to the kitchen, where my gaze skirted to the patio doors and the pool, glistening with the midmorning rays.

"Want to go swimming?" he asked.

"I didn't bring a bathing suit."

"Not a problem." He opened the door and stepped outside. "We're completely secluded. You don't need one."

I bit my lip, craning my neck right and left for proof of seclusion.

"The only people who can see you are skydivers with good binoculars and God." When I didn't move from my spot, he dipped his foot in to test the temperature, let his shorts fall to the deck, and dove in.

Coming up to the surface, he swam over the edge, resting his chin on his hands, taunting me. "Come on, where's my bold Bronte?"

I liked being his anything, but if he wanted bold, I could do that too. I stripped off my clothes and cannonballed into the water. We spent hours in the pool and lazily sunbathed the day away.

Still feeling bold later that night, I found Chris flipping through a script and cleared my throat in the doorway to get his attention. He did a double take at me wearing one of his button-downs. It hit two or three inches below my hips, leaving nothing to the imagination.

"What are you doing?" he murmured, eyes tracking down my legs.

"Playing."

I scampered away to the game room, where I plugged in my cell phone, hitting his playlist. As I'd planned, he followed me and stood in the middle of the room, breathing a little too hard for a guy who was so in shape.

Without words, I pushed him to sit down on the black suede sectional before strutting to the stripper pole. I had no clue what I was doing but assumed if I shimmied around enough, I'd get the point across. Swiveling my back to him, I rolled my head and shoulders side to side, leaning into the beat.

I spun around to find Chris relaxed on the couch, arms spread wide along the tops of the cushions. He let out a wolf whistle, spurring me on to wrap my hands around the pole, grinding up and down. I tried every clichéd trick in the book, licking my lips and whipping my hair around. In my past life, I might have felt self-conscious doing something like this, but there was nothing Chris and I could do that would ever make me feel ashamed.

I only felt powerful with him. Especially when he shifted in his seat, his hand covering his tented sweats.

I slowly unbuttoned the shirt and used it like a boa around my shoulders and hips then tossed it on his head. He held on to it, his eyes never leaving my body as I strutted back to the pole, this time arching my back against it. I closed my eyes, but a moment later opened them when Chris came to stand in front of me.

Words weren't needed, and he took me there, bent over and leaning against the pole.

We sank down to the floor after we both finished. "Quite a show you put on."

"Tomorrow, it's your turn to dance for me."

He chuckled, throwing an arm around my shoulders. "I had to move some stuff around so we could have the whole day to ourselves today. I know you're only here for two more days, but

I have a few hours on set tomorrow, and then Saturday, I've got a photo shoot. Are you okay to tag along?"

"Yes, of course. I finally get to experience a day in the life of CJ Cunningham."

He kissed my temple. "My days aren't really that exciting."

CHAPTER THIRTY-SIX

Bronte

Chris's alarm chirped bright and early at five a.m. to meet with his personal trainer, Yanni. I had full intention of working out with him—moral support and all—but ended up napping on a lounge chair while the six-and-a-half-foot Greek god put Chris through his paces for two hours. The first being strength training, and the second all boxing sequences.

Then after a quick shower and breakfast, which was a frozen meal from a personal chef, Taco and I trailed Chris into one of his three cars to head to the studio. He explained that since Taco still wasn't used to a lot of people, he kept the dog home and hired someone to walk him every day, but since Taco liked me, we could hang out in the trailer together.

And hang out we did, for three hours while Chris filmed some fight scene, popping back to the trailer for five- or ten-minute breaks at a time. No matter how fake it was, I didn't want to watch Chris repeatedly get beat up. So instead, I'd met Amy, the makeup artist, Jericho, the hair guy, Deb, the costumer, Trevor, the fight coordinator, Dante, the director, and Ruthie, the costar. They were all lovely but busy and didn't have a lot of time for conversation, which was good, I supposed. I only had to sit in the trailer and not look as awkward as I felt.

Lunch was at three, and I dutifully followed Chris to craft services, where we took a seat at a table by ourselves.

"Do you always eat alone?"

Still in his makeup so he looked even worse than the other day, with a black eye, cut cheek, and battered nose, he explained, "I eat with whoever is free. Not everyone has lunch at the same time, and not all the actors are on set at the same time. I only have these two scenes today. But Ruthie and Winston have another one after, and the entire crew is always here before and after we leave set. It's long, hard days for everybody, but especially the crew."

I coasted my attention around the lunchroom where a few groups of the crew sat, scarfing down food. A woman poked her head in the door, asking for someone named Pete, who stood up immediately, taking his sandwich with him as he followed her out.

Chris raised his eyebrows as if to say *See?*

As we finished up our food, he told me he'd be filming a scene with Ruthie next, one where she finds him after the fight. When she would tell him it's too late; she's betrothed to another man.

Standing off in the back corner, I watched take after take of Ruthie, as Lillian, run into the ring after the fight Roy lost. She wiped his brow and kissed him tenderly as she broke his heart. Again and again. The scene unfolding was heart-wrenching, but seeing someone kiss my boyfriend wasn't as bad as I thought it would be. There were so many people around, so much movement, I could barely believe the actors were able to push all that aside and focus on their lines.

It wasn't Chris and Ruthie up there, it was Roy and Lillian, and it was obvious there was no way he could ever give this up.

Not that I'd ask him to. Just like I would never give up my kids and classroom for Hunter when he'd wanted me to move, I couldn't ask Chris for a "normal" life, when his career involved all this abnormality.

We were at an impasse.

When he finished filming, he showered and changed in his trailer, and I said goodbye to Dante and the crew, thanking them for allowing me to be on set. Dante hugged me then mumbled something to Chris I missed, but it was clearly positive about me from the way Chris grinned and Dante winked at me. Although it didn't make me feel any better about the situation.

As a surprise, Chris took Taco and Bronte for a drive up the coast. We ate a dinner of grapes, cheese, and crackers on the hood of his car while watching the sun set over the ocean, but that only mollified me until the next morning.

Saturday began much like the day before, early and with a workout. Wes and Jillian, Chris's publicist, showed up to go over details for the day. I listened as they talked business and described how next month was going to be crazy after filming wrapped up. Chris had a commercial and print campaign scheduled for a cologne, as well as some promo work the studio wanted him and Ruthie to do.

Jillian opened her laptop to show Chris some shots for the movie posters, and he motioned me over. They were various photos of Chris, all rough-and-tumble, next to Ruthie in an emerald-green gown, her dark hair spilling over her shoulders with pearls decorating a few strands.

"What do you think?" he asked, wrapping his arm around my hips.

"They're gorgeous."

"The studio wants to push up the release date for Oscar season," Jillian said.

"What? Really?" Chris swiveled back and forth between Jillian and Wes.

"You've seen the dailies." Wes nodded. "They're really good."

"Yeah, but the postproduction schedule would be shortened. By a lot."

Wes shrugged. "Dante told me the other day he doesn't think there'll be many pickups because you and Ruthie have great chemistry together. He said, and I quote, 'CJ's got his magic back.'"

Chris's face flushed, his fingers pressing into my thighs, though there wasn't any more time to celebrate. Jillian piled everyone, including Taco, into a big Escalade with a driver, and we were off to a *GQ* photo shoot at the Santa Monica Pier.

With Chris's nineteenth-century hair and sideburns, they decided his big comeback spread should be elegant and whimsical. I made a home in yet another trailer as two women pulled looks for him, all various combinations of pants, suspenders, suit jackets, and open shirts, even a derby hat. They had shut down parts of the pier for the shoot. It was fun to get a behind-the-scenes view of everything as Chris posed and pouted in front of the Ferris wheel, carousel, and on the beach, but it was almost impossible for me not to be in the way with all the moving pieces. I was a roadblock, always in the way of a set piece or light or a PA running around with coffee.

I headed back into the trailer, where Jillian camped out with her laptop. I may as well have been wallpaper. Chris finally reappeared after I wasted an hour or so playing on my cell phone. "There you are. I didn't know where you ran off to."

"I got bored," I said when he sat down next to me, running a hand over my head.

"I feel like I've been apologizing a lot this weekend, but I'll say it again. Sorry about that."

"It's okay. This is your job."

He kissed my cheek as someone knocked at the door. Jillian stood to open it, introducing the *GQ* journalist, who was going to interview Chris later on in the week. The man's eyes toggled between us, but Chris didn't introduce or even acknowledge me.

"I'm going to take a walk, I think." I got the distinct impression I was in the way. Yet again.

"Hey." He snagged my wrist. "Why don't you take Taco? We'll be here for another two hours or so, right, Jill?"

Jillian nodded, and I sighed inwardly, reduced down to CJ Cunningham's dog-wrangler. With Taco's leash in hand, I had one foot out of the trailer when Chris said behind me, "I appreciate you letting me reschedule. Had a few things come up I couldn't get out of."

Those words landed right in my solar plexus. I wasn't his girlfriend or partner or even dog-walker. No. I was a thing he couldn't get out of.

When it was finally time to go home, I was tucked up next to Chris in the back of the Escalade as I flipped through pictures I'd snapped while wandering the pier with Taco.

"I wish I could've been there with you." He took my phone in his hands to enlarge a selfie of me and Taco sitting on the surf. He grinned, tapping the screen a few times to text it to himself. When his cell phone buzzed, he made the picture his new home screen then showed it to me. "My girl and my dog. Everything a man needs."

I blinked away my blurred vision, refusing to cry. This day had been a roller coaster. Hell, this whole weekend. I'd come searching for answers, but what I'd found was more confusion. Chris didn't seem to be any better at managing his work and personal life. At times, I felt like a secret hidden in a corner, and at other times, as if I was the only other person on the planet with him. But at some point, one of those had to win out.

Once we arrived back at his house, he marched right into the shower. I followed him, sitting on the toilet lid, admiring his sinewy frame through the clear shower doors while he soaped up.

"Did anyone say anything about your tattoo? You have to have your shirt off for some scenes, don't you?"

He washed suds from his hair. "Yeah, and they can cover it with makeup. Amy was jealous. She said her husband never got a tattoo for her."

"You told Amy what it means?" Although it seemed churlish, I was pleased Chris had talked about me to other people. It was proof I was with him, on his mind, even when I wasn't so sure.

He wiped water from his eyes. "And why I got it." He slanted his head, his gaze colliding with mine through the glass door. "You're not some dirty little secret. I know that's what you're thinking. I told my friends, the people I trust, about you. I'm just not willing to share you with the rest of the world. It already gets so much of me. I don't want them to have you too."

My heart didn't merely reach the peak, it soared.

"You want to join me in here?"

As tempting as it was, I only had a few hours left with this man, and I wanted to treat him to a home-cooked meal. "I was thinking I could make us dinner. I saw you have some chicken in the freezer. You have mushrooms and lemon, so I could—"

"Dinner? No, baby, I have that meeting tonight. We have to leave in about an hour."

Then my heart plummeted. "*We* do?"

He pivoted so the water hit his back. "Yeah, didn't they tell you?"

"They who?" I huffed, storming out of the bathroom.

Chris wasn't far behind. "Bronte, hold on. I thought when we were going over my schedule this morning, Jillian or Wes would have told you."

I avoided his hand when he reached for me and kneeled down at my suitcase. "Jillian or Wes? Why didn't *you* tell me?"

"I don't know... I... Can you look at me for a second?"

I did, hiking my eyebrows expectantly, annoyed that after these past few days of nonstop action, *this* was how we were going to spend our last night together.

"I'm meeting Tom to go over some other possible projects. I'm sorry, I—"

I cut him off with an angry growl and dug through my clothes, tossing shirts and shoes on the floor.

"What are you doing?"

He was standing so close, drops of water fell onto my back. "What does it look like?" I pushed off the floor with a shirt crumpled in my grip. "I'm trying to find something to wear."

"I'm sor—"

"Don't say it, Chris."

He sounded like a broken record with all these apologies. He had a job to do, one that he loved; I knew that. I just didn't like it right now.

He stepped away and shut his mouth—smart man—and I slid past him to the bathroom to get ready for dinner.

When I finally made my way into the living room, Chris set down his guitar, a slow smile unfurling as his gaze swept over me. He was dressed in jeans and a blazer over a plain white T-shirt. Even with the ridiculous sideburns, he looked sexy and relaxed. It was infuriating.

"You look beautiful." Even through my anger, I couldn't help but lean into him when he kissed me.

The sky was dark on our drive, but floodlights brightened

up the well-known sights of Beverly Hills as we cruised down Rodeo Drive. It's funny how someone might think they knew what Los Angeles was like from television, movies, or books, but no one really knows what it's like until they see it with their own eyes. They don't know how beautiful and ugly it could be.

My pulse spiked as Chris slowed at the valet station. People with cameras and cell phones lined the sidewalk in front of Spago.

"What's going on?" The question left my mouth right as the answer strolled out of the restaurant. I didn't know who they were, but each girl appeared as if she had stepped off the runway in heels and fancy tops. They were gorgeous, smiling and laughing as they made their way into their waiting car.

"Is that...?"

"Iris Moon," Chris supplied.

"The model? Didn't you hook up with her?"

"No, I did not."

"I thought—"

He rolled his head back with a sigh. "Don't tell me you read it somewhere?"

"It might've come up in the Google search I did when I first found out who you were."

"Well, it's not true."

Even if it wasn't true, I was still wildly out of my element in my ballet flats, jeans, and flowy top. Not exactly model material, and now the paparazzi had their lenses aimed at Chris's car.

"Keep your head down and walk fast," he instructed before opening his car door.

I did as I was told, reaching for his hand when he jogged around the front of the car, while trying to hide my face with the other. They peppered us with questions about who I was and made comments about Chris, obviously goading him for a reaction, but he kept his head down, speeding into the restaurant. My heart beat a mile a minute, barely keeping up as I bodies closed in on me.

A man in a suit held his arms up, putting some space between us and the cameras. He shepherded inside and introduced himself as one of the managers of the restaurant. I didn't pay attention to his brief exchange with Chris. I was too busy blinking away the spots in my vision.

"We have your table in the back, right this way."

Chris pressed his hand into my back, ushering me in front of him, and I took cautious steps forward. The walls were white, but the lighting was dim, casting a glow throughout the place. We were seated on a patio surrounded by brick walls, and twinkle lights strewn in the open space above us. There was a single candle lit on the table with small green plants on either side, while soft piano music was piped in.

It was really romantic. Too bad I was across from Tom, who never stopped talking. I didn't have anything to contribute to the conversation, but even if I had, it wouldn't have mattered. I was basically a piece of the scenery while Chris was busy playing CJ Cunningham.

"Excuse me." I slid my chair back, the sudden clarity the situation closing in on me until I was claustrophobic. Chris shot me a worried glance, but didn't say anything when I rushed away from the table, heading for the bathroom.

Leaning against the sink, I texted the girls.

I don't think I can do this.

Surprisingly, a response arrived within seconds. Even though it was after midnight at home, it was only nine here for Laney since she lived in the Bay Area.

267

> LANEY
>
> Do what? Be with Chris?

> Be with CJ.

> LANEY
>
> Aren't they the same?

Back at the table, I pasted on a smile, scraping the bottom of the barrel for a smidgen of enthusiasm as we finished our meals, but it was evident Chris saw right through it. Once we were out of the restaurant and on the road, he curled his fingers around my knee. "What'd you think of dinner?"

"It was good."

"Sorry about Tom. He's a bit of a humblebrag."

I got that. "Yeah."

"Did you have fun?"

My emotions were too raw to answer, and I stared out the window. "Mm-hmm."

He huffed, removing his hand from my leg, tension settling between us like a summer storm. I crossed my arms to ward off the chill and braced myself for the coming crack of lightening.

When we arrived back at the house, he slammed the car door, the sound ringing in the garage. He threw his keys on the kitchen counter and they sailed across it, landing with a smack against the wall. "You're going to give me the silent treatment?"

He stripped off his jacket and tossed it on the sofa across the living room. I rolled my eyes. "You want me to throw a tantrum like you?"

"Yeah, sure. Go ahead." He circled his hand, bending into a deep patronizing bow, but when he stood up, he finally must have seen the tears I barely held back. He cut the distance between is in a few steps, wrapping his hands around my arms. "What's wrong?"

How could I begin to explain? I loved him but this weekend proved we couldn't have a future together. I wasn't interested in living here, where it took an hour to get anywhere, and I especially wasn't interested in being some kind of trophy wife while he worked. "Everything and nothing."

"What are you talking about?" He examined the room as if he could find the answer. "I know you go silent when you're trying to find your words, but I'm losing my patience."

I pulled away from his grasp, trying to come to terms with what my brain wanted while my heart pulled in the opposite direction. "I came here to see you. To see if we could make this work." He nodded in agreement, and I held my hand up. "What I got was a nice vacation with gorgeous weather."

He stopped me when I took a step toward the bedroom. "What's that supposed to mean?"

"It means I wanted to be here with you. You, Chris. But I came here for what? To hang out in the back and be invisible while you worked?"

He stood rooted in his spot, mouth gaping, and I rushed by him, this time making it to the bedroom, where I picked up the mess I'd made earlier with my clothes.

"You can't say something like that and then run away from me." He caught up to me, looming in the doorway, chest heaving.

"I enjoyed being here—I loved seeing you do what you love, but I'm not naive enough to think I could truly fit in here."

"Fit in here? Of course you fit in here."

I turned to look at him but fell off-balance and ended up on my butt. He met me on the floor. "What does that have to do with us?"

"It has everything to do with us," I nearly shouted, throwing shoes into the luggage. "You're CJ Cunningham. Your job is here, in front of cameras, and on set." He opened his mouth to interrupt, yet I barreled on. "I know all of this, all this glitter and shiny stuff is part of the package, but I don't want it. I'm not cut out for it."

He mashed his lips together like he didn't want any words to escape as his cheeks filled with color, and I folded the last of my things before zipping up my suitcase. "I think I'm going to go to the airport now." I stood on unsteady legs. "My flight leaves at six anyway. Might as well sleep there."

"No." He scrambled to stand up too. He was trembling just as bad as me. "You can't leave."

"Yes, I can. I have to."

"No. You can't. You said you wanted to make a plan. So, let's do that. Let's talk this out and figure out how to make it work."

I didn't know whether to laugh or cry. The last time we'd had this conversation, it was in reverse. "You can't be mad at me for this. When you left, you didn't give me a choice. You didn't give me a say. At least I came here and tried to work it out. I tried, but it's not possible."

"It's possible! It's fucking possible!"

His eyes were wide and hysterical, and I wanted to comfort him somehow. "I love you, Chris. I do. But it's too complicated."

"It won't always be this hard." He held my hand to his chest. "My schedule is crazy right now, but it'll slow down. Then we can—"

"Then what?" I whimpered, the last of my will to be strong crumbling. "Then we can be together? So I have to wait while you finish whatever project you're working on so we could be together for a few weeks, and then you go back and we do this all over again?"

"No." His heart beat riotously under my palm as he said, "I'd never ask that of you."

"There is no other way. I don't want to live here perma-nently, but I also don't want to be apart from you for months at a time. And I won't ask you to give this up." I traced the line of his wrist then slipped out of his grasp. "I want you to be where you're meant to be, where you need to be. Your dream is to inspire people with your work. That's what you always say, so you need to be here, making movies.

"What I need is you."

There was a fine line between need and want. I didn't *need* Chris to survive—I'd wake up every day like I had the day before—but I didn't *want* to do it without him. "You told me once I should never apologize for asking for what I want. What I want is to teach, to get married, and have a family. I won't stand in the way of your dream. Please, don't ask me to change mine."

An eternity passed before he nodded, his voice hoarse. "Okay."

"I'll meet you outside," I said, and too many emotions flashed over his features to count: shock, hurt, frustration, confusion, and anger among them. His jaw was clenched but his eyes were hollow, and I turned away, unable to endure his gaze any longer.

He let out a heavy breath. "Make sure you get your glasses. They're in the bathroom."

Then he left the room, and I finished packing. Taco had come out from his hiding place, and I scratched his head before heading outside. Chris was already in the driver's seat, staring out the window. He didn't acknowledge me as he started the car.

The forty-five-minute ride to LAX was the longest forty-five minutes of my life, nothing but silence for miles of highway. I reminded myself that I was doing the right thing, even if it felt like I was being ripped in two.

Finally arriving at the airport, Chris idled at the drop-off curb, his eyes never straying from the windshield.

"I did have a good time, Chris. Please know that."

He nodded.

"I was thinking..."

Still, he didn't look over at me.

"If we could live that plane ride all over again, I wouldn't want you to tell me who you were."

His head snapped toward me.

"I wouldn't change anything between you and me." I finally understood what it meant when people said they would relive their hurt all over again if it meant they got to experience the joy of a relationship one more time. I'd never give up what I experienced with Chris.

His lips turned down at the corners, though he still didn't say anything. He didn't even try to touch me.

This was it.

The end.

"Goodbye, Chris."

CHAPTER THIRTY-SEVEN

Chris

I kept my eyes on Bronte's retreating form until she passed through the automatic doors.

She didn't even spare me a backward glance.

My hope had walked away from me. Again.

"Fuck." I released the strangled sob I'd been holding in, slamming my fists into the steering wheel. "Fuck!"

A horn honked behind me, and it spurred my anger. I rolled down my window to flip the guy off, adding a few curse words for good measure, and jerked the steering wheel, cutting another car off in the process, leaving a flurry of angry horns behind as I sped east on the 105.

I may have deleted all the phone numbers of the guys I used to race with, but that didn't mean I still didn't need to get it out of my system. I needed to drive, to feel the gear shifts, hear the hum of the engine. I needed to go *fast*. I sped down the highway, weaving in and out of traffic, other cars honking their displeasure, but I didn't care. I drove and drove and drove with nowhere in particular in mind.

Syd's was a piece-of-shit bar located in the middle of Koreatown that I used to frequent. It was cash only and the sole place in the whole of Los Angeles where you could buy a shot and a Pabst for five bucks. It stank of stale beer and had a layer of smoke you could barely see through most nights, so much so that you didn't know what sticky substance you were stepping on since they probably only cleaned the floor once a decade.

I was so used to driving there, I could probably do it with my eyes closed, even after a year. I didn't make any conscious decisions to take the exit then make a right and a left. It was as if my body knew what it wanted before my brain. I was split open, bleeding out until there was nothing but pain left, and I needed something to numb it.

Turning off the ignition outside Syd's, I could already taste the whiskey. And as I took my first steps toward the bar, I could already feel the oblivion set in.

However, as I reached for the door, I froze.

A year ago, I'd been labeled as Hollywood's latest disaster. I was a fuckup, a drunk, a playboy. I'd become more famous for my off-screen shenanigans than my on-screen work, and if I stepped into the bar, I could slide right back into that life. I stomped away from the door.

Yet with the picture of Bronte walking away from me burned in my brain, I didn't care about what everyone thought of me. What was the point of being a better person if I didn't have her? I pivoted back, the blinking neon sign in the window beckoning me inside.

Back when my parents disowned me and I was faced with the prospect of turning my back on my career or moving forward without my family, Wes told me, "It's okay to look back to your past, but you don't have to stare." I whirled away from the OPEN sign to peer into one of the dirty windows, all the people lined up at the bar.

Well, I was staring at my past now, and it didn't seem so bad. Not when my other option was living with this goddamn wound in my chest. I moved back to the door, once again stopping abruptly.

I yanked at my hair, yelling incoherently into the night. I probably looked wild and irrational, but I didn't care. I felt that way, ready to burst out of my skin. I punched and kicked at the air until I was flushed and out of breath then plopped down on a parking block, my head hanging between my knees.

I didn't know how long I sat there, memorizing the pores in the macadam, although it was long enough for the door to bang open behind me. A guy staggered out, burping the alphabet to his own delight, then George came stumbling out. He was a regular, like I used to be. The guy looked terrible, even worse than I remembered, and I was suddenly glad the neon sign shut off moments later.

The weekend hadn't gone how I would have liked, but I never would've guessed it'd end up with Bronte in the airport, me on the ground outside a bar, and our future together completely obliterated.

I waited until the lights in the parking lot blinked out, and then another hour as the traffic slow down until the street was silent. Then, finally, I got back in my car.

The temperature had dropped with a cold wind blowing, but by the time I arrived home, I couldn't stand the thought of sleeping in the bed Bronte had been in mere hours ago, so I lumbered out to the deck, where Taco curled up at my feet on one of the lounge chairs. At least while I was awake, I could control my thoughts. My dreams, on the other hand...I wouldn't risk seeing her there.

———

I dumped the last of the Cocoa Puffs into the bowl and poured in enough milk that it sloshed over the top when I picked it up, but as I sat back on my sofa, there was a pounding on my front door like the SWAT team had arrived with a battering ram. Curious, I placed the bowl down and leaned over, peeking around the corner to see through the semitransparent window by the door.

"You better be dead in there, Chris!" Wes unlocked the door with his spare key and filed straight toward me. "What the hell, man?"

I crossed my legs on the sofa. "Nice to see you, too."

"Don't give me that. What the fuck are you doing?"

I swallowed a mouthful of Puffs and motioned to the TV with my spoon. "Watching *Judge Judy*."

"*Judge Judy*? You don't answer my calls or return my texts because you're too busy watching *Judge Judy*?"

"I'm sick."

"What the hell is wrong with you? The last two days, you've fallen off the face of the earth." He knocked the side of my shoulder so I spilled some of my cereal in my lap.

I clucked my tongue. "Come on."

"There better be a good reason I've been covering for your ass. I've been getting calls every day asking when you'll be back on set." He held up his phone as evidence. "They've had to rearrange the filming schedule. So much for that stellar reputation you've been working on. You know how much is riding on this, and you're throwing it all away!"

"Bronte left. She left me."

With that, he leaned back, crossed his arms, and threw his gaze out the windows. "What happened?"

Merely remembering what she'd said made a crater open up in my chest. "She told me it was too hard. All of this—" I circled my spoon around to encompass my life "—was too hard." Her words echoed in my ears, and the anger and frustration came back full force. "She said she didn't fit in here, that she felt invisible."

Disgust with myself bubbled up at the idea that Bronte could ever feel invisible, that I contributed to it in any way. I threw my head back. Her anger I could handle, but her hurt? That was too much.

I have not broken your heart—you have broken it; and in breaking it you have broken mine.

"I need a recap here," Wes said, his hands up in a time-out signal. "Start from the beginning with you two."

I did. I recounted how we met by chance on the plane and explained the roller coaster that was our relationship. I listed the reasons why I fell in love with her, and how, in spite of everything, she loved me back, and how I stupidly believed we could make it work, even when days went by without being able to speak to each other.

When I finished narrating the last conversation we had, Wes reclined back against the sofa. "It must have been tough for her to be dropped in the middle of everything."

I dropped my spoon in my empty bowl. "You know Bronte. She was so logical about it. One plus one equals two. I need to be here, she needs to be there, ergo we can't be together. She was so sure of everything. I couldn't argue otherwise."

"Why couldn't you argue? Because you're afraid she's right, or because you can't do math?"

"You're a dick."

"I'm going to take a wild guess and say it's because you're afraid. You're so afraid of screwing up, you'd rather walk away than take a chance. Am I right?" I didn't answer, and he grinned like the smug bastard he was. "What's holding you back?"

I shrugged. I didn't want to admit the truth.

"As your manager, I can tell you that something changed

for you while you were out there. You were always talented, but you came back, and the work you've been doing on this project has been so, *so* excellent."

I didn't need to be told. I knew I was good as Roy.

"As your friend, I've never seen you healthier and happier than last week. It's obvious she's lit something inside you."

Not just something, everything. She made me brand-new.

"You said it yourself, that life was easier for you there, nobody chasing you around or stressing you out. People do the bicoastal thing all the time, and after you finish this project— finishing this project being the key because you cannot fuck this up any more than you have these last two days—you can do whatever you want. Pave your own way on this. You're in the driver's seat of your career. We could finally open the production studio, and we could make movies from your base- ment if you really wanted to. So, I ask again, what's holding you back?"

I scrubbed my hands over my face before dropping them to my lap. "I don't want to ruin her like I do with everything in my life."

There. It was out.

Finally.

"Could you be any more of an arrogant asshole?"

"What?" I raised my gaze to an angry Wes.

"I know you can be a bit of a dick, but really? You really think you could *ruin* her?"

The guy used air quotes, and I threw my arms up. "That's not arrogance. That's me being honest."

He stood up, shaking his head. "I'm disappointed in you. You say you love her, but you deny the very basic element that makes Bronte *Bronte*. She may not look like it, but she's got a steel spine. No one is ruining her. She knows what she wants, and she wants you. All you need to do is show her you deserve her."

He had a point. A really good point. Bronte deliberated everything she did, sometimes to the point of exhaustion. Every decision was made with her eyes wide open and both feet on the ground, absolutely positive it was the right thing to do.

Looking back on our relationship through her eyes, I recognized how scary it must have been to accept her feelings for a person she hadn't known for very long, and one who was a celebrity on top of it all. She'd gone against her own grain and was probably very much afraid of the possibilities between us, yet she took the jump anyway.

Then at the first sign of trouble, I pulled away.

When she came back to me for a sign, for hope, I let her go.

She'd taken such a huge risk, while I hadn't given up anything.

"You're right," I said after a while. "I left my family back in PA. There's nothing left for me here anymore. I need to go home."

Wes grinned as he offered his hand to me. "You know how I know you're from Pennsylvania? You just said PA." He tugged me off the couch with a slap on the back. "Let me know what the plan is when you figure it out, but in the meantime, you get your ass to set at six a.m. tomorrow. I don't want any more phone calls where I have to make an excuse about you having food poisoning. You've got two weeks left. After that, we'll figure the rest out."

CHAPTER THIRTY-EIGHT

Bronte

I had had one of those BFF heart necklaces when I was a kid. It was split in half so Callie, my best friend at the time, and I could each have a piece. The broken heart was cut in clean zigzag lines with a silver edge.

The adult kind of broken heart was very different.

It was ugly and raw. I couldn't even say his name, I missed him so bad. And to make matters worse, there was no way to avoid him.

He was in magazines and on television.

In my dreams.

Everywhere.

The only place I was safe was at school, and I spent a lot of extra hours hiding there.

"Hey, are you heading out of here anytime soon?"

I picked my head up from where it was cradled in my arms and glanced at the clock on the wall. Cartoon hands pointed at the time, 4:40.

"I think I'm going to work a little bit more," I said, waving Rachel inside her classroom.

"On what?" She made a show of turning in a circle. "You have all your paperwork done for the rest of the year and all your lesson plans organized. If you're really itching for something to do, why don't you come across the hall and clean out my storage closet?" When I smiled, she pantomimed tugging me with a rope. "You know you want to."

"Maybe next week."

She propped her hands on her hips. "I wish I could make you feel better. What can I do?"

I shook my head, hoping she didn't see how my bottom lip quivered.

"Are you sure there's nothing?"

"I don't think so." I hiccupped in a breath and reached for a tissue. One tissue turned into two and then three, and I pitched them at the garbage can, missing by a few inches. After picking them up to throw away, I fixed my glasses on my nose, turning my attention back to Rachel.

Except Rachel wasn't five foot nine with bulging arms and legs meant to wear dark ripped jeans.

It was Chris.

Standing in my classroom.

I gawked at him for a moment before finding my words. "What are you doing here?"

His mouth quirked up in the corner. "Detention."

I pinched my wrist and closed my eyes. Wouldn't be the first time I'd dreamed of him.

"I'm here, Bronte. I'm real."

Opening my eyelids, I found him a few feet closer. "Wh— How? I'm... Is this what a stroke feels like?" I slumped against my desk and moved one hand to my throat, searching for a pulse. "I think I'm having a stroke."

"You're not having a stroke." He took two more steps closer, and I swore my heart beat thudded to a complete stop. His black V neck showed off the contours of his chest. The same chest that I knew was tattooed with words for me. He was clean-shaven, his sideburns gone, his hair cut short on the sides and long on top, waving into a dangerously attractive curl on his forehead. If I didn't know better, I would have assumed somebody dressed him to look this good, but no, it was his natural state.

And it was completely unfair.

I hadn't dried my hair this morning, and my wrinkled purple shirt didn't match my pastel orange skirt. I was a drunk Easter egg and would've been embarrassed if the shock of him in front of me hadn't overpowered every other possible emotion.

He raked his gaze over me, from head to toe, and when his dark eyes met mine again, they softened. "I had to see you in person when I told you that you were wrong."

I could barely wrap my brain around the fact that he was here, let alone blaming me. "Huh?"

"You fit in. You fit with me."

I struggled to comprehend what he was saying through my astonishment and confusion.

"The best day of my life was the day I met you, and I'll be damned if I let you get away without putting up a fight."

"You want us to be together?" I squeaked out the question since I hadn't heard a word from him since he dropped me off at the airport.

He frowned. "Of course I do."

"But how— You're...you?"

He closed the gap between us, and I stood up straight. "I got caught up trying to hide you from my insane life, and then I tried so hard to make you love that life, I forgot we already had one. My life is with you, wherever you are. You're my home, Bronte."

I swallowed the lump in my throat, my heart threatening to burst out of my chest.

"After you left, I didn't go to work for two days."

"What? Chris, no, you didn't—"

"I know." He shook his head. "Wes covered for me, and they were able to rearrange the schedule, but they did worry. Dante, and the producers, they took a chance on me, and I disappeared for two days."

I huffed out a breath. "You can't do that. When you've been working so hard to prove you aren't like that anymore."

"I know. I know." He took hold of my hands. "I was out of my mind for you. I had trouble getting it together, but then Wes came over and kicked my ass in gear."

"Maybe he should come over here and kick mine too."

He pressed my palms together and trapped them against his chest, pulling me so close there was nowhere else to look but right into his eyes. "I made some plans. Since you're so fond of them."

The hopeful tilt of his growing smile had the corner of my mouth climbing up too. "Really?"

He took a breath, as if still contemplating what he wanted to say, and then his words tumbled out in a flurry. "I sold my house in LA. I didn't really like it anyway, and I'm hoping we can pick out a new one. One you'll love so that when we're there, you'll never feel out of place or invisible."

"I don't... I don't understand."

"Your dream is to teach and have a family. My dream is to act and help you fulfill your dreams. I figured, if you agree, we'll stay in Allentown during the school year. I may have some small events or jobs here or there, but nothing that I have to be away from you for long periods of time or that you won't be able to travel with me when you have days off from work."

He was speaking so fast, it was hard to get it all in my head. "What about your movies?"

"I'll film during the summer so you can be with me in LA.

At least for a few years. When we have kids, we could make new plans. Rearrange the schedule."

"I...uh...what?"

He bent his knees so I'd meet his eyes. "I was thinking two, but if you want more, we can talk about it."

"Chris, I...what the fuck?"

A big burst of laughter erupted from him. "I love it when you curse. You never do, and it sounds so filthy coming out of your mouth."

"You want kids with me?"

"Of course. Eventually." He shrugged. "If you're okay with that."

"And you want to get married."

He grinned. "I figured you'd want to do that first. Since you're big on following the rules and all."

My stomach flip-flopped, bubbles of excitement stirring up that I felt like I might puke. "I can't believe that you want all those things."

"I want you. And I want everything you want. Including blue-eyed babies who can quote the Brontë sisters and who will be the stars of their third-grade plays. We can have a house on each coast, summers in LA, the rest of the time here. What do you think?"

"I... Uh..."

"I realize this is a lot of information, but I want you to know that I will not give up or settle. You're it for me." He stroked my knuckles with his thumbs as I blinked at him like an empty-headed owl. "Bronte, I really wish you'd say something here."

I blurted the first thing that came to mind. "I'm surprised they let you in here without a badge."

He kissed a chuckle into my palms. "I was aiming for something about us."

I tried to come up with any reason to turn him away. My fears and insecurities had taken over in California, and I'd thought our lives were just too different. Then I'd spent nights alone in bed, assuring myself I had made the right decision, but none of those mental lists and supposed rationales made me happy.

Because, as Chris waited for my response with a tender gaze and patient smile, I knew there was no textbook for this, only instinct. And from the first second I'd laid eyes on him, I had loved him.

I was in love with him. Overwhelmingly, irrationally, madly in love.

I skimmed my hands up the planes of his chest until I hooked them around his neck. "You'd be giving up an awful lot."

He wrapped his arms around my waist. "I'd be giving up everything if I lost you."

"CJ Cunningham living here in Allentown?"

"Reminds me of a song." He hugged me close, dipping his face to hum Billy Joel's "Allentown" into the slope of my neck. "Does that mean you're in?" He nipped my throat.

"I'm in."

He lifted me up, swinging me around. "You and me, doing it for real this time. Dates and fights and make-up sex and movie nights on the couch and brunches at your parents' house—"

"Do they know about this?"

"Oh yeah." He put me down, waving his hand behind him as if they were all there. "They all know. Even your girls. I got Shelley to give me their numbers. They helped me plan this, but Gemma gave me a lot of shit."

I bit back a smile, imagining it all, but with so much

emotion in only a few minutes, it all came crashing down in a flood of tears.

"Baby, don't cry." He wiped away the tears before kissing my cheeks.

"I never thought we could be together." I sniffled. "I didn't think we could be a reality."

"I'm here now, and I'm not going anywhere." Then he checked the time on his phone and sucked in a breath. "Except to pick up Taco from Fitz's house. He'll start to rip things apart if he's separated from me too long."

"I know how he feels." I fixed my glasses on my nose.

He smiled at me, and I returned it with one that just about split my face in two. "Let's get out of here. We have our whole lives to get started on."

Epilogue

CHRIS

"This is quite the housewarming party," Gemma said, strutting alongside the pool in her retro bikini. "Margaritas and vegan snacks. It's almost like you're trying to impress me, Christopher."

I held up my beer bottle in a cheers to her from my seat on a lounger.

After school ended in June, Bronte and I flew to LA to find a house. She fell in love with a little bungalow in a gated community in Studio City. She liked the views of the canyon and the courtyard with the twinkle lights. I liked that I wouldn't have to drive far to film sets. The first thing Bronte decided we *had* to do was invite her girls to officially meet me. Delaney, Samantha, and Gemma—along with her baby, fiancé, and pack 'n play in tow—had arrived yesterday.

"I was hoping to match with an internship in Texas, but maybe I need to rethink," Samantha said from her spot on the steps in the shallow end of the pool.

"Oh, so you'll move here, but not San Francisco?" Delaney sniffed from over by the makeshift bar.

"LA is better for my emotional state. It's sunny all the time." Samantha laughed, tossing her rainbow-colored hair over her shoulder, and tipped her chin to where Delaney refilled her glass from the margarita pitcher once again. "You want to just stick a straw in there? Why pretend that isn't *your* pitcher?"

"I have some class, Sammy, darling." Delaney made a big show of slurping up her drink.

"Anyone want to take bets on what time Laney's asleep tonight?" Bronte asked, slathering more SPF lotion on her shoulders.

"I have the strongest constitution out of all of us," Delaney huffed before reconsidering. "Well, maybe not Chris."

Again, I raised my bottle. "Not anymore. I am happy to relinquish that title. One or two drinks are enough for me."

"What happened to CJ Cunningham of old?" Gemma heaved out a sigh. "He settled down and got so *boring.*"

I pointed to Bronte. "She ruined me."

She held her thumb and index finger an inch apart. "Only a little."

She wore a black one-piece, totally demure and covering all her good bits, but I liked it anyway. "Come here, Bunny. I'll do your back."

"Bunny?" Samantha snickered. "You call her Bunny?"

"I think it's cute." Delaney leaned down to boop Samantha on the nose. "You jealous you've got nobody to call you pet names?"

"Absolutely not," she said firmly, and Gemma covered up her dubious laugh with a cough.

Bronte glanced over her shoulder at me as I rubbed her down with lotion, and she nodded ever so slightly, her eyes dancing with laughter. Samantha *was* jealous. She also wasn't a great actress. It was pretty evident in the way her shoulders hiked up to her ears. Maybe I'd give her pointers later.

"But, seriously," Gemma started, dropping down to the pool deck to stick her feet in the water. "It's gorgeous here."

"Yeah, it's pretty okay. This one makes it better." I patted Bronte's ass when I finished my job, but before I could cop another feel, she scurried away, muttering something about the cookies burning in the oven.

Jason, Gemma's fiancé, swam over to her, their baby next to him in a tiny inner tube. "And thanks for letting me and this little chicken tag along," he said to me. "Will's still attached to Gem. She can't go anywhere alone."

"Literally." Gemma playfully scowled at Willow as she tugged her from the inner tube. "Just call me Elsie the cow."

I didn't understand until she held the baby up and unsnapped her top. I darted my gaze away as she breastfed Willow and cleared my throat. "Well, Bronte said you guys are practically family, and her family is my family, so…"

Jason hoisted himself out of the pool and towel-dried before sinking down into a chair next to me. "Laney," he called, raising his arm. "Water, please."

She chucked him a bottle of water, with incredible accuracy across the pool, and he caught it with ease. Jason and I had gotten off to a bit of a rocky start yesterday, with him being so reserved at first, but he'd loosened up after we'd headed down to the media room to watch a movie while the girls gabbed away in the kitchen.

"Hey," he said quietly, knocking the side of his fist into the arm of my chair. "What we talked about last night…"

I shook my head. We had talked about a lot of things: my rise to fame and his history of partying. And that led into a whole other conversation when Jason told me his parents had been killed by a drunk driver. I, in turn, apologized for getting behind the wheel after drinking because that could have been me killing someone's parents.

"About the ring," Jason clarified. "I know this is supposed to be your weekend, but would you mind if...?"

He had explained that when he'd proposed the first time, it was in the hospital after Gemma had just given birth to Willow. She had, of course, said yes, but in the newborn panic of the last few months, they hadn't talked about it at all besides that they'd be married eventually.

"You want to do it now? Yeah, yeah, go for it." I arced my arm wide, as if the backyard was a stage. "The floor is yours."

Jason nodded once, downed a few gulps of water, then strode off into the house, a man on a mission. He returned a minute later behind Bronte, who carried a tray of cookies.

"I can't get the hang of this oven. It doesn't heat evenly." She put the plate of homemade chocolate chip cookies next to the other food. "Look at this one," she said, holding up a cookie with a dark brown bottom.

"You want a new oven?" I asked, standing to throw my arm around her shoulders.

"You're ridiculous."

I feigned pain when she needled her bony elbow into my side. "What?"

"The oven is fine. You have to stop buying me things. I don't need anything else."

"I like buying you things. You don't *need* a new oven, but if you want one..."

She smiled indulgently at me, wrapping her arm around my waist as Jason made his way to Gemma on the other side of the pool.

"Sam, you mind holding Will for a minute?" he asked with one hand behind his back. Gemma threw him a suspicious eyebrow but handed the baby over anyway. When Samantha had Willow settled against her shoulder, Jason held out his hand to Gemma to stand up in front of him.

"Gem, this last year has been crazy," he started, his voice even and sure. "Building a life and family has been the hardest and best thing I've ever done, and I'm so grateful to be able to do it with you."

Next to me, Bronte realized what was happening and let out a gasp, pressing her hand to her chest. I squeezed her tighter.

"You gave me my daughter," Jason went on, "and you're the most amazing mother. There is nothing I want more than to be by your side forever, so I'd like a redo on my proposal." He opened his fist, revealing a ring in his palm, and knelt on the ground. "You are everything I could ever want. You're wild and amazing and the absolute worst," he said, eliciting a laugh from not only Gemma but everyone else except for me. I didn't get it, yet as this scene unfolded, I couldn't wait to be in on the joke. To make a life with these people as my friends, my family.

"I want to spend the rest of my days with you, experiencing all the wild and amazing things life has in store of us. Marry me?"

Gemma nodded, and Bronte hiccupped next to me. I towed her in for a hug. My beautiful little empath, she couldn't ever contain her emotions.

Jason slipped the ring on Gemma's finger, and she held it up to get a good look before saying, "What a tremendous waste of resources."

He tossed his head back to laugh, and the girls squealed in delight, attacking her. I, for my part, gave Jason a hug and pat on the back.

"Congratulations."

"Thanks." He swiped a knuckle across one eye, his grin so wide.

I knew the feeling. That one of gratitude and bliss. Of knowing he had the rest of his life to show the love of his life exactly how much he loved her. It would never be enough time, but it would be fun trying.

Jason grabbed Willow from Samantha in one arm and wrapped his other around Gemma. Delaney captured the moment with a photo on her phone, then ducked her head next to Samantha for a selfie of the two of them. Last, she pointed it at me and Bronte. She draped her arm across my chest, her front pressed exquisitely against my back. Delaney snapped a picture as Bronte kissed my cheek then whispered in my ear, "Be with me always. Drive me mad."

"Oh, don't worry." I swung my arm around to capture her to my side, smothering her neck in kisses before pressing her palm to my chest. "You're never getting rid of me." I tapped on my tattoo, where the words written by her namesake were imprinted on my heart. "I signed the contract."

Then I bent her backward for a kiss worthy of a Hollywood ending.

Acknowledgments

Indie publishing is a wild ride. Thank you, reader, for coming along with me.

I wouldn't be able to put out these books if not for the encouragement of my friends, especially Ellis Leigh and Brighton Walsh, and the help of my editors, Libby and Lisa. I'd especially like to thank my street team for helping me spread the work about my books. I'm forever grateful.

If you'd like more information about me, you can find it at: https://sophieandrewsauthor.com.

About the Author

Sophie Andrews is a contemporary romance author who writes steamy books that will leave you smiling. As a millennial, she's obsessed with boybands, late 90s rom-coms, and will always be team Pacey. When she's not writing, she's most likely trying to wrangle her children or drinking red wine. Or both at the same time.

Also by Sophie Andrews

Tangled Series

Tangled Up

Tangled Want

Tanged Hearts

Tangled Beginning

Tangled Expectations

Tangled Chances

Tangled Ambition